prejudice
& pride

LYNN MESSINA

potatoworks press
new york

ACKNOWLEDGMENTS

As a friend said during one of a dozen email exchanges discussing edits for *Prejudice & Pride,* it takes a small red-brick Georgian village to write a novel. Huge thanks to my villagers: Dawn Yanek, Mark Leydorf, Ariella Papa, Roell Schmidt, Jennifer Lewis, Karen Lanza, Ann-Marie Walsh, Joyce Kehl and Donna Levy. And a special shout-out to Chris Catanese for holding down the fort. All would be in ruins without you.

CHAPTER ONE

Bennet Bethle is heartily sick of universally acknowledged truths. He appreciates the value of hard-earned knowledge and the usefulness of insights gleaned from years of experience, but the pronouncements his boss makes fall into neither category. They're opinions elevated to aphorism wrapped in the shiny gloss of established fact.

Today's assertion, uttered while buttering a bagel with a spoon, because Mr. Meryton can't find a knife, is simple: Any young woman in possession of a good fortune must be in want of a social committee to chair. Whether the heiress is actually interested in the organization's cause—be it cultural, ethical or political—is immaterial to the designs of museum directors everywhere. At once impervious to reality and beleaguered by it, professional fundraisers have an overdeveloped sense of entitlement to other people's money: It already belongs to them; it just needs to be routed to the correct bank account.

Knowing that Meryton can never say in one sentence what can be vigorously enthused in eight, Bennet doesn't glance up from his computer. Rather, he opens an email from the manager of community affairs at Venture Marts, confirms an upcoming meeting, enters the date into his calendar and files the message in the appropriate folder for future reference. The blond-haired man at the desk across from his also continues to type, and for three minutes, Meryton's loquaciousness is scored by the muted clack-clack-clack of both their keyboards.

And then suddenly he's silent, and the cramped, little room fills with expectation.

Now Bennet looks up.

Meryton's dark brown eyes, round like walnuts, are glittering with excitement and impatience. "Didn't you hear what I just said? Netherfield on the Park has been rented."

Bennet pictures the lovely beaux-arts tower along Fifth Avenue, with its high, arched windows and graceful balustrades, and wonders at Meryton's sense of urgency. Although the Netherfield had the unfortunate timing to open three days before the stock market crash of 1929, it somehow managed to weather the Depression and in the years since has developed a following among an international clientele seeking an old New York flavor and elegant afternoon tea. Now it perennially tops lists of the best places to stay in Manhattan. "Oh, yeah, I read hotels were doing that now—renting rooms," he observes. "It's this newfangled thing called guests."

This flippant remark does little to amuse Meryton, who's disappointed once again by his young employee's inability to see the infinite in a grain of sand. When one hears the Netherfield is rented, one should immediately envision the magnificent three-story penthouse crowning the august hotel. In an instant, one should call up the layout of the thirty-three-room accommodation: the three bedrooms on the first floor, along with the library, living room, kitchen, dining room, and north and south reception halls; the second floor, with its grand salon that used to be the hotel ballroom, its additional two bedrooms and wraparound terrace; the third-floor bedrooms each with an adjoining dressing room larger than a studio apartment in Red Hook.

"The penthouse," Meryton says with breathless excitement.

"The penthouse at the Netherfield is rented at last. It has been empty for ages."

The blond-haired gentleman, perceiving the significance of the development and uninclined to make jokes at his employer's expense, leans back in his chair and stares thoughtfully. "Who's rented it?"

Meryton takes a deep breath, savoring the moment, and announces with obvious relish, "Charlotte Bingston. Yes, of the Boston Bingstons. Her father patented a process for mass-producing lithium-ion batteries. Reliable Energy's third-quarter earnings were up fifteen percent, and its market cap is $1.2 billion. Charlotte and her two brothers are Bingston's only heirs, and her net worth, not including real estate holdings in London, Telluride and Los Angeles, is conservatively estimated at $450 million."

At this concise breakdown of Charlotte Bingston's wealth, Bennet smothers a smile. Even after seven years in the development department of the Longbourn—seven years of Meryton's gross calculations and tabulations and speculations—he's still amused by the way his employer follows fortunes as if they're sports scores. Several times a day, he consults the Bloomberg Billionaires Index for shifts in ranking, and every morning he combs the obituaries of several major international newspapers for familiar names. There's nothing he relishes more than the unexpected death of a little-known industrialist.

As executive director of the Longbourn Collection, Meryton feels a keen sense of ownership of the institution he has overseen and safeguarded for twenty-three years. His tenacity is remarkable, and as much as Bennet admires his employer's relentless devotion to the cause, he knows he'll never be able to emulate it. His intentions are good, his commitment is sincere, his work ethic is strong and his faith in the mission is absolute, but at the end of the day, his job at the Longbourn is simply that—a job, not the source of all meaning in his life. For Bennet, it's a satisfying way to cover the rent on his apartment and pay for drinks at Minetta Tavern and buy suits that don't make

3

him look like he just got off a bus from Michigan. Meryton knows this about his employee and has accepted, through years of the slow dissolution of hope, that he'll never make a great executive director. A fine one, maybe. A competent one, without question. But he will never be truly great, and he'll certainly never be transformative, for he just isn't calculating enough. As Meryton once observed with a regretful sigh, Mr. Bennet Bethle has a heart where his spreadsheet should be.

His older brother, John Bethle, who also works in the development office, is likewise too soft for Meryton's comfort, but his physical beauty—the chiseled jawline, the thick blond hair, the lush pouty lips, the brilliant blue eyes—more than compensates for his lack of calculation. His perfection is startling and disconcerts even the most methodical mind. Before a donor gathers her wits enough to realize what she's agreed to, she's already sitting down with him in a meeting. To Meryton's delight, the benefits are not limited to the female half of the species. Men are also caught off guard by his employee's appearance, trying, he supposes, to find flaws amid the perfection.

The first moment Meryton spotted John—hunched over the Xerox machine making copies of board minutes—he recognized the young man's potential. Not even the harsh green glare of the old copier could dim his stunning beauty. What heiress wouldn't want to hand over her checkbook to such an Adonis?

Naturally, when he assigned the young man to the development department, run, at the time, by the sister of a successful movie director, Meryton left out all mention of Greek gods and refrained from uttering the phrase *physical perfection*. Rather, he spoke of the challenges of insulating an esteemed institution from the vagaries of fate.

Money, he explained, is the only thing that can guarantee security.

And the Longbourn Collection needs security. Housed in a Venetian mansion built in 1902 by art lover and industrialist Cyrus Reginald Longbourn, who made his fortune in steal manufacturing, the collection suffers from Disinterested Heirs Syndrome. None of the millionaire's four great-grandchildren and ten great-great-grandchildren are the least bit interested in preserving his legacy, which they consider the folly of an old man seeking immortality. Setting up an art museum in a provincial backwater like Forest Hills! It had been an utterly ridiculous proposition in 1913, when the trust was established, and it's an utterly ridiculous proposition now. And to expect the latest crop of Longbourns to continue to throw money at the crumbling old monstrosity, with its second-tier assortment of paintings, is the most utterly ridiculous proposition of all.

The contempt is palatable but not entirely appropriate, as the assortment of paintings is hardly second-tier. The Longbourn has one of the finest collections of Impressionists in the world. Monet, Pissarro, Renoir, Manet, Cézanne, Degas, Sisley, Cassat, Morisot and Bazille are all represented and represented generously. Every year, hundreds of scholars, historians, critics and artists walk its rooms in awe and delight.

The charge of being a backwater, however, isn't as easy to dismiss, for few self-respecting New Yorkers relish making the extended journey out to Queens to look at art. Tucked at the end of a quiet, tree-lined street, the Longbourn is a long way from the glamour of the Upper East Side or the practicality of midtown. It does a brisk business with tourists, who don't see the East River as the great impediment the locals do, but a healthy international business doesn't equal local respect. Perhaps if the mansion were on Madison Avenue like the Frick, its heirs wouldn't be so eager to sell it to developers.

Or perhaps they would. As much as Cyrus's great-great-grandchildren would welcome the prestige of an important Manhattan cultural institution, they would probably welcome the purchasing power of a large check more. The only thing saving the Longbourn from becoming eighteen luxury condos with granite countertops and steam compression dryers is a property-tax exemption, the generosity of Cyrus's last remaining grandchild and the sweat of Mr. Meryton's brow.

As valiant as Meryton's efforts are, they cannot prevail

over the greatest hurdle of all: time. The clock is running down, and Meryton always hears the tick.

This year, their benefactor, Henry Cortland Longbourn, turns 86.

"Four hundred and fifty million," Meryton enthuses again, his eyes focused on an unseen mound of dollar bills piled as high as the Flatiron Building. "John, you must go over there at once and introduce yourself. There's no time to lose. The vultures are circling."

"Vultures?" Bennet repeats with a wry smile. "You mean the men and women who do exactly what we do at other institutions?"

Meryton immediately dismisses the sentiment, on the grounds that nobody else does exactly what they do, and grumbles under his breath about inappropriate levity. Then, as he contemplates the competition, he begins to pace back and forth, his short, round frame—oddly matronly, as if he'd given birth to five daughters in rapid succession—maneuvering awkwardly around the desks, chairs and file cabinets that fill the tight space.

An office is never as large as its mission.

Now, there's a universally acknowledged truth, Bennet thinks.

"I bet you anything, Mr. Lucas from the Frick is already en route and Mr. King from the Morgan is hailing a cab as we speak. You must hurry, John."

Bennet glances at his computer and sees that it's only nine-fifteen. "Isn't it a little early for morning calls? Maybe John should wait until noon before bursting in on her."

"Do you think Mr. Lucas is waiting? Or Mr. King?" Meryton asks before knocking his knee against John's desk.

Sadly, bumping into furniture is an occupational hazard for all employees of the Longbourn, as the offices are housed in the former servants' quarters, a warren of tiny rooms at the very top and the very bottom of the faux palazzo. The development department, with its array of file cabinets and secondhand color printer, is squeezed into a maid's bedroom, while publications and special events share the coachman's bedroom on the other side of the building. The curators are consigned to the basement, in the former kitchens that still smell faintly of coal and ash. Meryton, who, like the original owner of the home, rarely visits the scullery, likes to say the curators are in the kitchens so they can "cook up" their excellent ideas. Having heard this clever quip dozens of times, the curators can barely drum up a grimace at each new repetition—though, to be fair, they were hardly amused the first time Meryton uttered it.

For his part, Meryton works in the old housekeeper's quarters, a lopsided trapezoid dignified by a small closet and a pair of generous windows overlooking the back garden. Located next to development, the office sits at the top of a winding staircase far too narrow for the installation of an elevator. To partake of that modern convenience, one has to walk down two long corridors to the east end of the building.

John and Bennet rarely make the trek; Meryton rarely does not.

Rubbing the painful spot on his knee, the executive director insists they move on Bingley immediately. "I'm sure she's an early riser. How can any woman sleep when she knows she has all that money to spend?"

"Bingley?" John asks, while his brother imagines a horde of dollar bills jumping on a bed like unruly children yelling, *"Spend me! Spend me! Spend me!"*

"Yes, Charlotte Bingston," Meryton explains impatiently. "She goes by Bingley. Do neither of you read the tabloids? What do you do all day while you're not comprehensively following the industry in which you're employed?"

This time Bennet doesn't bother to hide his smile. Although there are many frustrations in his job as director of corporate giving, including the disconcerting fact that he has no staff to direct, he's genuinely entertained by his boss's antics. Meryton is one part CEO and two parts court jester.

"Why don't I send flowers from our garden now and follow up this afternoon?" John proposes calmly.

Although this suggestion is perfectly reasonable, Meryton is appalled. "Flowers from our garden? Are you mad?" he asks, his voice growing shrill. "Can you not imagine how anemic our sad little bunch will look next to the Met's towering bouquet of red roses or MoMA's immense assortment of orchids?" He shudders with horror. "Absolutely not."

The shudder, like most things the fiftysomething Meryton does, is needlessly dramatic, but Bennet concedes his boss's point: The Longbourn doesn't have the resources to compete with the heavy hitters who play in the next league up. It does have a few natural advantages, though. "I think John is onto something with the local angle. We have some of the best bakeries and artisanal foods in the city. Quinny was just named the best small-batch brewery in New York by *Time Out,* and Whitestone Baking Co. has topped the list for best black-and-white cookie three years running."

"HBO recently aired a documentary on the Astor Pickle Factory," John adds. "We could make a basket of Queens delicacies. Great idea, Bennet."

Meryton nods slowly, reluctantly conceding the wisdom of leveraging their local advantage. The Longbourn would never win on strength alone; it has to be wily and clever. "Let's do it. Pull something together and have it on her doorstep by noon. Include a personal note offering a private tour of the collection at her convenience and an invitation to next week's gala."

"Yes, of course," John says mildly, as if Meryton isn't treating him like a newbie who's never courted a prospective donor before. At thirty, he's been in the department for more than nine years and the director of individual giving for almost five. He knows exactly what to do. But he also knows his boss has a hard time believing anyone is as competent as he is. "I'll also invite her to lunch in the trustees' dining room."

"Yes, yes," Meryton says, leaning against Bennet's desk as the plan to win over Charlotte "Bingley" Bingston falls into place. "That's a nice touch. And don't forget to mention the committee she's to chair."

John looks up from the note he's writing to himself and wrinkles his brow. "Which committee?"

It's a very good question. Meryton taps his fingers against the desk as he thinks. "How about the Diamond Circle Committee?"

John shakes his head. "We gave that to Gloria Carlsberg last month."

At once, Meryton recalls the teenage daughter of one of their board members, a financier who lives in South America. He pictures her strong chin and stronger bank balance. "Ah, yes, Gloria. She's doing a wonderful job."

"What about gold circle?" Bennet offers, although he has little hope of prevailing. Handing out meaningless and hastily conceived social chairs is something the Longbourn does on a bimonthly basis. Meryton believes vanity is the greatest motivator: Convince a socialite to put her name on an event, and she'll move heaven and earth to ensure its success. It's also an excellent way to get your hands on her list of contacts. Socialites don't often sponsor events for the Longbourn Collection, but when they do, the museum usually nets thousands of dollars' worth of free press and several sizable donations. Newcomers tend to be more generous than old standbys, who are tired of being tapped every time a brick falls off the facade.

As expected, John rejects his suggestion on the basis that another heiress—Shia Haines—already chairs the Gold Circle Committee.

Bennet tries again. "Platinum?"

Meryton shoots it down just as abruptly. "Josie Chow."

Bennet tries to think of a metal they haven't used before. "Titanium?"

Appalled, Meryton shakes his head. "She's an heiress, not a golf club."

"Silver," Bennet offers.

"You might as well make her chair of the Very Muddy Mud Society," Meryton insists impatiently.

Amused as always by the challenge, Bennet decides

switch gears. "How about the Patrons Circle Centennial Committee, which is planning the celebration for the collection's one hundredth anniversary. It will be a huge bash."

"It *was* a huge bash," John reminds him. "We had that two years ago."

His brother shrugs. "She'll never know."

"Your opinion of heiresses is appalling," John observes. "They're not all airheads."

Bennet pictures the last heiress he met—Ms. Haines, whose hairless Chihuahua has its own personal assistant and a weekly standing appointment at the Woofdorf-Astoria for a puppy pedi. Although he's not inclined to concede the point, he knows his brother is determined to see the best in everyone and admits he might be overly harsh in his estimation. "But the vast majority of them are too busy Instagramming selfies or creating vanity perfume lines to come up with a useful idea. And if one of them has had the good sense to hire an actual professional as her admin and not her dear friend Bitsy from Theta Phi, I've yet to meet her."

Impatient with the chatter, Meryton knocks on Bennet's desk three times. "Tick-tock, tick-tock, gentlemen," he says and strides in three easy steps to the door. "Figure it out and get that gift basket to the Netherfield immediately. We don't have any time to waste. And don't disparage the Theta Phis, Bennet. That illustrious organization has supplied us with some of our best committee chairs."

With that, he returns to his office and sits down at his computer to make sure Charlotte Bingston's father has retained his ranking on the Billionaires Index. Ah, yes, there he is—holding steady at 395.

CHAPTER TWO

The basket from the Longbourn arrives first. Although fund-raising isn't entirely a race, it's mostly a race—the first one to the credit line wins!—and Meryton is delighted to know they've established contact with their quarry before any of the competition.

"A bellman delivered the basket at 11:45," John says, "and I've been assured by Larissa, the front desk manager, that ours is the only one she's received since checking in last night at 7:39 p.m. I was just about to follow up with a call, but if you'd rather take a meeting to discuss our next move, I'd be happy to put it off until later."

Meryton would love nothing more than to provide John with a script for his conversation with Ms. Bingston, but he knows the value of momentum and doesn't want to lose it. "No, no, proceed as planned. Time is of the essence."

John nods and picks up the phone. To his delight, Larissa answers, and he has a breezy conversation with her about bird watchers in Central Park. The mid-March weather always brings them out.

Meryton, listening from just a few feet away, knows the advantage of having the front desk manager from the Netherfield in one's corner and doesn't protest when the conversation switches to the boat pond. Rather, he grabs a pen, jots down a few words—new polar bear, zoo, children giddy—on a Post-it and hands it to John, who looks at it briefly and nods.

Having been fed many such communications during his tenure, Bennet knows how easily the executive director can conduct proxy conversations via scraps of paper. To buy his brother some breathing room, he says, "I had a meeting with Martindale from Venture Marts this morning, and I'm not sure if I've got the tone right for the follow-up. Should I gush a little or keep it entirely businesslike?"

At once, Meryton dashes to Bennet's desk, dislodges its occupant with a firm shove and sits down to address the question. Rather than ask for permission, he jumps right in, rewording the missive to suit his own fundraising approach. Amused, Bennet watches his hands zip across the keyboard. Of course he'd known exactly what he was doing: Meryton has supreme faith in his own abilities and would never let an employee do well what he himself can do perfectly.

He's so immersed in Bennet's letter to the representative from the big-box retailer, he doesn't notice when John puts down the phone.

"Gush a little?" Meryton asks scornfully. "Try gush a lot. Funders want us to be tripping over ourselves to express our enthusiasm at their potential involvement. Trust me, that's the trick to winning them over. Devote the first paragraph to your excitement and your second paragraph to stroking their ego: Their participation is necessary to the success of the project, their interest is more than we'd hoped for and so forth. Then get down to business in paragraph three. It's always best to bury the ask, so they don't see the request for money coming."

Bennet, who had saved the original draft of the email before soliciting his boss's advice, nods appreciatively. "I'll keep that in mind."

"Yes, do," Meryton says, standing up. Only then does he realize John's no longer on the phone. He pounces.

"Well, what did she say? Is she coming? Has she met Mr. Lucas? Does she want a private tour?"

"That was her assistant, Mitzy," John says with a wry look at his brother.

Bennet smiles and murmurs, "Mitzy, Bitsy and Cottontail."

"Her assistant?" Meryton echoes, visibly deflating at the news.

"Yes, but," John rushes to add, "she said Ms. Bingston is looking forward to the gala next Wednesday and will be bringing several guests with her. She doesn't know the exact number yet."

Meryton instantly reinflates. "The more the merrier," he croons happily, his smile stretching so wide Bennet thinks it might split his face in two. "I wonder who her guests will be. She's been seen palling around with Zoe Saldana in Paris. And last month she sat next to Rania Al-Abdullah at the Mosaic Foundation benefit dinner."

Although Bennet doubts very much that the queen of Jordan will attend their gala fundraiser, he lets Meryton have his fun and doesn't say a thing when, excited by the possibilities, he wonders if the king will accompany his wife.

Meryton is planning the seating arrangements—do the king and queen have to sit at the same table or could they be strewn about the room like rose petals?—when the department intern walks into the office.

No, Bennet thinks, he *saunters* in. His gait is light and carefree and reflects no concern for the lateness of the hour. In his right hand, he holds a cup of coffee, which he's about to dip his nose into when he spots Meryton. He stops in his tracks.

Not so cocky now, Bennet observes with more than a little satisfaction.

So far, the great Lydon Bethle internship experiment hasn't been the stunning success their mother had promised when she'd pleaded with Bennet and John to help their brother get the job. He understands why she had been so optimistic: Seven years ago, when she'd made the same entreaty to John on his behalf, the arrangement had turned out beautifully. Bennet had thrived in the development department, working his way up to his current position in only four years, an accomplishment that delighted his parents, who, as a personal injury attorney (Dad) and a comparative literature professor (Mom), prize financial security and professional stability.

But Lydon isn't cut from the same cloth as his older siblings, and finding himself gainfully employed at a New York museum hasn't been the sobering experience his parents had intended when they discovered their newly minted philosophy grad had spent six months running up bar tabs at campus haunts. They'd been *told* that he had an office job entering data at a large pharmaceutical company, but the only data he'd entered were women's numbers into his phone.

Although banishment to an obscure outpost in Queens to work for little money had felt like punishment, Lydon quickly recognized it for the reward it was. Not only are there more bars in New York City than Ann Arbor, but they stay open later. Bunking at his brothers' apartments isn't exactly ideal—he's either on John's futon or Bennet's pullout—but both men keep grown-up food in their cabinets (good-bye, ramen!) and their showers have a steady supply of hot water. On a scale of one to his best friend Steve's frequently backed-up toilet, he'd give couch surfing at his brothers' a solid doesn't totally suck.

As a guest, Lydon rates somewhat lower, at pretty sucky, and Bennet is tired of picking up after his youngest brother at home and at work. Because the internship pays a marginal day rate, Lydon's commitment to it is marginal as well. He strolls in every day some time after noon, heads out a little before five, and spends the hours in between reading reviews of the latest technical gadgets he can't afford and texting his friends. Sometimes he'll make a run to pick up office supplies, but he never returns with anything. He simply uses it as an excuse to cut out early on a job he's barely showing up for.

To say that Lydon is driving his brother crazy is to

vastly understate Bennet's tenuous connection to sanity. Having slid past crazy a month ago, he's well into sign-me-up-for-intensive-therapy-with-a-Danish-Jungian territory. In another few weeks, he'll enter lock-me-in-a-padded-room-and-throw-away-the-key country.

That Lydon is lazy and careless comes as no surprise to Bennet, who had lived in the same house with him for thirteen years before leaving for college. The youngest Bethle was always around when there was fun to be had and long gone when it was time to clean up. But it's only in this last month that Bennet's fully grasped the depth of Lydon's irresponsibility—and it worries him. Blowing off this internship is one thing, but sooner or later, Lydon will have to get a proper job in a proper office with proper coworkers, and they're going to expect proper results, not hot air and buffoonery.

To be fair, Lydon isn't entirely without skills, as the young man is remarkably proficient at manipulation. With his easygoing smile and ingratiating personality, he effortlessly wins people to his cause, even their parents, who should know better. Honestly, in what universe is an all-expense-paid trip to New York City a punishment for drunken vagrancy?

Quickly recovering his composure, Lydon turns his talents now to the executive director of the Longbourn. "Mr. Meryton, sir," he says with an easy smile, "just the man I was hoping to find. I have your favorite: iced mocha latte with extra cream."

This information disconcerts Meryton, who's surprised to discover not only that he has a favorite drink from Starbucks but that it's a concoction called an iced mocha latte. Rather than demur and risk bruising the young man's feelings or dampening his enthusiasm, he accepts the cup. "Thank you, Lydon," he says. Cautiously, as if suspicious of the frothy beverage, he breathes in deeply and, finding nothing untoward, takes a sip—and then another and another. If mocha latte with extra cream wasn't his favorite drink before, it certainly is now. "Mmm. Lovely. Just the thing for a pleasant March afternoon. You're doing an excellent job, m'boy. Keep up the good work."

Lydon dips his head modestly. "Thank you, sir. I do my best."

The sad thing is, Bennet knows this exchange does represent Lydon's best, and he doesn't doubt that his feckless brother could make a very good living as a grifter. The legal version of grifting is raising funds for an institution or cause, so it's fitting—or ironic—that Lydon is in the perfect place to get the experience he needs to succeed in the profession for which he's most suited.

Swallowing another large gulp of mocha latte, Meryton marvels at how resistant he'd been to taking on another Bethle brother. Having two already in his employ had seemed sufficient to him, as no executive director of a small cultural institution—or, indeed, a large one—wants to be outnumbered in his own office. But the lure of cheap labor was too tempting to resist and the Bethle track record was too impressive to dismiss, so he agreed to an interview. The meeting had gone well, mostly because Lydon had been savvy enough to answer every question with a compliment and had had the good sense to congratulate Meryton on his Award for Excellence from the National Association of Executive Directors. None of the museum's other staff had noticed the accolade, which, having been hung on his wall in August, could hardly be described as a recent addition to his office.

"As you know, I had my reservations about employing three Bethles, but Lydon here has worked out so well, I think we should hire more," Meryton says, his eyes sparkling with either mischief or the profound happiness that comes from ingesting excellent whipped cream. "If your two remaining brothers are interested in fundraising, please tell them to schedule an appointment with me as soon as possible."

While Bennet shudders in horror at the thought of his whole family crammed into the airless space, Lydon thanks Meryton for what's surely the nicest compliment he's ever received.

"I mean it," Meryton assures him, "one hundred percent."

"We appreciate it," John says, "but our brothers are settled into careers. Mark teaches piano at a boys' school in Detroit, and Kit sells cars at the leading Toyota dealership in Evanston."

"Well, if anything changes, do let me know," Meryton says, taking his new favorite drink into his office.

As soon as he leaves, Bennet turns to Lydon. "You're late again."

"Sorry," Lydon says as he flashes his signature smile—brash and bold with just a hint of bashful. He brushes his dark hair, which falls to his shoulders, behind one ear as he blinks his bright brown eyes innocently. "I was doing some market research in the café. You know, furthering the cause."

"Flirting with pretty tourists only furthers your cause," Bennet says. Even without John's classic good looks, Lydon attracts women like flies. They're drawn to his easygoing manner and flirty bonhomie.

Lydon winks. "Isn't that what I just said?"

Bennet, feeling his temper snap, closes his eyes for a moment and strives for patience. As a brother, Lydon has always been difficult to deal with, but as an employee, he's next to impossible. Nothing would make Bennet happier than sending him home to their parents in disgrace, and the only thing stopping him is the disappointed look his mother would give him—as if Lydon's failures are somehow his fault.

Knowing how close Bennet is to the edge, John jumps in. "Hey, Lydon, can you call Hannah in special events and add Charlotte Bingston to the gala guest list? Let her know she might be bringing as many as eight guests."

"Charlotte Bingston," Lydon repeats thoughtfully, as if the name might mean something to him. "Charlotte Bingston."

Bennet rolls his eyes at this affectation. "You don't know her. She's a socialite, not a reviewer for Gizmodo or C-Net."

"But Bingston. Bingston Reliable makes batteries," he

says with a triumphant snap of his fingers. "Any relation?"

"Yes, actually," John says. "Her father founded the company."

"Ah, then they're rolling in it," Lydon says as a calculating look enters his eye. "Is she pretty?"

"And how is that piece of information relevant to your calling Hannah as John requested?" Bennet asks irritably.

"You can't very well expect me to dance with an ugly heiress," Lydon explains, affronted by the notion. Then he pauses and replays the sentence in his head. "You know what, scratch that. An heiress is an heiress is an heiress. Who am I to quibble? Count me in. I'll totally take one for the team."

Bennet sighs deeply and wonders how upset their mother would be if he strangled her youngest son. Distraught, naturally, but surely some part of her would understand. "For the hundredth time, you're not attending the gala; you're working it. Your job will be to check people in. That means you'll take the list of all the people who R.S.V.P.'d and mark them off as they arrive."

"Yeah, yeah, bro, sounds like a blast," Lydon says with a dismissive wave. He's not even pretending to listen. "Now, if you gentlemen will excuse me, I have an errand to run."

Bennet doesn't know how he can still be surprised by his brother's audacity and yet there it is—amazement. "But you just got here."

"I know. But I gots no coffee." He raises his empty hands as if presenting evidence to a court. "The old man took mine. You saw it," he says before breezing out of the room.

Although the café in the museum's courtyard serves excellent fair-trade, single-origin coffee from an upscale Seattle roaster, Lydon will walk the fifteen minutes to hit the Starbucks on nearby Continental Avenue. "You realize that's the last we've seen of him today," Bennet observes wearily.

John nods. "He just needs a little more time to settle down."

"A little more time?" Bennet asks scornfully. "It's been twenty-three years. How much time do you think he needs?"

"Be fair," John says. "He's only been working with us

for a month. Don't you remember your first month? It's not easy to adjust to the rigors of an office after the freedom of college."

Of course Bennet remembers his first month at the Longbourn. It had been the longest four weeks of his entire life, waiting and hoping and fearing he'd be fired at any moment for various incompetencies, such as emailing their donors list to a journalist at *New York* magazine and spilling iced coffee on the silk dress of the chairwoman of the Patrons Circle Anniversary Committee.

Yes, he'd screwed up royally during his first month—to his lasting mortification—but at least he'd tried to do things right. Despite his inexperience, he made every attempt to perform the tasks assigned to him correctly, and when everything went horribly wrong he apologized profusely and resolved to do better.

The learning curve had indeed been steep for an English literature major who never actually completed his honor's thesis ("Hard Thyme: The Symbolism of Herbs and Plants in the Works of Charles Dickens"), but after a few months, he got the hang of it and stopped embarrassing his brother. That was the most important thing to him—to ensure John never regretted recommending him for the department assistant job. He knew his brother had gone out on a limb for him, for it was highly unusual for siblings to work for the same organization, let alone the same department. If Bennet had continued down the path of ineptitude, things might have become very uncomfortable between the two, but luckily the arrangement had worked out to everyone's benefit.

"It's probably harder for him to see it as a real job because he's getting only a small stipend," John adds.

Bennet has heard the small-stipend argument before—from his mother. "Nobody forced him to take the internship," he says.

Now John smiles. "What else is a twenty-three-year-old with a degree in philosophy going to do? He needs the experience to fill out his résumé. Don't worry. He'll get better.

You'll see."

Bennet shakes his head but doesn't comment, because he knows it's useless to discuss it further—John's Pollyanna spin will hold up under questioning. It always does.

Instead, he swivels toward his computer to read the changes Meryton made to his letter. Bennet is trying to convince Julian Martindale, head of community affairs of Venture Marts, to underwrite a Bauhaus exhibition the museum is planning for next spring. The show will feature the Longbourn's small but significant collection of Werner Drewes prints from the twenties. Gropius, Breuer and Mies Van der Rohe pieces borrowed from other collections will round out the story of the famous German design school. Venture, the second-largest discount retailer in the United States, is the ideal sponsor because its philosophy—good design for the masses—draws on the tenets established by the Bauhaus.

Meryton's draft, with its flagrant disregard for moderation, is like a bright neon sign flashing WE LOVE YOU! Bennet promptly deletes it and opens the original. The executive director's unrestrained style, the way he fawns and flatters, doesn't really work for Bennet, but he understands the appeal and knows that people like Henry Cortland Longbourn respond well to his effusiveness. Rich people like praise and expect attention, which is why Bennet prefers to work with the Julian Martindales of the world, folks who oversee vast sums of money on behalf of corporations. More often than not, they have the same middle-class background as he.

Bennet finishes the letter, attaches a photo of the lone Drewes silkscreen from the proposed exhibition and enters Martindale's email address. As he hits SEND, he hears John pick up the phone and say hello to Hannah in special events.

Once again, it falls to the two responsible Bethle brothers to get the work done.

CHAPTER THREE

The Longbourn Collection's annual gala fundraiser is held every year in the soaring courtyard at the center of the stunning fifteenth-century Venetian-style palace Cyrus Longbourn built at the turn of the twentieth century. Latticed Palladian windows and ornate loggias overlook a tranquil garden of roses and geraniums, giving the spacious enclosure the unreal air of a fairy tale. At any moment, Bennet expects to see Cinderella run across the stone patio in her bare feet.

By every account—*Time Out, The New York Times, The Village Voice,* Mommy Poppins, Fodor's—the courtyard is one of the top ten hidden treasures of New York, and it's Bennet's favorite spot in the entire city. A stillness hangs over it, a silence so pervasive and deep it's hard to believe you're still in New York, even with the incessant chatter of tourists drinking tea at the next table over. During his first month there, he spent every lunch hour on one of the marble benches lining the rose beds, eating egg salad sandwiches and watching people gaze in bemusement at the gorgeous stone edifice, so out of place on the edge of a modern metropolis. He loves their awe, their ability to be surprised and humbled by the unexpected. A Venetian palazzo in the middle of Queens—of all things!

It's this wide-eyed wonder, this bewildered astonishment at Longbourn's beauty and incongruity, that keeps him in Forest Hills despite offers from larger institutions. Bennet could raise money anywhere—he knows the circuit and has the skills—but saving an absurd dream, preserving a ridiculous inconsistency, can only be done here.

Because the museum is so off the beaten path, the board of directors talk every year about moving the gala to a more central location, such as the Starlight Roof at the Waldorf-Astoria. But the best advertisement for the Longbourn is the Longbourn. Few Manhattanites are willing to make the trip, but those who do agree it's worth the effort. The intimacy of the galleries—art displayed in an intensely personal setting—charms visitors, who are used to the austerity of white-box galleries and the intimidating grandness of art museums. This reaction is exactly what Cyrus had intended, for he had designed his museum to contrast sharply with the marble mausoleums of Europe.

Despite its unappealing location, the annual Venetian ball draws a respectable crowd, with many of the guests coming from Long Island to enjoy a glittering night under the stars. The food is always excellent and plentiful, thanks to their caterer, a formerly unknown chef from Bayside who recently opened a restaurant on Prince Street. He's built his reputation on *fegato alla Veneziana* and *seppie col nero*.

The music is also sublime, supplied by twelve industrious Juilliard students who hope to one day play for the New York Philharmonic. Since at least one guest is a trustee of that rarefied institution, the musicians consider this gig to be something of an audition, or an audition for an audition. Couples dance on the patio as music wafts from the second-floor balcony.

Observing how smoothly the event is going—no gate crashers, no drunken brawls, no yipping Maltese smuggled in under the hoop skirt of the borough president's wife, like last year—Bennet allows himself a glass of champagne. Even the weather, which can be chilly in late March, is behaving like a gracious guest, supplying a light northeasterly breeze that's warm enough to make the dozens of heat lamps unnecessary. Gratified, he smiles and snags prosciutto-wrapped melon from a passing tray.

As he eats it, he notes that the elbows on his black tuxedo are starting to fray. He pulls the same one from the back of his closet every year, and despite the care he takes of it, he suspects it's time to invest in a new one.

Thoughtfully, he takes a sip of champagne and surveys the crowd, noting several familiar faces he has yet to greet. What he said to Lydon last week goes double for him—he's not attending the event, he's working it—and in order for him to consider this a good day at the salt mine, he still has to talk to half a dozen contacts.

For the moment, however, he's happy to stand off to the side, drink champagne and people watch. He spots Hannah by the bar, her expression stern as she shakes her head with increasing urgency at the bartender.

"What do you suppose that's about?" he asks his older brother when he joins him along the south wall. John is wearing a tuxedo that's almost identical to his, save for the threadbare arms, but it looks different on him, better, more like a second skin than a costume donned for an evening's performance. With his smooth good looks, John is everything you'd expect from a man in a tuxedo: international playboy, elegant spy, runway model.

John follows his brother's gaze and smiles. "You don't want to know."

"Oh, but I do," he insists, watching Hannah paste a smile on her face as she turns to greet a trustee. She darts a look at the bartender, warning him that their conversation is far from over.

"Olives," John says. "More specifically, the pimientos in the olives. Hannah feels the pimientos are deficient and need to be replaced. The bartender—and here's the surprise twist—agrees that the pimientos are straggly looking and would happily substitute a fresh batch but since these are all they have, he contends they're good enough."

"So really it's an argument about the compromises one is willing to make," Bennet says. "A battle for one's soul, if you will."

"Or, as Hannah sees it, a dispute over who's responsible for picking a substandard supplier."

23

Bennet nods and turns his gaze elsewhere. "Which one is Ms. Bingston?"

John gestures to the ornate balcony, under which five figures in elegant evening wear are observing the proceedings with varying degrees of interest. "In the pink dress."

Bennet nods and zeros in on a pretty blonde with rose-petal lips and wide blue eyes, who is, at that very moment, studying a tray of arancini. She considers her options carefully, selects one and eats it, patting the corners of her mouth daintily with a white napkin. Then she darts after the waiter to get a second.

"She's lovely," Bennet says, charmed by her obvious enthusiasm. Most of the heiresses he meets at museum functions have a jaded air, as if they've done it all before with better service. And to be fair, they probably have, for the Longbourn's annual gala is a staid affair—reliably entertaining, of course, and genuinely pleasant, but without the elaborate trimmings that cause weary hearts to flutter. Mermaids don't frolic in the fountain and waiters don't juggle knives and fairy dust doesn't fall from the sky.

Ms. Bingston's companions seem like the more familiar variety of glitterati. They glance around the courtyard with mildly disdainful looks that indicate a determined unwillingness to be impressed by anything, least of all their surroundings.

It must require some effort, Bennet thinks with sly amusement, to sustain that much contempt.

"Who are the others?" he asks, his attention caught and held by the dark-haired woman behind Charlotte Bingston. Tall, with raven curls that spill over porcelain shoulders, she would be stunningly gorgeous if not for the partial sneer that seems permanently affixed to her face. Even with it, she's beautiful enough to stop traffic.

"The two men are her brothers, Carl and Hurst Bingston. Hurst is the taller one. Next to him is his wife, Lucy, and behind Ms. Bingston is Darcy Fitzwilliam, a friend of the family," John says.

"Darcy Fitzwilliam," Bennet repeats softly. "Why does that name sound familiar?"

"Because she's wealthy, sought after and famous," John says mildly. "Her great-grandfather was nineteenth-century land magnate Earl Fitzwilliam. She owns a large mansion on Fifth Avenue, along with several other properties, and is reputed to be worth around $900 million. Her aunt Catherine de Bourgh is a great patron of the arts. She's never paid any attention to us but gives millions to the Met and the American Ballet Theatre."

Accustomed to lavish wealth and the privileges it affords, Bennet takes another look at Darcy Fitzwilliam and decides her scorn is perfectly in keeping with her person. He's never met her aunt—indeed, he hasn't been afforded the pleasure—but he has heard a great deal about her from colleagues at other institutions. A notoriously difficult woman who demands graciousness and affability but offers neither in return, she considers the vast majority of the human race to be well beneath her notice.

Bennet watches Darcy tilt her head to the side to hear Carl Bingston more clearly. She nods twice, then flashes a smile, and for a brief moment, the sneer is gone, replaced by a mischievous grin. To his surprise, Bennet finds himself smiling, too.

"Does Meryton know?" he asks, imagining the joy with which the executive director of the Longbourn would greet the news. Luckily, the courtyard is too crowded for cartwheels.

Before John can answer, the gentleman in question appears beside them, his eyes glittering with an excitement he can barely contain. "Have you heard? Nine hundred million."

Meryton speaks slowly, for emphasis, and just loud enough to make Bennet cringe. Yes, everyone knows a fundraiser is about raising funds, but nobody is so gauche as to actually discuss money. That business is left to the administrative assistants and the lawyers.

"Nine hundred million," Meryton says again, as if he can scarcely bring himself to believe it. The good fortune of the Fitzwilliam fortune seems too serendipitous to be true. "The scion of the Fitzwilliam real estate empire at our humble little fête! Fitzwilliam Company owns 25,000 apartments, 262 office properties, twenty-three shopping centers, twelve golf courses, five marinas and one hotel. I'm speechless with wonder."

But of course he isn't. Meryton has much more to say, and he insists on introducing himself to Bingley's party at once, so he can get on with saying it immediately.

Bennet glances at the small group, which, aside from Ms. Bingston, appears self-contained and forbidding. "They arrived only recently. We should allow them a few minutes to get their bearings."

Meryton scoffs. "Get their bearings? What nonsense. They're attending a party, not a wilderness training course. Look, they're coming our way. They must want to introduce themselves."

Although this statement is patently false—the group is walking in the opposite direction, toward the marble benches of the rose garden—Meryton scurries after them with his hand raised in greeting. With a helpless look at his brother, Bennet follows. John trails two steps behind.

By the time Meryton catches up with the Bingston party, he's out of breath and panting heavily. His portly frame isn't made for long dashes across courtyards.

"Ms. Bingston," he gasps, laying a hand on her shoulder as he interrupts her conversation, "it is a huge pleasure. I'm Mr. Meryton, executive director the Longbourn." He pauses briefly, inhales sharply, then continues. "Ever since your assistant said you were coming tonight, I've been looking forward to this moment with such enthusiasm. Some people cautioned me to keep my excitement in check, but I knew you would not let me down and here you are, exceeding my expectations with your illustrious self and your guest. Such a guest! I'm thrilled to meet you."

Although taken aback by this forceful and unexpected intrusion, Ms. Bingston smiles brightly and offers her hand. "I'm pleased to meet you as well."

Meryton beams. "Please allow me to introduce my colleagues. John Bethle and his brother Bennet. They're the directors of individual and corporate giving, respectively."

The young blond man standing to Bingley's right sighs loudly and rolls his eyes, and Bennet, knowing exactly what he's thinking, wonders why he bothered coming to the gala at all. There are two dozen things to do in New York City on an early-spring evening that don't require a tedious trek across the East River.

Ms. Bingston shows none of her companion's disrespect. Rather, she tilts her head to the side and raises an eyebrow speculatively. "John Bethle? Aren't you the one who sent me the remarkable gift basket?"

"I am," John says, surprised that she not only saw the note but read it as well. "I'm glad you liked it."

She smiles widely, revealing a dimple in her left cheek that John finds very endearing. "Liked it? I adored it. I'm still working on the truffles, but the rugelach are entirely gone. We ate the whole box in one sitting. I'd never had rugelach before, and as soon as I took the first bite, I looked at the box and said, 'Where have you been my whole life?' Didn't I, Darcy?" she asks, turning to her friend, who doesn't appear to be listening to the conversation. "I don't usually address comments directly to the pastries, but I couldn't resist, they were *that* delicious. Oh, how remiss of me. I haven't introduced anyone. This is my friend Darcy Fitzwilliam, and these are my brothers, Carl and Hurst and Hurst's wife, Lucy."

Although the members of Bingston's party are too well-bred to flat-out ignore their hosts, they immediately avert their gazes after the niceties are performed, and an awkward silence follows. Meryton, whose chatter can usually be relied on to fill a void, any void, is busy retrieving the data he has on the Bingston brothers. They both, if he's remembering correctly, purport to be men of business, investing in various concerns that have caught their eye. Hurst, the elder, owns stock in a company that helps businesses keep track of their legal bills, and Carl holds shares in Sutton & Grey, a custom clothier. Although they have liquid assets, the majority of their wealth is tied up in investments—unlike their sister's.

While Meryton calculates the Bingstons' relative value, John says, "The rugelach are from a bakery down the block. Bonelle. It's on Ascan, right off Austin. I'm sure you could arrange delivery to Manhattan. Or, better yet, why don't I send you another box?"

Ms. Bingston's smile widens as she shakes her head. "You don't have to go through the trouble of all that."

But John is already one step ahead of her, making a notation in his phone. "I assure you, Ms. Bingston, it's no trouble at all. In fact, it's my pleasure."

"All right, but if you're going to be my rugelach dealer, then you must call me Bingley."

"Thank God that's sorted," Carl says with more vehemence than Bennet would expect from a man working so hard to appear uninterested in the conversation. "Maybe now she'll talk about something other than the rugelach. The way she's been going on, you'd think it was caviar from the very last Beluga whale on earth. They were just cookies."

Bingley laughs at her brother's tantrum. "He's dismissive now, but he fought me over the last piece."

"I was hungry," he says peevishly, "and the croissants were stale."

As his sister declares the croissant story a red herring, Bennet looks at Ms. Fitzwilliam, who, like Mr. Carl Bingston, has perfected the glassy-eyed stare of the outrageously bored. Bennet doesn't question the sincerity of her tedium, for he imagines it runs very deep indeed, but he still resents its blatant demonstration. It's a measure of her disrespect, he thinks, that she doesn't even try to hide it. If the Met Gala bored her to tears, she'd paste a smile on her face and insist she was fascinated.

Determined to draw her into the conversation—mostly out of spite, he readily admits—Bennet pastes on his own smile and says, "What about you, Ms. Fitzwilliam? Did you like the rugelach?"

Without raising her eyes to meet his or even tilting her head in his general direction, Darcy says no. The single syllable hangs in the air, heavy and flat, for several seconds, creating an uncomfortable silence. Bennet knows he should say something to break the awkwardness, but he's too irritated by her rudeness to make the effort. He holds his peace and waits to see what she'll do next.

But Meryton, with a confused, sideward glance at his director of corporate giving, acts first. "Your enthusiasm is refreshing, Ms. Bingston. We could certainly use someone with your energy and ideas on our Golden Diamond Circle Advisory Board. We host many wonderful events attended by some of the most important and influential people in New York, and we're always hoping to enlist enthusiastic newcomers. If you're interested in chairing the committee, we'd love to discuss it with you in greater depth."

Bingley dimples charmingly and, assuring Meryton she'd love to hear more, instructs him to call her assistant Mitzy to set up an appointment. Then she turns to John. "Mr. Bethle, 'It Had to Be You' is one of my favorite songs. Would you be so kind as to indulge me?"

The look of surprise on John's face is almost comical, and he stares at her outstretched hand as if not sure what to do with it. Should he shake it? Give it a high five? Finally, he says, "Yes. Yes, of course. I'd be delighted."

Jubilant, Meryton watches the pair cross to the dance floor, so elegant in their finery, so well matched in their beauty. Glowing with triumph, revving with expectation, he turns to Darcy to win her over as well.

"I cannot tell you what a thrill it is to meet you, Ms. Fitzwilliam," he says fawningly. "Had I known you were in New York, we would have sent you a welcome basket, too. At the Longbourn, we're very fond of the esteemed de Bourgh family. Your aunt Catherine de Bourgh, a majestic woman if I ever saw one, is a dedicated patron of the arts. No doubt you'd like to continue the great family tradition. I'm happy to discuss your chairing a committee as well."

Darcy's expression doesn't change—her brow doesn't wrinkle, her lips don't purse—but Bennet can feel her disgust. It's as if she's radiating repugnance. How dare this upstart beggar have the impudence to talk about her family?

"Excuse me," she says stiffly and walks away. The

remaining members of the Bingston party follow closely at her heels.

"Of course," Meryton says to her receding back. "We'll pick this up later."

But the executive director never does pick it up later, because even he is daunted by Darcy's unfriendliness. Instead, he contents himself with one triumph for the evening, for what a triumph it is. John and Bingley dance together for twenty-two minutes. Almost a full half hour! They only stop when the Juilliard students take a break.

"I have a good feeling about this," Meryton says to Bennet as he watches John hand a flute of champagne to Bingley.

Although his boss is prone to having good feelings about things that never come to pass, Bennet must concede that the relationship between his brother and Bingley seems inordinately promising. John's handsome face and unassuming nature make him a favorite among their female patrons, but he's always treated them with a sort of indifferent kindness—easy smile, amiable conversation, affable banter.

But now he's different.

Pleased by the development on a personal level, not professional, Bennet scans the courtyard for Julian Martindale, with whom he has yet to connect, and finds him by the grand marble staircase that leads to the second-floor loggia.

"It's from a piazza overlooking the Rialto," Bennet explains as he approaches the director of community affairs at Venture. "They had to bring it over in three parts. If you stand on the fourth and ninth steps, you can see the seams."

Julian runs his hands over the smooth balustrade. "It's gorgeous. Actually, the whole place is. I was just exploring the galleries on the first floor. The Degas over the fireplace is magnificent."

Bennet knows it: a trio of ballerinas in startlingly bright pink dresses standing to one side of the stage.

"There are more Degas ballerinas on the third floor," Bennet says. "I'd be happy to show them to you."

"I'd love to see them. I was just saying to my assistant

that we should come back for the ten-cent tour during business hours to get the full experience."

Bennet thinks this interest is a very good sign, but he doesn't let himself get excited. There are still a dozen steps between the ten-cent tour and a generous check. "Excellent. I'll arrange it with your office in the morning. I can show you some sketches for our show on Impressionism, fashion and modernity, which is opening next month. It's in a different space than the Bauhaus exhibition but will still give you a sense of how our curators work."

"Sounds great," Julian says as the orchestra, returning from its dinner break, plays the opening strains of "I've Got You Under My Skin."

"I was about to get myself another drink," Bennet says, noting the other man's empty glass. "Can I interest you in a refill?"

"That would be wonderful," he says. "I'm drinking gimlets. Vodka."

On the way to the bar, Bennet passes the mopesy twins, who are brimming with disapproval on the edge of the dance floor.

"Does this even rise to the level of Venetian kitsch?" Carl asks Darcy with dismissive scorn. "I mean, all this fake Italian architecture is so sincere it makes my teeth ache. I want to laugh, but it's too sad. All I can manage is a sigh of pity."

During his seven-year tenure, Bennet has heard the building described negatively on many occasions. Paul Goldberger of *The New Yorker*, reviewing the renovation that had wrapped up in the late aughts, lamented the lack of canals sufficient to the grandeur of the Longbourn and suggested the building be relocated to the Gowanus, a former industrial waterway so polluted it had been deemed a Superfund site.

But there's something about Carl's derision that makes his comments harder to swallow than Goldberger's proposal to move the museum to a toxic waste dump. It's his blanket superiority that's so galling, Bennet thinks as he turns abruptly to confront the supercilious young man. It's the smug knowingness of his tone and its elemental meanness.

Bennet's hand is in the air, his index finger only inches from Carl's shoulder, when the inappropriateness of his intentions strikes him. He can't go around castigating guests for their opinions.

Mortified, he pretends to swat a fly and drops his hand.

By the time he reaches the bar, he's calmed down, but seeing Lydon hanging on the arm of a petite redhead in a diamond choker irritates him all over again. Carefully, Bennet extricates his brother from the fortysomething donor's French-manicured grasp and sends him back to the door. He realizes it's unlikely Lydon will stay there, but short of posting a guard at the front table, which the Longbourn hasn't budgeted for, he doesn't know what he can do to make him stay put.

Worse comes to worst, I can always have him thrown out of the party, Bennet thinks as he orders a vodka gimlet for Julian. Although he knows it's not a viable solution, simply having the option improves his mood, and he spends the next hour energetically mixing with donors. With his quick wit and memory for detail, he finds conversing with acquaintances and strangers to be the easiest part of his job.

He's asking a real estate developer about his recent safari in Tanzania when he hears Bingley's elegant alto: "Seriously, Darcy, you have to dance. You can't stand here by yourself all night glaring at everyone. You look ridiculous."

Having observed the sulky heiress's glare for more than an hour, Bennet is amused by her friend's entreaty, and he glances around to discover their location—four feet in front of him and off to the right. Immediately, he turns back to the mogul and compliments his daring in climbing Kilimanjaro.

"It wasn't very daring," Roberto says before launching into a detailed explanation of the many hazards he'd faced. Bennet nods attentively but keeps one ear trained on the other conversation.

"I certainly will not," Darcy says. "I hate dancing with strangers, which you very well know. And, really, look at this crowd."

"What's wrong with this crowd?" Bingley asks, genuinely mystified.

"It's scruffy," Darcy says.

"Scruffy?"

"Scruffy," she says again before deigning to explain. "Half the women are wearing last year's couture, and the other half aren't wearing couture at all. Take that woman over there in the tartan skirt."

"That's a man in a kilt."

"Exactly," Darcy says with satisfaction. "Kilts went out with goatees. Where are we? In 2005? Let me get my peasant top and chunky highlights."

"Kilts are timeless," Bingley says. "You're just being difficult. There are dozens of attractive men you could dance with."

Darcy snorts—at least, Bennet identifies it as a snort. "Easy for you to say, you're dancing with the only handsome one here."

"Omigod! Is he not the most beautiful creature you've ever seen?" Bingley asks with a delighted chuckle. "What about his brother? He's behind you. I think he's very good looking."

"Which do you mean?" Darcy asks and turns around to look at Bennet, who, unwilling to be caught eavesdropping, quickly averts his gaze. But the pull of curiosity is too strong and he raises his head again to find himself staring into Darcy's eyes. Immediately, she turns away and says, "He's all right, but not handsome enough to interest me. And even so, I'd probably have to listen to another Golden Diamond Precious Metal Very Important Committee pitch, and I can't imagine anything more tedious. Development types are always begging for something. You might as well give up, as you're wasting your time."

Bingley sighs and follows her friend's advice.

"Ultimately, altitude sickness is what does people in," Roberto says, drawing Bennet's attention back to their conversation. "I wasn't bothered by it, which is no great surprise—last year I climbed the Inca trail and didn't notice the altitude. I think a lot of that comes from preparedness training. Too many people hop on a plane without thinking about the rigors of adventure travel."

Bennet nods as if he himself has noticed this particular trend, and, encouraged, the developer recounts the many challenges of climbing the Inca trail. Midway through the retelling, Meryton interrupts to thank Roberto for his generous donation to their summer program, and Bennet excuses himself to check on Lydon. As he walks to the entrance area, he passes Darcy and, feeling particularly uncordial toward her, darts her a peeved look. He can't care less about what one rude heiress thinks of him, and yet he feels the sharp sting of irritation at her comments.

It's ego, he thinks.

Bennet's ego is still feeling the prick three hours later when he sits down with John in the quiet courtyard to have a celebratory beer. The caterers are carrying out the last of their crates, and the cleanup crew is sweeping the floor. Hannah, her auburn hair pulled back in a sturdy bun, is directing the effort.

"To us," John says as he clanks his beer bottle against Bennet's. "Another gala fundraiser over and nobody tried to scale the wall to the balcony."

"Here, here," his brother says, taking a long sip of the cold brew. "And Lydon didn't elope with a divorcee."

John smiles. "That's right, he didn't."

"And Meryton didn't ask a single woman to donate her diamond earrings."

"Another check in the win column," John says.

"And you met a fabulous woman," Bennet adds.

John opens his mouth to cheer again, but nothing comes out as the substance of his brother's remark hits him. Although his instinct is to protest, he shrugs, smiles and turns slightly pink. "She's great, isn't she? Funny, smart, clever, down to earth."

"Rich," Bennet adds, rounding out the list, "beautiful."

John doesn't hear him. "I was shocked when she asked me to dance. I mean, yeah, the rugelach was good, but it wasn't that good."

Bennet laughs. Even after twenty-eight years, he's still

amazed by his older brother's lack of vanity. "I don't think she asked you to dance because of the rugelach."

Uncomfortable with the implication, John dips his head and examines the label on the bottle. "Her brothers seemed nice, a little standoffish at first but all right once you got them talking."

Bennet shrugs, unable to conceive what it would take to get the disdainful Carl talking. He doesn't doubt that his brother could do it—John's good nature and sincere enthusiasm can overcome even the most entrenched churlishness—but it seems like an awful lot of effort for very little reward.

But he would bite off his own tongue before offering any criticism of Bingley's family. He doesn't want to dull the luster in his brother's eyes.

"Did you talk to Darcy?" John asks.

Now Bennet speaks freely. "Did anyone? She swatted away all comers with a scornful flick of the wrist. She even swatted me away before I could make the mistake of approaching," he says, giving his brother a rundown of Bingley's conversation with Darcy.

By the time he's done, they're both laughing.

"Clearly, she didn't recognize Mickey Kiminski in his finery," John says, naming the famous stand-up comedian whose trademark fashion statement is a kilt.

"No, but even so, I don't think she would be very impressed. New money."

John shakes his head and admits he didn't have any luck with Darcy either. "It's strange that Bingley is friends with her. She's so outgoing and affable, and Darcy is quiet and withdrawn."

"If by quiet and withdrawn, you mean moody and sullen, then I wholeheartedly agree," Bennet says before suggesting they head out—Meryton will soon return from collecting his things in the office. Neither brother has the energy or the inclination for an immediate and longwinded debrief of the evening. The morning is soon enough.

CHAPTER FOUR

The first thing Darcy Fitzwilliam noticed about Bennet Bethle was his eyes. Golden brown and fringed with long, dark lashes, they seem to hold an expression of perpetual amusement, as if everything makes him laugh.

There were, she concedes thoughtfully as she climbs into the black town car waiting for her by the curb in front of Pemberley, her ancestral home on Fifth Avenue, many funny things at last night's gala. The building, for example: how strange to turn the corner of a leafy New York street and see the Ca' d'Oro, with its delicate crenellations and inflected arches, towering over suburban basketball nets and Range Rovers. She can't imagine anything more out of place, except, perhaps, herself.

It's just like her friend to insist they attend a Venetian-themed party at a faux palazzo on the other side of the river, to not consider—or not care—about the tacit commitment her attendance implied. Bingley, with her outgoing nature and her adventurous spirit, is always game for a new experience. She doesn't mind fussy little men making claims on her money, time and connections.

Darcy does, and as she stood on the edge of the dance floor, she'd counted the many ways the event displeased her. Where Bingley had looked and seen a crowd of friendly, interesting people, she'd seen only a collection of unremarkable bores: provincial climbers with social aspirations as high as their hair, sporting Jackie O pearls and estate sale diamonds.

Naturally, that fussy little man—oh, what was his name, Merydale, Meryvale, Merydon?—had asked Bingley to chair some ridiculous social committee. Fussy little men, with their hunger and unquenchable desire for more money, always do. This one had been particularly absurd, with his inconsequential chatter and nervous twitter. The details of the actual conversation escape her now. All she can remember is being ambushed almost immediately upon arriving by the usual assortment of development types and being bored out of her mind. Rugelach. Blah, blah, blah.

And that, perhaps, was the funniest thing from the previous evening: how quickly she'd become fascinated by a man she had no recollection of meeting. When Bingley suggested she dance with the other Bethle brother, Darcy had had no idea whom she meant, and when she turned to look—without admiration—she found nothing familiar about his face or form.

But no sooner had she written him off as another mindless lackey than she'd noticed the keen intelligence in his dark eyes. Other disturbing observations followed. She noted his broad shoulders and tall, lithe build. His face, which she'd dismissed as plain, suddenly seemed to be a beguiling combination of hard angles: the strong jaw, the high cheek bones, the straight nose. She liked the sound of his laughter, deep and vibrant and alive.

She began to follow him around the courtyard. She told herself it was a game to alleviate her boredom, but the real reason was, she wanted to know more about him. His conversations were enlightening. He had a lively sense of humor and gave his opinion freely without wondering how it would be received, something she admired and didn't expect from a perpetual supplicant. Sticking to your guns and pleading for money rarely go hand in hand.

At one point, he approached a beleaguered-looking redhead and offered to remove all the pimientos from the olives, listing, as proof of his qualification, a childhood skill at the game of Operation. He then held up a pair of tweezers and asked to see the patient.

"I mean, patients," he amended, "unless the offending pimiento acted alone."

The woman laughed and assured him surgery was not necessary.

Darcy didn't understand the substance of the conversation, but she liked the tone with which it was conducted, and by the time she left the party, she was well on the way to being enthralled.

But that was then, Darcy tells herself as her car pulls up in front of the Netherfield, and this is now. Now she refuses to let herself dwell on the baffling events of the night before. Whatever strange magic was in effect— whatever bewildering mix of champagne, moonlight and Forest Hills air had created the sensation—it's in the past.

As she waits in the lobby for the elevator, she settles into this thought, for surely her fascination with Bennet Bethle is as much of an anomaly as the Longbourn itself. He certainly has none of the traits she looks for in a date—worldliness, urbanity, professional success—and if they were to, say, go out for dinner together, she couldn't imagine what they'd find to talk about. The conversation would be stiff, stifling and awkward.

Pleased to have dismissed Bennet Bethle entirely, Darcy enters the penthouse with a cheerful hello and drops her bag by the front door. She finds Bingley in the front parlor, a gracious room with gilded mirrors, mahogany bookcases and handmade Persian rugs. Although Darcy is also staying at the Netherfield while her Fifth Avenue mansion undergoes renovations, she's the only occupant who's been up since the break of dawn. She's already had two business meetings—one with the contractor working on Pemberley, one with the management company that oversees her Manhattan real estate holdings—and inspected a work site on the Lower East Side.

"Darcy," Bingley says, her voice ringing with excitement, "was that not just the most wonderful party last night? We were just talking about how much fun we had."

Her brother Carl, who's sitting next to her on the sofa, scowls at her description of their conversation. "You were talking about how much fun you had. I was politely holding my tongue, Hurst was reading the newspaper, and Lucy was texting with her chiropractor."

"I was reading the paper and holding my tongue," Hurst says from the comfort of a deep, leather armchair by the window. "I'm multitalented."

His wife, who's perched on the ottoman by his feet, concurs. "As am I," she explains, holding up her phone. "I was texting with Sarah and playing Words with Friends. On the matter of last night, I have no thoughts to hold back, as I've already forgotten everything."

"Ignore them," Bingley says as she slides over on the sofa to make room for Darcy. "Carl is grumpy because the model he was moving in on shut him down at the end of the evening. He gave her his searing your-place-or-mine look, and she laughed." She lifts a silver tray with an assortment of pastries. "The croissants are excellent, as are the Danish. I think the apple strudel is a little off."

"It was a cough," Carl says defensively. "The woman had a cold."

Bingley pats him on the back. "Of course she did, darling."

Carl darts his sister a dirty look and stands up, while Darcy tears off a piece of a croissant. "I thought the party was a dead bore," she announces.

"Brava, Darcy," Carl says with an approving nod.

"Since even Darcy is piling on, I now feel compelled to admit I didn't have the worst time in the world," Hurst says, "and Lucy liked the bright purple drink. What did they call it? The Loggia? The Doge?"

"That's right, I did like it," his wife says wonderingly. "I had five or six."

Bingley smiles. "I think we've gotten to the bottom of the mystery of why you can't remember anything."

Carl shakes his head. "Impossible. They were watering down the drinks, I'm sure of it. Places like that are always cutting corners. Lucy is a lightweight. If they weren't skimming on the alcohol, she would have been dancing in the imitation Trevi fountain by the end of the night."

"Trevi?" Lucy asks. "I thought it was a copy of the Fontana delle Rane."

"If she was seeing frogs on that fountain," her husband

says thoughtfully, "the drinks had more rum than Carl is giving them credit for."

"You jaded grumps can grouse all you want," Bingley says, reaching for another cheese Danish, "but I had a marvelous time and I'm very glad we went."

Carl leans against the back of the sofa and lays his hand on his sister's shoulder. "Miss Sunshine over here can't see beyond the nose of her handsome new man."

"And can you blame her? It's a remarkably handsome nose," Lucy says. "One rarely sees a nose more handsome. Don't you agree, Darcy?"

Darcy nods. "As far as appendages go, it's quite perfect, as is the face it's attached to. But he smiles too much."

"Excuse me?" Bingley asks, her jaw almost dropping at this observation.

"He smiles too much," her friend says again.

Finding the observation entirely childish, Bingley responds in kind and sticks out her tongue.

"She's right," insists Carl, who, in his never-ending quest to earn Darcy's favor, rushes to validate her statement. The more he agrees with her, the more likely she is to agree with him, and eventually they'll make their way to the altar in agreeable cordiality. Although the plan has yet to deliver results after several years, Carl remains optimistic. "Every time I looked over, he had a wide grin on his face. But I liked him. He follows soccer. He knew the name of every starting player for Tottenham."

"And he has a good grasp on finance," Hurst adds. "He had some surprising insights on how Basel III will affect international markets."

"I appreciate your approval," Bingley says sardonically to her brothers, "even if Darcy withholds hers."

"You have mine, as well," Lucy says, "and I think you should make your move immediately. A straight man who wears a tuxedo that well is a hot commodity in this city."

Bingley dimples and leans against the sofa cushions. "I was thinking of sending him clam chowder from the Summer Shack, because, you know, he sent me all those lovely foods from Queens. Or is that pushy?"

"You slut," Darcy says mildly.

"No, it's good," Lucy says. "Putting a condom in with the chowder—that's slutty."

Hurst rustles the paper he's reading. "Really, Lucy, you must stop talking about my sister and condoms in the same breath. This is the third time in a week."

His wife smiles. "You want her to be safe, don't you?"

As much as Bingley appreciates her sister-in-law's feedback, it's Darcy's opinion she values the most, and she turns to her friend. "Truly, what do you think?"

Darcy lifts the coffeepot and fills her mug with the rich, steaming brew. "There's no harm in having a little fun. Send the chowder," she says, causing her friend to squeal with delight and leap to her feet. "But don't do it now. I've reserved a court for ten, and it's already nine thirty."

Bingley wrinkles her brow consideringly. "Are you sure we can't push tennis back twenty minutes while I make some calls? If I want the chowder to arrive today, I don't have any time to lose."

"Absolutely not," Darcy says with a firm shake of her head. With the renovations on Pemberley hitting an unexpected snag—damn those nineteenth-century water pipes!—she's in New York sooner than she'd planned, and business matters that had been back-burnered while she was in London are suddenly front and center. Although she's not involved in the day-to-day management of the family business, she's required as a shareholder to attend several meetings a year and to vote on an ongoing slate of business issues. In addition to Fitzwilliam's and her own properties, she oversees half a dozen initiatives to alleviate poverty around the world. Every day isn't jam-packed with appointments and obligations like they are for her real-estate-tycoon cousins, but many days are—and today in particular. "I have a meeting with my lawyer at eleven-thirty. If you throw enough money at them, the Shack will have the chowder here by noon. You can figure it out with Mitzy in the car. Now go change."

"All right," Bingley says, throwing the rest of the Danish into her mouth before running off.

Carl watches his sister disappear up the stairs and sits next to Darcy. "Thank you for taking her away. She's been intolerably chipper all morning."

Knowing how easily her friend falls in and out of love, Darcy shrugs. "It'll pass."

"I suppose," Carl says, "but how often will we have to visit that crumbling eyesore before it does? How many times will we have to meet with that awful man he works for? Have you ever heard so much nonsensical blather in your life? And the way he looked at Bingley—and you, for that matter—with such an avaricious gleam in his eye. It was as if he were taking a bath in your money."

Darcy both smiles and shudders at the image Carl's description calls forth. She knows a proper museum would never suffer a fool like that, and the fact that the Longbourn does counts against it and its other employees. They must all be cut from the same cloth, she thinks, even Bennet Bethle.

"I googled them," Carl announces. "I got enough information from John to look them up. His father is a litigation lawyer specializing in personal injury. His firm has a garish website announcing how much money they've won in settlements for their clients. He's currently running an ad to scare up more plaintiffs in a class action suit related to mesothelioma and asbestos. Classic ambulance chasing. And get this: One of the uncles is a used-car dealer. He's fairly successful, with several locations in Illinois and Indiana, but still: used cars." He shakes his head with wonder.

Darcy nods absently as Carl continues to report on his findings—"The mother teaches a comp lit course on nineteenth-century pornography at a small college in Michigan"—but finding it oddly difficult to listen to him, she excuses herself to change into her tennis whites. She already knows Bennet Bethle is unsuitable and doesn't require a catalog of his shortcomings to confirm it. He's nothing to her anyway.

Nothing at all.

And yet, as Darcy climbs the stairs to her room, she can't help picturing his fine brown eyes.

CHAPTER FIVE

The arrival of the clam chowder changes everything. Before the messenger knocked lightly on the door to deliver the insulated foam package, Meryton had been content to rest on his laurels, reviewing the triumphs of the previous evening in glorious detail.

Bingley: "Such a delightful young lady."

Bingley and John: "Her eyes lit up the moment I introduced him. The spark of interest—I always know it when I see it."

Bingley and John again: "Every time I looked over, the two of them were dancing. She didn't dance with anyone else for so long or so often, although once I spotted her dancing with Mrs. Long's son. However, that was to 'Moon River,' which, as you know, is an inordinately short song."

Bingley and John some more: "What a gracious departure! I do believe she kissed him twice, once on each cheek, European-style, and only shook hands with Mrs. Long's son."

Darcy: "Horrid."

But the moment Meryton discovers that the package is from Bingley, he sets his sights on the future. "You must strike while the iron is hot, my boy. There's no time to lose. Call her right now and thank her for the present and suggest a meeting to discuss her work on our committee. Don't mention a specific dollar figure yet. Let's gauge her interest before settling on an amount to solicit."

"Naturally, I'll thank her right away," John says as he removes several dozen packing peanuts and two frozen gel packs.

Lydon picks up the note card, which his brother had dropped on the desk. "It's not rugelach." He tilts his head and furrows his brow as if deciphering a great mystery. "What does that mean?"

Amused by Bingley's piquant sense of humor and the eagerness on John's face, Bennet snags the card from Lydon's hand and tells him it's none of his business.

"Au contraire, mon frère," Lydon says with a smug grin. "I work here. This is a work establishment, wherein we work—a fact I've been reminded of a hundred times, even though last night John was allowed to dance, an activity expressly forbidden to me, a worker in this work establishment. Instead, I was forced to stand by the entrance watching for gate crashers, of which there were none. Zilch. Zero. It was so boring, I actually started begging neighbors who were passing by to come in. There were no takers, by the way. You guys should do more community outreach."

Meryton listens to just enough of Lydon's speech to gain further respect for the boy's work ethic—he's a worker indeed!—but his attention is quickly diverted by the contents of the box.

"Clam chowder," he marvels as John extracts two quarts of creamy New England clam chowder. "What can it mean? Is it code? Is Ms. Bingston trying to tell us something?"

Bennet examines the label on one of the containers and says, "I believe she's thanking him for the basket of homegrown treats with a homegrown treat of her own. It's from a little shop in Boston."

John stares bemusedly at the package, a quizzical furl between his brows, and then he stands up. "I have to thank her."

For a moment, Bennet thinks John intends to walk over to the Netherfield to express his gratitude in person, but then he realizes he's merely going into the storage closet to make the call in private. Accustomed to the tight workspace, the brothers easily conduct museum business well within earshot of each other, and that John feels compelled to speak with Bingley in private strikes him as an interesting development.

While Meryton draws up an equation to figure out how much money Bingley should donate for the Diamond Gold Circle Advisory Board position—a mathematical formula as complex as the algorithm for breeding cattle—Lydon grabs one of the soup containers and opens the top drawer of John's desk.

"What are you doing?" Bennet asks.

"Having lunch," Lydon says, removing a clipboard to get a better look at the drawer's contents. A moment later, he holds a spoon aloft triumphantly. "It's after two, right? I'm allowed to eat." In the bottom drawer, he finds a red melamine bowl.

Bennet puts the quarts of chowder back into the box they arrived in and places the package on top of the file cabinet. Lydon eyes his brother sullenly. The soup is a work dividend, he argues, i.e., the product of John's efforts on behalf of the museum the night before. "The spoils of our toils," he adds with an impish grin. "The perks of our works."

Although Bennet doesn't doubt that John would happily share the chowder, he thinks he should have the opportunity to offer. "I have a sandwich if you're really hungry."

"What kind?"

"Egg salad."

Lydon scrunches his nose. "Uh, no. The only thing worse is tuna fish. I'll check out the café downstairs. Tell John not to finish the soup while I'm gone."

Given that his brother's lunch breaks are typically two hours long, Bennet thinks it's highly unlikely there will be soup left when he gets back. But all he says is, "You got it."

Before Lydon leaves, however, John steps out of the closet and gently closes the door. "I'm going to go over there now," he says with a hesitant smile. "To the Netherfield. Bingley would like to hear more about the committee. She asked me to bring information."

As the director of individual giving, John has a packet

of neatly organized, professionally laid-out brochures and fact sheets with color pie charts and graphs, and he quickly pulls one of these from his middle drawer. Meryton, convinced that too much is never enough, runs to the row of file cabinets and pulls together a stack of all their exhibit catalogs and floor plans from the last ten—no, fifteen—years. He hands them to John, who pretends to put them into his briefcase but dumps them into the garbage can under his desk as soon as his boss looks away. Then he catches Bennet's eye and says, "Later, can you…?"

John trails off suggestively, but his brother knows exactly what he means and promises to take care of it. Oblivious to the byplay, Meryton insists on including five years' worth of invitations, both to gala events and exhibition openings, and rummages haphazardly through the file cabinets.

Although John's packet already contains a thoughtful selection of invitations, as well as program guides and the collection's quarterly magazine, he accepts the new stack from Meryton and thanks the executive director for his diligence. Then he tosses them into the trash bin with the others and winks at Bennet.

By the time John leaves fifteen minutes later for Netherfield on the Park, half the contents of the file cabinets are under his desk, Meryton is glowing with excitement, and Lydon, having accurately assessed the level of distraction getting his brother out the door would provide, is finishing his second bowl of chowder. The empty container is next to the microwave.

Annoyed, Bennet waits for Meryton to return to his office and holds out the garbage can filled with assorted publications. "Refile these."

"Seriously, bro?" Lydon asks, his tone caught between disbelief and disappointment. "That's your retribution? Making me file the trash? Doesn't that strike you as a little petty?"

"It's not trash. John had nowhere else to put it," Bennet explains.

"Nowhere else?" Lydon repeats doubtfully, as he looks at the wall of file cabinets.

"Never mind. Just file everything."

Recognizing his brother's stubborn tone, he says, "Sure. After I finish lunch."

Bennet takes the remaining quart of clam chowder and stashes it in his desk drawer with the frozen gel packs it came with. "You're done with lunch."

"Cool," Lydon says with a smile. "Then I'll go get a fresh shot of espresso to fire me up for my very important task."

His brother shakes his head. "File."

"Yeesh," Lydon says, rolling his eyes. But he takes the can, filled with brochures, invitations, magazines and program guides, and starts looking through the files for the right month and year of each publication. He closes the drawers with more force than necessary, but Bennet doesn't rise to the provocation. Instead, he sits at his desk and begins writing follow-up emails to all the current and potential funders who came to the party. Even though it's almost three in the afternoon, he's barely had a chance to glance at his email all day. Every time he'd settled into a task, Meryton had interrupted with another fond remembrance.

It always amuses Bennet how quickly his boss's ruthless calculation can give way to gloating frivolity. The two traits strike him as mutually exclusive.

The loud clanging of the drawers is distracting, especially when Lydon puts on his headphones and adds off-key Jay-Z lyrics to the clamor, but Bennet doesn't let it disturb his concentration. There are three dozen new emails in his inbox, many of which are thank-yous for a great evening, and he slowly and methodically works his way through each one.

"It's five-thirty," Lydon says suddenly.

His brother finishes the sentence he's typing and glances up briefly. Then he resumes writing. "OK."

"It's five-thirty," Lydon explains with meaningful emphasis.

Bennet has no idea what his brother is trying to imply. As far as he can tell, the only remarkable thing about the hour is that his brother is still in the office to toll it.

"It's five-thirty, and John isn't back yet. He's been gone all afternoon."

"He's working."

Lydon scoffs. "That's what you said last night."

"He *was* working last night," Bennet points out.

"C'mon," Lydon says, lowering his voice as he leans his head closer to Bennet's. "The old man's not listening. Let there be a little honesty among men. John is trying to hook her, isn't he? Marry rich and blow this popsicle stand. It's a good gig, amiright?"

Bennet is spared the necessity of a reply by the loud trill of his cell phone, and he reaches for the device gratefully because he really doesn't know how to respond to Lydon. Obviously, his cynical take is way off the mark—their brother would never be motivated by greed—but the implication that what John's engaged in isn't all work isn't entirely wrong. The spark between him and Bingley is real.

He answers his phone with a curt hello.

"I have a ridiculous favor," John says quickly, "and I'm only asking it because I can't think of another option."

"OK."

"Is that John?" Lydon asks. "If it's John, tell him it's five-thirty."

Bennet swivels in his chair.

"Hannah just called to say she has the box of rugelach I ordered," John says, his voice picking up speed as he rushes to explain. "There was some mix-up at Bonelle and they delivered it to the Longbourn instead of the hotel, and apparently the box has been bouncing around the building all day, and Hannah just figured out who it was supposed to go to. Do you think you could bring it here? I know a trip into Manhattan is the opposite of on the way home, but it's too late to call a messenger, and the rugelach will most likely go stale by tomorrow morning, and I told Bingley it would be delivered today, and I would like to be a man of my word."

"No problem," Bennet says. "I'll leave now."

John exhales with surprising force. "Thank you. I'm in the bathroom. Actually, in the shower stall in the bathroom, because I couldn't be certain sound wouldn't travel. I feel like an idiot, but I didn't know what else to do, and I really appreciate your helping me out."

Bennet laughs as he imagines his usually dignified brother crouching in the corner of the Netherfield's elegant glass stall, with its rain-shower head and ornate fixtures. "Hang tight, act normal and don't forget to breathe. I'll be right there."

Perceiving a grave injustice in his immediate future, Lydon takes off his headphones and says, "You're going to the Netherfield, aren't you?"

"I'm just running an errand," Bennet says, putting his computer to sleep. "It's nothing glamorous."

"If it's just an errand, why can't I do it?" Lydon asks. "I excel at running errands. Every day, I run to get coffee. Twice. You never get coffee."

Although silently Bennet appreciates the sly reasoning, he knows acknowledging it will only encourage his brother to argue further. "It's getting late. You should go home."

Now Lydon wrinkles his brow, suspecting a trick. No family member has ever told him to work less before. "No, thanks. I'll stay and file. One of us has to be responsible."

Bennet smothers a smile at his indolent brother's display of moral superiority. "Suit yourself," he says, slipping his phone into a pocket as he slides his messenger bag over his shoulder. "See you at home. Don't stay too late."

Lydon grunts in response, puts on his headphones and turns the music up so loud the entire neighborhood can hear Jay-Z clearly. Then he takes an exhibition brochure out of the garbage can, which, even after three hours, is still half-full, and resumes loudly opening and closing cabinet drawers.

Watching the display, Bennet smiles and wonders when his little brother is going to grow up. The kid still acts like he's fifteen years old.

Although he knows Lydon can't hear him, Bennet says good-bye and heads over to Hannah's office to pick up the misdelivered pastries. The special events department is located on the other side of the building, down two long corridors and past the elevator, and Bennet is more than halfway there when he remembers the clam chowder. When he returns to the office a few minutes later, the box of rugelach tucked firmly under his arm, Lydon is elbow-deep in his bottom drawer. The quart of soup is on Bennet's desk—indisputable evidence of his brother's intentions—but the files he had to rifle through to find it have distracted him from his original purpose. Now he's reading budget reports and resource distribution spreadsheets, amazed and impressed by how much money passes through his brother's hands on an annual basis.

"Dude, is this for real?" he asks when Bennet enters the room, his eyes bright with surprise. He's not the least bit disconcerted to be caught rummaging through his brother's folders. "You raise this kind of cash all the time?"

Bennet doesn't know how to respond. Without question, he's appalled by his brother's lack of respect for his privacy and his inability to follow even the most basic office protocol. Although nobody had actually told Lydon in clear, decisive language that colleagues do not poke through the files of other colleagues, he knows his brother knows it. You can't grow up in a house with four brothers and not learn the value of privacy.

At the same time, he's pleased to see the boy finally showing interest in the world around him. "Yes, this is for real," he says, withholding the lecture that's on the tip of his tongue. Better, he decides, to encourage his curiosity than deflate it with rules and regulations he won't follow anyway. "No museum can survive on admissions alone. If you're lucky, you can cover your staffing needs with the take from the front desk, but every other operating expense comes from grants, donations or the endowment. That's why the development department is so necessary. We can go over it in the morning. I'm happy to sit down with you and run through the figures."

Lydon nods. "Yeah, all right. That sounds good."

"Great," Bennet says, resisting the urge to remind his brother that *morning* means before noon. But he can't stop himself from neatly stacking the folders, returning them to their correct file and locking his desk drawer. Then he picks up the quart of clam chowder, reminds Lydon not to stay too late and texts John that he's on his way.

CHAPTER SIX

The train from Forest Hills takes so long—*earlier incident at a station, we apologize for the delay*—that Bennet could have walked to the Netherfield faster. By the time he emerges from the 59th Street station, it's after seven o'clock. It seems unlikely his brother is still at the hotel. If that's the case, he'll simply leave the box at the reception desk and go home.

"Nope, I'm still here," John says cheerfully when Bennet calls to confirm. "We're picking a date."

"Picking a date?" Bennet asks as he enters the hotel through the Fifth Avenue entrance, where two liveried doormen stand at the ready to help guests carry packages or hail a taxi.

"I'll tell you all about it when you get here," his brother says.

Although Bennet has been to the Netherfield several times for various functions, including a gracious afternoon tea that Henry Cortland Longbourn's wife hosted before she had the stroke from which she never entirely recovered, the grandeur of the lobby, with its soaring triple-height ceiling, never fails to impress him, and he takes the elevator up to the penthouse genuinely eager to see the lavish apartment he's only read about in *Us Weekly*.

A gentleman in a navy suit answers the door. Tall, with

broad shoulders and curly hair just starting to turn gray, he looks to Bennet like several people at once—butler, man-servant, steward, uncle—and rather than give unintended offense, he introduces himself. During his tenure as director of corporate giving, he's learned that nobody takes exception to an excess of good manners.

"Hello, I'm Bennet Bethle," he says as he offers his hand.

Carl, rounding the corner of the foyer, calls out, "Who's there, Mulberry?"

"Mr. Bethle," Mulberry says, neatly avoiding the issue of the handshake by opening the door wider to admit their guest. "I have yet to ascertain his purpose."

Amused to have discovered the only situation not improved by an excess of good manners, Bennet steps into the foyer, which is large and ornate, with gilt moldings, a coved ceiling and deep, rich red walls. Several feet beyond the entrance is an informal living room with mahogany trim and large windows facing Central Park. Darcy, looking equally informal in a ponytail and light-colored capris, is sitting cross-legged on the couch opposite a marble fireplace. She has a computer on her lap, but she stops typing when she hears his voice.

Bennet nods to her in acknowledgment, then looks at Carl and Mulberry as he holds up the box from Bonelle. Clearly, John had failed to mention he was coming. "I'm making a delivery. Rugelach. In case the croissants are stale again."

Carl eyes the bakery carton with such displeasure, Bennet is tempted to assure him the pastries don't contain cyanide or rodent droppings. Instead, he says, "If you would point me in the direction of my brother, I'll leave this with him and get out of your way."

A brief, awkward pause follows this statement as Carl fails to assure his guest that he's not in the way. It falls to Mulberry, who comes with the penthouse apartment like the chandelier in the dining room and the teapot in the kitchen, to break the uncomfortable silence. "Your brother is in the library with Ms. Bingston," he says. "This way, sir."

"Of course, Mr. Mulberry. Thank you," Bennet says with a glance at Darcy, who's watching the scene from her perch on the couch. Silently, he nods at her again and smiles pleasantly at Carl, whose disapproving sneer has yet to recede.

Like the rest of the first floor—and, no doubt, the entire penthouse—the library is turned out in the style of a nineteenth-century English country house, with red walls, dark-wood shelves and elliptical arches. In the center of the gracious room is a round pedestal table at which John and Bingley are sitting with their heads close together. They're so engrossed in their conversation, neither one hears them enter.

"Mr. Bethle to see you, ma'am," Mulberry announces.

No, not announces, Bennet thinks with wry amusement, bellows. The library is empty save for the pair at the table, and yet the butler speaks as if he's addressing a room full of dignitaries.

Bingley looks up with delight. "Bennet, what a pleasant surprise."

"I was in the neighborhood, so I thought I'd drop this off," he explains, holding up the box as Mulberry silently leaves the room.

She recognizes the logo for the bakery immediately and shrieks in delight. "Oh, you wonderful, wonderful man. I've been craving those."

Bennet places the box on the table and unties the string. "John's the one who ordered them. I'm just the delivery boy."

Bingley immediately drops a rugelach in her mouth and smiles at John. "You're a wonderful man, too."

John turns a light shade of pink at the praise, but Bingley is too busy selecting another pastry to notice. Softly, he says to his brother, "I really appreciate this."

Bennet shrugs nonchalantly. There's very little he wouldn't do for his brother, and hopping a subway to midtown is hardly an act of heroism.

"Coming or going?" Bingley suddenly asks Bennet.

He looks at her in confusion. "Hmmm?"

"You said you were in the neighborhood," Bingley explains as she takes a picture of herself holding the box of rugelach with her phone. "Are you coming into the neighborhood or are you going out of it? If it's the latter, then you must stay for dinner. Right, John? John is staying for dinner, so we can have another planning sesh after we eat."

Bennet watches in amusement as Bingley posts the selfie (#yummy, #heaven, #dontyouwishyouwereme). "Planning session for what?"

"The wonderful, absolutely amazing ball I'm going to throw here at the Netherfield for your museum," she says, smiling brightly. "Did I forget to mention that part? It'll be the inaugural event of the Gold Circle Diamond Society."

"The Gold Circle Diamond Society?" Bennet asks, darting a glance at his brother.

"The party was Bingley's idea," John volunteers.

"And it's going to be a tremendously elaborate affair with too much champagne and too much dancing, and it won't end until the first light of dawn creeps over the horizon, because I was desolate to see the party break up so early last night," she says.

"Naturally, we have to run it by Meryton," John says.

Bennet smiles as he imagines the look of unabashed joy on the executive director's face when he finds out an heiress wants to throw a lavish and unsolicited party on the Longbourn's behalf. "I don't think he'll have a problem with it. Have you picked a date?"

"We were just looking at our calendars when you arrived," Bingley says. "John suggested we coordinate the ball with the opening of the *Art & Style* exhibit, which is set for the last week of April. At first I thought four weeks wouldn't be enough time to pull an extravagant event together, but now I'm convinced the last-minuteness will give the party a bit of a pop-up feel. What do you think?"

"I think you've got everything well in hand," Bennet observes, meaning his brother as much as the party. Despite the several relationships John has had, including one that lasted almost a year, Bennet has never seen him so smitten. Something about Bingley makes him glow from inside. He's like a house with every light blazing.

It's wonderful to see, and yet Bennet has his reservations. Bingley is the genuine article—sensible, good-humored, lively, beautiful—and he doesn't doubt she would make John, whose temperament matches her own, very happy. But the differences in their situations cannot be ignored. Bingley throws parties; John works them.

Bingley claps merrily. "I think so, too. All right, then, let's each resolve to have one more rugelach and then go have dinner. I'm starving."

Although Bingley is the only one whose willpower necessitates the enactment of a resolution, the Bethle brothers comply and, finishing their duly allotted portion of rugelach, accompany her to the living room, where Carl is pouring red wine from a decanter. Lucy and Hurst are resting quite comfortably on the couch, her head against his shoulder, and Darcy is ensconced in the far corner talking on the phone.

"Dinner," Bingley calls brightly.

It takes fifteen minutes for the entire party to gather—Darcy is the last one to sit down—but Mulberry brings out the food as soon as Bingley appears. The meal is a simple preparation of salmon in a sesame-soy sauce with sautéed spinach and buttered new potatoes, and Bennet, whose usual dinner consists of one of three short-order-cook specialties (grilled cheese, hot dog or omelet) prepared by himself in his one-bedroom apartment in Queens, enjoys the fresh flavors. John, too, sends his compliments to the chef, and Mulberry promptly informs him that he'll pass on the message to the kitchen staff downstairs.

While they eat, Bingley, pen in hand, brainstorms a guest list. Her ball, she insists, will be a big opportunity to move the Longbourn Collection beyond its usual crowd of stuffy millionaires and reliable standbys. "Let's break new ground!"

"We can invite Tully," Lucy suggests. "I haven't seen him since Rome, so he's due for a visit."

"Tully it is," Bingley says as she adds his name to the list. "Who else?"

"I don't see why—" Carl begins.

He's summarily cut off by his sister, who has now interrupted him three times. "Uh-uh. No complaints, only suggestions. Hurst, you summered on Martha's Vineyard last year. Who can we invite from the beach?"

Hurst furrows his brow and thinks. "Muriel Watson, perhaps. She once went to the Tibetan Museum of Art on Staten Island, so she's very open-minded like that."

Bingley nods with firm approval. "Good thinking, Hurst. Ms. Watson is also on the list." Then she turns to Carl and speaks with exaggerated calm as if conversing with a small child. "See how easy it is to contribute productively to the discussion? I'm sure you could do it if you tried."

Carl grumbles, "I'm sure if I wanted to aid and abet your plan, I could suggest several excellent guests, but as I said before, I don't see why you're hosting a ball. It's madness."

"Madness is renting a three-story penthouse with a ballroom and not hosting a ball," Bingley says.

"Darcy agrees with me," Carl says as he wipes a speck of sauce from the corner of his lips. "You think it's a terrible idea, too, don't you?"

Bingley waves her hand dismissively. "Darcy doesn't count. She's still sulking about having to return to New York because of misbehaving pipes. She'd much rather be in London than dithering with the toilets at Pemberley."

"Ah, yes, London," Lucy says with a grin. "Such delightful theater, shopping and men. Europe's the only place where one can find a true gentleman anymore, isn't that what you said, Darcy?"

"I believe the adjective she used was *well-rounded*," Bingley says. "A well-rounded gentleman."

Although Darcy recognizes the flippancy in her friend's tone, she chooses to address her comment seriously. "I did say well-rounded, yes, because the word *gentleman* itself has been devalued to mean any man who holds a door open for a woman. I don't consider that to be a sufficient qualification—and not simply because I can open my own door, thank you very much. In truth, I haven't met more than maybe six men who I would consider to be really well-rounded."

"That sounds about right," Carl says.

Bennet, who has watched Bingley's deft dinner performance with silent admiration—the effortless way she takes her brother to task while compiling one of the most impressively aspirational guest lists in the history of New York institutional fundraising—looks across the table at Darcy. "Your definition of *well-rounded* must be very extensive."

Darcy shrugs.

"Well, naturally," Carl insists. "Otherwise, we all sink to the lowest common denominator, which is, I assure you, the last place I want to be—except, perhaps, Bingley's ball. But to Darcy's point: A gentleman should have a thorough knowledge of music, literature, art, theater, wine and cigars. He should be well-traveled and speak at least three languages, one of which has to be Mandarin if he has any hope of remaining relevant in the modern world. He should know how to tip a maître d' without arousing attention and have a clear understanding of his financial portfolio. Plus, he should have a certain athleticism about him—that is, how to pull off a bicycle kick, how to get out of a greenside bunker at St. Andrews and how to return a rolling nick shot in squash."

"And," Darcy says with a firm nod, "he should keep up with world affairs through extensive reading and be able to communicate complex ideas in simple terms."

Bennet considers her thoughtfully over the rim of his wineglass, not entirely convinced she isn't joking. Surely, nobody's standards are that high. "If that's really your definition of a well-rounded man, then I'm no longer surprised you know only six. I'm shocked you know any at all."

"Do you have so little faith in your fellow man as to believe none of them could be so accomplished?" Darcy asks.

"On the contrary," Bennet says, "I have enough faith in my fellow man as to know that not a single one would be so insufferable as to have all those qualities at once. Honestly, I can't imagine a more unpleasant human being."

Both Carl and Hurst protest what they consider to be an unjust characterization—insufferable!—and insist they know many very pleasant men who fit this description.

"Jefferson Cartwright," Hurst says, "whose father owns several Swiss banks. He plays rugby, collects stamps and knows exactly how to grill a steak to get that perfect contrast between the charred outside and the warm, juicy center."

"Matthias Ferrar has won the Dressage World Cup three times," Carl adds, "and is preparing to compete in the games again this year. He also earned the master sommelier designation from the Union de la Sommellerie Française and can dismantle and reassemble a rifle while blindfolded."

Hurst is about to list the accomplishments of his dear friend Lerner Williamson—British ambassador to Argentina and actual rocket scientist (though his work is more theoretical than practical)—when Lucy shrieks. "Oh, my God, are you two going to seriously list your entire graduating class at Harvard? Unless these gentlemen will be in New York next month for Bingley's party, I don't want to hear another word about them."

Bingley tips her head to the side. "Are any of them going to be in New York next month?"

Carl mumbles no, while Hurst shrugs petulantly.

"Then let's keep the conversation to locals," their sister says. "I believe we were going around the table brainstorming. Hurst came up with the last name. Carl, it's your turn."

But Carl, whose objections to the party have not been overcome, refuses to add anything to the list and sits silently while his sister, pen perched over paper, stares at him expectantly. Lucy, however, is a game player and suggests many excellent prospects, several of whom her husband seconds because he hasn't seen them in a while and it would be nice to have a visit in the comfort of his own apartments.

Delighted, Bingley dimples and calls to Mulberry to bring out dessert, which, being strawberry shortcake made from the very first of the season's strawberry crop, is as fresh and lovely as she.

CHAPTER SEVEN

Meryton requires a site inspection immediately. Planning for the Netherfield ball is still in its infancy and John's photos render every aspect of the room in crystalline detail, but Meryton remains emphatic.

"I must know exactly what I'm dealing with," he insists, dismissing John's suggestion that they hold off on a visit until next week. "When Mr. Longbourn or one of the other board members asks me for information, which can, you understand, happen at any moment, it's imperative that I be able to supply it in vivid, firsthand detail."

He prevails upon John to arrange the inspection for the very next morning, even though the latter already has a breakfast appointment with a high-level donor scheduled. Bennet, horrified at the prospect of the executive director meeting with Bingley alone, volunteers to go in his brother's stead.

Upon their arrival, Mulberry leads them up the stairs to the ballroom, which, in the hundred years since the hotel was built, has been repurposed as an overly large living room. Although the hotel officially calls it the grand salon, the space, with its assortment of period furniture arranged in discreet conversational groupings, is curiously ungrand. Filling the ballroom with couches, armchairs, ottomans and end tables gives it a remarkably mundane appearance, like the clubhouse of a high-end gated community for people over fifty-five, and not even the six art deco chandeliers, lavishly decorated with crystals, add gravitas.

"Don't judge," Bingley says, suddenly appearing at the top of the staircase. "It's uninspiring now, but imagine it without the hideous furniture. Remove all the settees—they're too hard to sit on anyway, and their backs are ruthlessly straight. Remove all the end tables and lamps, which may or may not have come from Macy's. Now close your eyes and picture the floor, miles and miles of golden, gleaming oak. See yourselves twirling in the arms of your partner as the orchestra plays a waltz. It's perfect, isn't it?"

Meryton, whose imagination doesn't extend to picturing himself doing anything to a waltz, keeps his eyes resolutely open as he stares calculatingly at the space, trying to figure out how many people they can squeeze in comfortably. There must be a legal limit established by the fire department—despite being a private apartment, the ballroom is also a public space—but government bureaucracies are always extra cautious. No doubt, whatever the figure is, they can safely add fifteen percent.

"It's absolutely perfect," Bennet says.

Bingley grins and insists on giving them the deluxe tour, which starts at the north end of the room, where a beige pool table sits in the center of an alcove set off by the same elliptical arches as in the library. She shows them the terrace to the east, which overlooks the river and Bloomingdale's. After twenty minutes, she suggests continuing their discussion over coffee and pastry.

"But no rugelach, I'm afraid," she says. "I finished the last one just minutes before you arrived."

"We can fix that, can't we, Bennet?" Meryton says jovially as they follow her down the grand staircase to the foyer. He thinks if he keeps Bingley hooked on butter and sugar, she'll continue to be putty in John's hands.

At the bottom of the staircase, they turn left into the

breakfast parlor, a comfortable room with yellow curtains, daffodil wallpaper and bright rays of sunshine pouring in through the windows. The only thing casting a pall on the cheerful setting is the ferocious scowl on Carl's face as he looks up from his newspaper. Even Darcy's customary frown seems welcoming in comparison.

Meryton, perceiving the cinnamon-pecan bun on the silver serving tray to be the last of its kind, bumps Carl's coffee with his elbow in his enthusiasm to reach it.

"Whoops," he says as he wipes the small spill with a cloth napkin as yellow as the walls. "Do accept my apologies, Mr. Bingston."

Carl's nod of acknowledgment is a study in cold civility, but Meryton interprets it as an invitation to speak and sits down next to him to discuss the ball, assuming, wrongly, of course, that the young man must be as excited about the upcoming event as he is.

Bennet takes the seat next to his boss, which puts him once again across from Darcy. Engrossed in the business section of the newspaper, she tilts her head in general acknowledgment of the visitors from the Longbourn and sips her coffee.

"You have a lovely room here, Ms. Bingston," Meryton says as he stirs sugar into his coffee, "and the terrace has a breathtaking view. I don't know anywhere in New York that's as lovely as the Netherfield. I hope you're not in a hurry to leave."

"I do everything in a hurry, and if I did decide to leave Netherfield, I'd most likely be gone in a matter of minutes. At the moment, however, I'm happily settled."

"That's exactly the vibe you give off," Bennet says, thinking she has a lovely, mercurial quality, like a hummingbird hovering over the petals of a flower.

Bingley turns toward him. "Am I really so obvious?"

It's impossible not to laugh at the archness of her tone. "Well, yeah," he admits.

"I want to be flattered," she says with a sigh, "but it's

pitiful to be such an open book. I'd much rather be dark and mysterious."

Bennet scoffs. "Dark and mysterious doesn't necessarily mean depth of character or interesting. Sometimes it just means silent and brooding."

"You speak from personal experience?" Bingley asks.

"A lifetime of study. Dark and mysterious can be entertaining to observe for anthropological reasons," he says, "but not so much fun to go to the movies with."

Across from him, Darcy arches an eyebrow a mere fraction of an inch and silently turns a page of her paper.

Although Meryton appreciates the value of small talk, especially for the unexpected financial commitments it sometimes draws forth, he has far more respect for pointed conversation, and rather than let the discussion meander its way over to the ball, he wrenches it back. "We must get the invitations out as quickly as possible. There are several social events in New York on any given night, and we want to get a jump on the competition."

"I'm finalizing the guest list as we speak," Bingley says.

Darcy finally raises her eyes above the paper. "I assure you, your usual concerns about competition do not apply to this event."

Her condescending smirk and the implied insult to the Longbourn offends Meryton, who throws off decades of obsequiousness to snappishly reply, "And I assure you, our usual concerns about competition are minor. We're a very well respected institution."

His curt tone surprises everyone, even Bennet, who knows how protective his boss can be of the museum he leads. Darcy examines the executive director for a moment, then resumes her perusal of the paper. Meryton, interpreting her silence as retreat, doubles down on his defense of the Longbourn. "I can't see what advantage a large museum has over a smaller one, except for the international reputation and high-profile donors. Working with a small institution is a vast deal more pleasant—isn't it, Ms. Bingston?—because you don't get lost in the shuffle."

"I like working with both," Bingley says diplomatically. "Each one has its advantages."

"That's because you're so thoughtful and kind, but other people"—he purposefully does not look at Darcy so the insinuation is twice as clear—"seem to think the Longbourn doesn't have any advantages."

Bennet is horrified. He knows Meryton is a man of excess, but his extravagance always tips toward effusive praise, and Bennet doesn't know what to make of this sudden dip into combativeness. It's no secret to the Longbourn staff that Meryton doesn't like Darcy, but as the executive director of a fragile and sometimes desperate institution, it behooves him to separate his personal feelings from his professional obligations.

Hoping to salvage something—if not Darcy's goodwill, then Bingley's good opinion—Bennet rushes to say, "You misunderstand. Ms. Fitzwilliam only meant that fewer people are inclined to take the trip out to Forest Hills to attend events at the Longbourn, which you know is true. We talk about that all the time in the office."

"It's a concern, certainly, but not one we spend every minute of the day agonizing about. Our events are excellently attended. The Pushkins come to everything, as well as the McCarthys and the Rivingtons and the Sanfords," Meryton says, launching into an inventory of the museum's wealthiest supporters. His tone, officious and self-important, readily conveys his high expectation that his audience will be bowled over by the quality of the list.

Listening to the extensive catalog of unfamiliar names, Bingley manages to keep a straight face only out of respect for Bennet. Her brother is less considerate and rolls his eyes at Darcy with a very expressive smile.

"Oh, and I mustn't forget Lady Williams, who is particularly devoted to the Longbourn. As you've no doubt concluded on your own, she's a member of the British peerage. And her title is real. It goes back generations and isn't one of these baubles bestowed recently by the queen for some charity work or another. What a lovely woman Lady Williams is. So kind and so easygoing—you'd never know she has $300 million. She always has something nice to say to everybody. *That* is my idea of good breeding. People who consider themselves too important to make polite conversation know nothing about it."

Bennet resists the urge to lay his head down on the table and bang it a few times. Instead, he introduces a new subject, "I think we should set up the orchestra along the north side of the ballroom, where the pool table is now."

"Just what I was thinking," Meryton announces, sufficiently engaged by the topic to forget about his list. "The south wall is too close to the staircase. We'll need to build a stage, of course, to raise the orchestra. It's vital to the acoustics."

At these words, Bennet smothers a sigh. Yes, he agrees elevating the orchestra a foot or two would improve the sound, but it's not Meryton's place to request modifications that will cost their host money. He doesn't doubt Bingley's taste is impeccable, and he's more than confident that whatever changes she decides to make will be perfect. Before he can say that, however, Bingley assures Meryton that she'll accept nothing less than a stage made of the finest cherrywood.

"I found some old pictures online of what the ballroom used to look like before it was turned so morosely practical," she says, tapping her phone, "and I thought it would be fun to restore some of its former glory. Alas, we can do nothing about the track lighting except turn it to dim. But look"—she holds up her screen for Bennet and his boss to examine—"at the lush valances over the window and the gorgeous candelabras. I've already spoken to the hotel and they're happy to indulge me in my request. The manager even thinks the original drapes are in storage in the basement. She's promised to send someone down to have a look."

Meryton is duly impressed with Ms. Bingston's industriousness. "It seems you've already thought of everything. How wonderful. Naturally, your standing at the hotel—that is, your status as an heiress who can afford to lease the penthouse of the Netherfield—makes the staff much more amenable to your requests. But that's the advantage of having money, is it not? It clears the way of all things. Lady Williams wanted to have the Empire State Building lit up yellow and blue in honor of her son's wedding to a Swedish royal. It was a very elaborate affair, with horse-drawn carriages for the entire party and fireworks. The flowers alone cost $145,000."

Bennet knows that the recitation of Lady Williams's wedding expenditures will take them well into the night, and in hopes of preempting that disaster, he says firmly, "And Lady Williams made a large donation to the Empire State Building's children's fund and the building was lit the desired colors. Money is wonderful and is the source of all good things."

"I thought money is the root of all evil," Darcy says with a twitch of her lips, amused by either him or Lady Williams's ability to bend the Empire State Building to her will.

"The *love* of money, as I'm sure you know," Bennet says, impatient to be gone before Meryton offends or bores them out of a ball. "But that adage is largely arbitrary. I find the love of tequila to be far more destructive."

Darcy's only response is a smile, and a brief silence follows, during which Bennet tries to come up with something to say to bring their meeting to a swift and courteous end. Meryton, however, speaks first, thanking Ms. Bingston once more for her generosity in hosting the party. Bingley assures him again that the pleasure is all hers and even shames her brother Carl into saying something nice, which clearly does not come naturally to him—he has to cough several times before getting the words out.

Delighted with the morning's progress, Meryton wraps a cheese Danish in a cheerful yellow napkin and slides it into his coat pocket before suggesting Bennet and he take their leave. Bingley shows them to the door, leaving

Carl to marvel over the behavior of the two fundraisers for the Longbourn Collection.

"Pilfering a napkin right under our noses!" Carl says. "The tedious man didn't even have the decency to ask if we'd mind his stealing the linens. He's so irritating. The insipidness and yet the noise, the nothingness and yet the self-importance. No doubt, Darcy, you're thinking how unbearable it was to have to suffer through that ridiculousness during breakfast when all one wants is a little peace and quiet to enjoy one's paper. Trust me, I know exactly how you feel."

"You don't, actually," Darcy says as she finishes the last sip of her coffee. "I was just thinking how the morning sunlight brings out the gold flecks in Bennet Bethle's eyes. And now, before you wish me joy—because, yes, I know how quickly your imagination will jump from admiration to love to matrimony—I must excuse myself. I have a meeting with my estate agent."

Although Carl is disconcerted by how easily Darcy anticipated his response, for he prides himself on being at least a little bit opaque, if not entirely impenetrable, he takes comfort in her composure and decides her comment was intended to provoke. Rather than rise to the bait, he reaches for the coffeepot.

CHAPTER EIGHT

Planning the ball is time consuming, but it doesn't take up every minute of John's life, and to his boss's dismay, he continues to show up for work each morning. Meryton would much rather he stay at the Netherfield around the clock, sorting out details and drawing ineffably closer to their benefactor. He blames modern life, with its endless string of technological advances—elevators, subways, non-leech-based medicine—for making it impossible to contrive a disaster severe enough to require John taking up residence at the penthouse. In the good old days, a touch of catarrh would have kept him bedridden there for a week.

"No, don't sit down," Meryton says as John pulls out his chair. He's just returned from a late lunch with the Sheffield sisters, who have agreed to underwrite an exciting new lecture series hosted by one of their curators. "You need to bring these documents over to the Netherfield. The board is insisting Bingley sign them immediately."

Surprised, John takes the stack of papers from his boss and examines them. Then he glances up with a confused look. "Articles of integration for the Golden Diamond Patrons Society?"

"Yes, it's a new requirement for all committees," Meryton explains. "I told the board it wasn't necessary, but they insisted. So you need to bring those documents over right now. Since it's already four o'clock, you shouldn't feel like you have to rush back to the office. Stay and plan."

"Or," Bennet says, smothering a smile at his boss's blatant machination, "he could stay and scan. Emailing the documents would be much more efficient. I think the board would appreciate that."

Damning the intrusiveness of modern conveniences—why can't anything be difficult anymore!—Meryton shakes his head regretfully and explains that the scanners are broken.

"What? All of them?" John asks incredulously.

"Every single one in the building," Meryton says with a regretful sigh. "As you know, most of our office equipment is cheap and old. If Bennet here could convince some corporation to donate top-of-the-line equipment, we wouldn't be in this fix."

"And yet somehow I think we would," Bennet murmurs, grateful that the executive director's estimation of their equipment is accurate. Meryton wouldn't have hesitated to disable brand-new machines in the pursuit of his goal.

Accepting this explanation, John slides the contract into his briefcase, pushes in his chair and leaves for the Netherfield. Bennet watches him disappear down the narrow winding stairs and returns to the grant application he's filling out for the Shubert Foundation.

"You shouldn't get too comfortable either," Meryton says.

"Why not?" he asks, unable of seeing how he could fit into the executive director's Machiavellian scheme.

"Because in about forty minutes, you're going to volunteer to bring John his phone," he explains as he holds up the device, which he'd discreetly removed from his employee's jacket pocket. "I need eyes and ears on the ground. Report back on how things are progressing and don't be stingy with the details."

Bennet knows exactly what details his boss would like, but he has no intention of supplying them, and by the time he arrives at the Netherfield two hours later, he's forgotten all about his boss's directive.

John is grateful to see him and clutches his phone as if it's a missing limb. "Thank you. I can't figure out how I forgot it. I really thought I'd put it in my bag."

His brother shrugs and assures him he doesn't mind playing delivery boy. "It rounds out my résumé."

"Come in. Sit down. We're having cocktails," Bingley calls from across the room as she holds up a silver shaker. "You can't have a party without a signature drink, which I know you know, so we're experimenting. On offer now is Lucy's entry, a kirtini, which is a martini made with crème de cassis."

"Which is the key ingredient of a kir," Lucy explains from her supine position on the couch, where she's flipping through a magazine. "Next, we're going to add champagne for a kirtini royale. Although I expect my love of the kirtini to be absolute, I think the kirtini royale might blow it out of the water."

"A mother should never play favorites with her children," Hurst says, briefly raising his wife's legs off the cushion to settle on the couch.

"Don't worry, darling," she says. "I'm entirely indiscriminate when it comes to alcohol."

Bingley laughs knowingly as she fills seven martini glasses with a burgundy-colored liquid and drops two raspberries in each. "Here we go. Round three: the kirtini," she says, distributing the first two drinks to Darcy and Carl, who are sitting at a round table next to the window. Darcy is typing quickly on her computer as Carl reads his phone and occasionally looks up to ask her a question about her email. Lucy sits up to take a glass.

To Bennet, who's still standing on the threshold of the room, unsure whether to enter or leave, Bingley says, "I'm sure you have a parcel of excellent excuses as to why you must run off, but I'm categorically denying you permission. Until you showed up, our numbers were even and we're in desperate need of a tiebreaker. So go find a seat and start drinking."

Amused, Bennet follows her order, sitting in the large leather armchair adjacent to the couch where Lucy and her husband are reclining.

"At the risk of sounding horrendously smug, it's as delicious as I expected," Lucy says.

Bingley agrees, as does John, who's leaning against the bar as he eats his raspberry, but Carl says the drink could use a bit more vermouth. Darcy takes a quick sip and raises her left thumb in approval as her right hand continues to type. When Bennet doesn't immediately offer an opinion, Bingley asks him what he thinks.

"It's good. A little on the sweet side," he says.

"That's two votes for more vermouth," Carl cries triumphantly. "Remember that for the next batch."

Lucy gives him a withering look and calls for kirtini royales all around.

Bingley rinses her cocktail shaker, pops a bottle of champagne and starts to measure ingredients for the next entrant.

"I'm sure your brother George will appreciate getting an email with so much detail," Carl says conversationally to Darcy, who makes no reply as her fingers dash across the keyboard.

He tries again: "You type so fast. Your fingers just fly across the keyboard."

Darcy tells him he's wrong. "I actually write pretty slowly. I just delete a lot, which makes it seem fast."

"I suppose you get a lot practice writing letters on behalf of your initiatives," Carl says. "Business letters are so odious. All those 'dear sirs and madams.'"

"Then it's a lucky thing for the poor that writing those letters is my responsibility."

Unable to smother a smile, Bennet hides his amusement in his glass and hopes the exchange, which is entirely in keeping with his opinion of each party, never ends. It's like a deliciously satiric one-act play performed in a black-box studio in the East Village.

"Be sure to tell your brother I hope to see him soon," Carl says.

"Already included, per your earlier request."

"It's getting rather dark in here. Maybe I should turn on the lamp."

"Thank you, no. I'll turn it on if I need it."

"How can you type for so long without your wrists hurting? If I type more than three sentences, I get carpal tunnel."

Darcy is silent.

"Don't forget to offer him my congratulations on graduating the conservatory," Carl says.

"Your congratulations will have to wait for my next email because I've already hit SEND," she says.

"That's all right. I'll tell him myself when I see him in September. Do you always write such long, informative letters?"

"Long, yes. Informative, I'm not so sure."

"You're too modest. People who write long letters easily always provide lots of interesting information. I know this as the recipient of many long letters."

Across the room, Bingley laughs. "Nice try, Carl, but that won't fly with Darcy, because she *doesn't* write easily. She struggles to find *le mot juste*. Am I right, Darcy?"

"We have different writing styles," her friend says as she closes her laptop.

Carl snorts. "I'm not sure you can call the nonsense my sister produces writing. She leaves out words, uses too many emojis and invents acronyms at will. ITBTWTS: I'm too busy to write this sentence."

"But I am," Bingley says in her defense. "My ideas come so fast and so furiously that if I don't record them as quickly as possible, they'll slip away. The result, I'm willing to concede, is a confusing letter that's difficult to decipher."

"Your humility is refreshing," Bennet observes. "People usually get defensive when criticized."

Darcy shakes her head. "No, no, don't fall for it. Bingley's the queen of the humblebrag."

"Lil' ole me?" Bingley asks, batting her eyelashes as she spoons ice into a row of empty tumblers. "However do you mean?"

"You appear to be owning the fault, but the truth is you're proud of your incoherent emails and texts. You think they reflect an agile mind too busy to waste time on niggling little things like details. It's the reason you use so many acronyms. ISICSDMTP: I'm sorry I can't slow down my thought process," Darcy says. "You like to think of yourself as unpredictable and spontaneous. It's like when you told Mr. Meryton that if you decided to leave the Netherfield, you'd be gone in a matter of minutes. You were complimenting yourself. And yet there's no reason to be flattered by the idea of skipping town with important business left unfinished."

Bingley pours a jigger of crème de cassis into the shaker. "Unfair! You can't possibly hold against me something I said a week ago. And anyway—I stand by it. So you can't accuse me of adopting an affectation just to show off."

"You can stand by it all you want," Darcy says, "but I know you, and your decisions are easily influenced by other people. I can totally see you on the corner of Fifth Avenue with your bags hailing a taxi to take you to Kennedy, and if a friend came up to you and said, 'Bingley, darling, stay until next week,' you'd drop your arm immediately."

"Oddly enough," Bennet says, "your description of Bingley is more flattering than hers of herself."

Bingley laughs. "It's lovely of you to interpret what my friend says as a tribute to my easygoing nature, but that's not at all what she means. Darcy would think better of me if, standing on the curb of Fifth Avenue, bags in hand, I abruptly said no and hopped into the first available cab."

Bennet cocks his head. "So as far as Darcy is concerned, a rash decision stubbornly held to is no longer a rash decision?"

"I can't say what Darcy thinks," Bingley says with a smile.

Darcy observes that Bennet is asking her to justify opinions that are not actually her own. Nevertheless, she's game and agrees to play along. "But you have to remember that the friend who tells her to stay in New York doesn't give her a single reason for the request."

"So giving in to the wishes of a friend without arguing isn't a good thing either," Bennet says.

"Giving in for no reason reflects badly on both of them."

"What about friendship and affection? Don't they count for anything?" Bennet asks. "When you care about someone, you're happy to give in to their request without needing to be wheedled or convinced. Forget this particular example and make it more general: If one friend asks another friend to change her plans, which weren't very important to begin with, would you really think less of the second friend for agreeing without an argument?"

"If we're going to do this, then we should really do it and fill in all the blanks," Darcy says. "Exactly how important is the request? How close are the two friends? These parameters should be established before we continue."

"Yes, yes," Bingley says gleefully, brandishing the cocktail shaker. "Let's do this properly and figure out all the particulars, starting with comparative height and size of the two parties, for that's a hugely important factor. Honestly, Bennet, if Darcy did not tower over me, I wouldn't pay her half as much deference. I can't think of a more awful object than Darcy on some occasions and in some places—at Pemberley especially, and on a Sunday evening when she has nothing to do."

Darcy smiles, but Bennet, seeing the faint color sweep her cheeks, realizes she's actually offended and resists the urge to laugh. Carl resents the insult on her behalf and takes his sister to task for talking so much nonsense.

"I know what you're doing, Bingley," Darcy says. "You hate arguments and want this one to end, so you're being ridiculous."

Emptying the ice from the tumblers, her friend readily agrees. "Arguments are too much like disputes. If you and Bennet could put yours on hold until I'm out of the room, I'd be very grateful. Then you can say whatever you like about me and each other."

"I'm happy to let it lie," Bennet says, "and I'm sure Darcy has more letters to write."

Thankful for the change in subject, Bingley pours a sample of the kirtini royale into each glass and asks for John's help in distributing round four.

Despite its potential—for what drink or situation has ever not been made better by the addition of champagne?—Lucy's newest contrivance falls flat. Carl immediately dismisses it as undrinkable swill, and Lucy, who'd assumed her capacity for sweets to be infinite, complains that it makes her teeth hurt.

"Excellent," Bingley cheers, pouring the remaining royale mixture down the sink. "We've finally managed to eliminate a contender. Now all we have to do is whittle down the other three. Since we didn't have a clear winner, I suggest we start again from the top."

This plan is generally held to be sound, and John slips behind the bar to scoop more ice. Bennet, with his parcel of excellent excuses as to why he has to run off, decides to stay for his brother's sake. The oldest Bethle sibling is certainly capable of holding his own—and no doubt has—among the snarky Bingston brothers, but Bennet sees no reason why he should have to. He leans back in his comfortable chair and catches the magazine Lucy throws at him, not in an attempt to share reading material but because that's how she disposes of publications when she's done perusing them: She tosses them into the air or across the room.

The magazine is the current issue of *Rolling Stone,* and Bennet is happy to flip through its pages while listening to Carl and Hurst dissect an acquaintance they'd run into that morning in Bergdorf. Their catalog of observations, at once minute and epic, is a duet of dislike sung in perfect harmony, and Bennet feels sympathy for the absent young man who had the terrible misfortune to shop for jeans that day.

As he scans headlines and Bingley presents drinks for their consideration, he can't help noticing how frequently Darcy's eyes are fixed on him. He knows it's not because she likes him—he's hardly an object of admiration for so impressive a woman—and yet it seems even stranger that she would stare at him out of dislike. No, the only thing he can imagine is there's be something more wrong and inexcusable about him, by her standards, of course, than about anyone else in the room. The assumption doesn't bother him. He likes her too little to worry about her approval.

After listening to Hurst discuss the prospects of an Italian programmer he'd met for lunch—sadly, very unlikely the man would get second-round funding for his app—Carl asks his brother about his friend in Brooklyn who makes small-batch Scotch.

"Small-batch whiskey," Hurst immediately corrects. "You can't call it Scotch if it's made outside of Scotland."

While Lucy protests her husband's nitpickery and Hurst defends the importance of nomenclature by listing inferior products that thankfully cannot call themselves champagne ("I'm looking at you, prosecco"), Darcy wanders over to Bennet's chair and glances at the positive review of Coldplay's latest release. Noting the effusive praise of the headline, she asks if it makes Bennet inclined to download the album immediately.

Bennet's lips twitch, but he doesn't say anything, and Darcy, unused to being ignored, repeats the question.

"Sorry," he says easily. "I was just trying to figure out the safe response. Clearly, you want me to say yes, so you can scorn my populist taste in music, and, obviously, I'd rather not give you the opening. So the answer is no, I don't want to buy Coldplay's new album. Now, judge me if you dare."

"I absolutely do not dare," she says with a surprisingly easy laugh.

Having expected to offend her with his honesty, Bennet is taken aback by her affable reply. What he doesn't know, however, is that he has a way of combining friendliness and archness that makes it difficult for anyone to take offense, and Darcy, who finds her interest rarely piqued, is thoroughly intrigued by him. She genuinely believes that were it not for the many disadvantages of his situation—personal as well as professional—she would be in danger of falling for him.

Carl sees, or thinks he sees, enough to be jealous, and after the Bethle brothers leave and everyone else turns in, he teases Darcy about her crush.

"I hope," he says as he refills her wineglass with a crisp pinot noir, "you will give your husband, when that happy event occurs, much-needed career advice. Use one of your connections to wrangle the poor man a job at a respectable museum. And explain to his current employer the advantages of holding his tongue. Also—and I realize this might be overstepping—see if you can't tone down his attitude; he's just a little too sure of himself."

"Any other dating advice?" Darcy asks, her voice remaining neutral as she sips the wine.

"You must hang a portrait of your father-in-law in the gallery at Pemberley. Put it next to your grandfather, the judge. They're in the same profession, you know, only in different lines. And you must also include a portrait of his uncle, the used-car salesman—in oils, naturally. As for Bennet's picture, you shouldn't even attempt to have it done. No painter could possibly do justice to those beautiful eyes."

"You're right," she agrees. "A painting might copy their color and shape and the eyelashes, so remarkably fine, but it would never capture their expression. Obviously, it will have to be a photograph."

At that moment, Hurst enters the room and asks if anyone has seen his phone. "I've tried calling it, but there's no ring, so the battery's probably dead."

"Rotten luck," Carl says, leaning comfortably against the wall. When Darcy gets up to help with the search, he straightens his shoulders and lifts up the sofa cushions.

CHAPTER NINE

A few days later, Bennet is surprised to discover the Bingston brothers have within their catty little souls the ability to be perfectly pleasant human beings when they condescend to make the effort. He doesn't share this finding with John because his brother, who rarely holds a negative opinion about anyone, already thinks well of the Bingstons. To him, however, it's a revelation to learn how easily they can hold a conversation and how accurately they can describe an outing and how humorously they can relate an anecdote and how kindly they can laugh at an acquaintance.

It is, he thinks as Carl offers him another beer, the first enjoyable hour he's ever spent in their company.

The reason behind their affability is simple: The women aren't there. Darcy, Bingley and Lucy are out at a food tasting, and with nobody to witness their posturing, they don't bother to pose. Instead, they reveal themselves to be excellent hosts, apologizing for their sister's tardiness and providing a variety of refreshments.

Bennet is at the Netherfield only because Bingley begged him to help her pick out the place settings for the ball. John is also there to aid and abet napkin selection, but no pleading was required to secure his presence. He's happy to comply with all Bingley's requests, and although their relationship is entirely circumspect—nothing to raise the eyebrows of the National Association of Fundraisers here!—it's clear to Bennet that both parties are equally infatuated.

After an hour, the women come home, and Carl instantly reverts to form, accosting Darcy with a question before she can even put down her handbag. She shrugs off her jacket and excuses herself to change out of her business clothes. Bingley, her arms brimming with packages, apologizes profusely for being so late.

"I want to blame the traffic," she says. "Can I blame the traffic?"

"Only if *traffic* is code for *paella*," Lucy says, taking a sip of her husband's beer as she sits on the couch.

Bingley lays the boxes on the round table by the window and says, "The traffic was so delicious I had to have more."

"By which she means, she liked the paella so much, she had the caterer make a second batch," Lucy explains.

"In my defense, the first batch was very small," she says.

"Yes, because it's a tasting," her sister-in-law replies, "wherein one tastes a variety of foods in order to decide which ones to serve at one's event. If one were meant to consume every crumb in sight, it would be called a consumption."

"Sounds like lunchtime at the sanitarium," Carl says.

Bingley scoffs and insists it sounds delightful. "Every crumb in sight is my favorite food group. But these attempts to distract me from the greater purpose at hand will not work." She holds up a book of napkin swatches. "We must decide on the table settings for the ball. Now who has what it takes to pick a color scheme and stick by it no matter how much I belittle their taste?"

Lucy, Carl and Hurst disqualify themselves immediately, claiming lack of interest, not lack of fortitude, and John happily throws himself into the fray. Bennet intends to help out, too, but just as he's about to stand up, he gets a text from Meryton asking for an update on Bingley and John's status and reiterating his preference for pastel table linens. "Strong colors compete w/ money," he writes.

Everything competes with money, Bennet thinks as he types a terse reply assuring the absent director that his voice will be heard. He doesn't address the matter of Bingley and John's status because there's nothing to say. Yes, they look as thick as thieves, their heads close together as they converse quietly, but a few speaking glances do not a relationship make and John is far too much of a professional to put the moves on a patron. If anything is to happen between the two, it will be because Bingley cannot stand the interminable flirting one second longer and attacks him.

Bennet can't wait for that moment.

Lucy grumbles about how full she is because she ate too much paella and asks if anyone wants to play Words with Friends. Carl eagerly takes her up on the offer, but before he can put out his first word (*warble,* 13 points), Darcy returns, requiring a redistribution of his attention. The object of his admiration observes the occupants of the room engaged in various activities, selects a novel from the bookshelf and sits down to read. Carl immediately follows suit, and although his efforts to appear literate seem sincere, he spends more time watching Darcy progress through *her* book than reading his own. He also keeps asking questions or looking at her page. His attempts to start a conversation, though manifold and creative, come to naught, for Darcy merely supplies the answer and returns to her novel.

Finally, Carl, tired of trying to immerse himself in a drawn-out tale of a slowly dissolving marriage, which he only chose because it's by the same author as Darcy's, stretches his arms and says, "What a unique experience it is to read a *book* book. I read on my phone so much, I'd forgotten how satisfying it can be to hold the actual object in my hands. When I have a house of my own, I'm going to have shelves and shelves of books. I'll even get an entire set of encyclopedias. Hashtag kitsch."

No one replies to his clever comment, and Carl drops

the book onto the couch and looks around the room for something to do. Hearing Bingley describe a fork as monstrous, he joins the Gold Circle Diamond Society meeting to offer a differing opinion, which is summarily ignored by the more established members of the committee.

Determined to attract Darcy's attention, Carl decides to strike up a conversation with Bennet and calls him over to the window. "You should really get a look at the view. You can see the whole park."

Although Bennet is surprised to be singled out, he's watched the other man's aimless progression through the room and realizes he's a last resort. The other man's level of desperation amuses him so much that even if he passes the entire evening at the Netherfield without so much as looking at a primrose-colored napkin or lobster fork, he'll consider the time well spent.

Nodding agreeably, Bennet joins him at the window and, observing all of Central Park laid out before them, says, "It's very impressive."

Darcy, who's also surprised by Carl's unprecedented friendliness, looks up and closes her book without thinking. Immediately, she's invited to join them by the window, but she declines with the assurance she can see the view well enough from the couch.

"Ah, but from here you can see everything," Carl says, listing the many features of Central Park: the zoo, the boathouse, the skating rink.

At the mention of Wollman Rink, Bingley looks up and says, "I love skating. I do a mean figure four."

"Figure four?" John says.

She dimples. "Half a figure eight."

"Isn't that a zero?" Darcy asks.

Bingley acknowledges the dig and returns to looking at china patterns.

Bennet asks, "Where does the ability to skate fall on the list of achievements for the well-rounded gentleman?

Does it come before or after reading *The Brothers Karamazov* in the original Russian?"

"Physical agility is important," Carl says thoughtfully. "I'd put it ahead of literature, wouldn't you, Darcy?"

She doesn't address the issue directly but rather says, "Bennet isn't interested in the answer. He's making fun of me."

Carl, as if genuinely stumped by the notion of making fun of Darcy Fitzwilliam, stares at Bennet with baffled eyes. You could sooner make fun of the Dalai Lama. "Darcy doesn't provide enough material for mockery. She's too smart and kind—you can't laugh at her and you'll only embarrass yourself by trying."

"You can't laugh at her," Bennet repeats. "Well, that's a rare superpower and I hope it stays that way—at least, among the people I know. I love laughing."

"Carl is giving me too much credit," Darcy says. "I can be laughed at. Anyone can be turned into a punch line by a person determined to mock them, even Superman himself."

"That's true," Bennet agrees, thinking Clark Kent is actually too easy a target to be worth the effort. "But I would never mock anything thoughtful, kind or clever. I'm amused by people's follies and their nonsense—when they say one thing and do the opposite and have no sense at all of the contradiction. But these sort of shortcomings, I suppose, are exactly the kind you lack."

"I have foibles," Darcy says. "I have many foibles. But I work hard to avoid the kind of weaknesses that would subject me to ridicule."

"Such as vanity and pride," Bennet says.

"Vanity is always a weakness, certainly," she concedes, "but if someone is clever, pride isn't a problem. An intelligent person can keep it in check."

Bennet turns away to hide a smile.

"If you're done cross-examining the witness," Carl says peevishly, "why don't you state your verdict so we can all move on to something more interesting. Have I mentioned the view yet?"

Although he's not convinced their brief exchange rises to the level of a cross-examination, Bennet says, "You're both right. Darcy is perfect."

"No," Darcy says firmly and impatiently. "I never said I was perfect. I'm quite imperfect. I have a bad temper. I'm stubborn. I don't let go of things. I'm not swayed by emotion. I'm resentful. I hold grudges. Once my good opinion is lost, it can't be regained."

Bennet is quiet as he considers her list. After a moment he says, "Implacable resentment is a significant failing, and it's a clever one, too, because there's nothing funny about it. You're safe from me."

"Everyone has a fault they can't overcome, no matter how enlightened they are, " Darcy says defensively.

"And your fault is a tendency to hate everybody."

"And yours," she replies with a smile, "is to deliberately misunderstand them."

"All right, then, let's turn on the TV," Carl says, tired of a conversation in which he has no part. "Tottenham played Arsenal today, and ESPN is replaying it at eight."

At the mention of the Spurs, Hurst reaches for the remote and turns on the screen. Darcy is grateful for the distraction. She's paying too much attention to Bennet for her own peace of mind.

CHAPTER TEN

Although the entrance foyer to the Longbourn is not as large and gracious as the original drawings intended, owing to a misunderstanding with the builder and an unexpected shortage of Carrara marble, it's rarely the site of head-on collisions, and Bennet stares in horror at the beautiful brown-haired woman sprawled on the floor. He drops to his knees to check for damage. "I'm sorry. I totally didn't see you there. Are you all right? Anything broken?"

His victim, whose bright blue eyes glint with humor as they inspect him, swears she's perfectly fine. "My ego has taken a beating, because I'd *thought* I'd mastered the art of walking and talking, but I'm otherwise uninjured. And, truly, you don't owe me an apology. It was all my fault. I wasn't looking where I was going at all, which is something I do quite a lot. But I resolve to get better. Let's schedule another pass for tomorrow at the same time and see if I can pull it off without a pratfall."

Charmed by her easy manner and endearing self-deprecation, Bennet insists on accepting half the blame. "I was in a hurry."

"Far be it for me to argue with a handsome man determined to absolve me of guilt," she says with a slow grin as she gathers the many files that scattered in her fall.

Bennet picks up several sheets of paper and straightens them into a neat pile. He looks at the logo of a crimson-colored shield with a gold crown in the center and reads the name of the company. "Redcoat Design?" he asks, handing her the stack.

She puts the papers into a large white binder with the same crimson logo, crumpling the edges in her rush to stuff them all in. "Yes, we're working on the Impressionism and fashion exhibit."

"I was just in the gallery," he says. "It looks wonderful. You've done a brilliant job."

The woman's cheeks turn a light shade of pink, and she looks down at the binder she's clutching. "Thanks, but I can't take all the credit. Who am I kidding? I can't take *any* of the credit. I'm not a designer. Well, I *am* a designer, but I only recently graduated from the program and am still establishing myself. So at the moment, I'm just a foot soldier in the regiment, so to speak. I do a lot of answering the phone, which I'm very good at, provided I'm not walking around the office at the time. And I photocopy and do the very important work of replacing the toner in the printer. Oh, and tripping, of course. I'm lead tripper on all Redcoat Design projects."

"Knowing how difficult it is to rise to any position of prominence in an office setting, I must congratulate you on your achievement," Bennet says with a grin. "And yet I'm more impressed by your ability to replace the toner, although the hard part isn't actually changing the toner."

"It's finding the cartridges," she says, finishing his thought. "They're always hidden in some obscure cabinet with the Post-its."

"Naturally," he says. "In the hierarchy of coveted office supplies, it goes Post-its, staplers, toner cartridges, Wite-Out."

She wrinkles her nose, her blue eyes alive with mischief. "Does anyone really use Wite-Out anymore?"

Bennet laughs. "Have I unintentionally revealed something deeply mortifying about myself?"

"Oh, indeed," she says with a giggle. "I believe it's now incumbent on me to suddenly remember a very important engagement."

Before Bennet can reply to her teasing remark with a teasing one of his own, John calls his name and he becomes keenly aware that the two of them are still on the floor. Coloring slightly because he usually has more finesse than to keep a woman on her knees, Bennet stands up and holds out his hand to help her to her feet as well. As he turns to introduce her to his brothers, he realizes he doesn't know her name.

"I'm Bennet Bethle," he says, holding out his hand.

Her grip is firm and warm. "Georgia Wickham. It's a pleasure to meet you."

"And these," he says with a gesture in their general direction, "are my brothers John and Lydon. We work in the development department."

"They work," Lydon says with the boyish insouciance that goes over so well with the tourists in the café. "I slave."

"He gets a stipend so the reports of his servitude are greatly exaggerated," John says, as he shakes Georgia's hand.

"Small stipend," Lydon says, pinching a whisper of space between his thumb and index finger. "Very small."

"Georgia works for the company that's designing *Art & Style*," Bennet explains.

"Redcoat?" John says. "They've done an excellent job. Everyone here is very pleased, especially our exhibition team, which is relieved to have the help. Like all nonprofits, we're understaffed."

"I'll tell that to my boss," Georgia says. "The praise part, not the understaffed bit. We're understaffed, too, and it might sound like I'm subtly hinting for an assistant."

"I could use an assistant," Lydon says.

"Like that," Georgia says, laughing. "Except, you know, subtle."

"Lydon doesn't know the meaning of *subtle*," Bennet says.

The youngest Bethle dips at the waist, as if sketching a quick bow. "I must apologize for my brother, whose manners aren't always entirely appropriate," he says, then smirks at Bennet. "And that, my friend, is what we in the biz call throwing shade. Deal."

Georgia laughs as John tries to ascertain from his brother what business he's referring to and Bennet questions Lydon's inclusion in any industry.

It's in the middle of this energetic discussion that Bingley and Darcy arrive. They enter through the lobby doors and stop briefly at the admissions desk before spotting the Bethle brothers near the brochure rack. Bingley greets them with a cheerful hello and Darcy with her customary reserve.

"Do note, Bennet, that I'm here in the capacity of delivery boy," Bingley says, waving a large manila envelope proudly. "You're not the only one charged with menial tasks."

"I'm sure nobody has ever charged you with a menial anything," Bennet says to Bingley's delight.

"True. True. I only charge myself. The invitations are ready and I couldn't wait to show John," she says, "and you and Lydon, of course. And I'm sure Mr. Meryton will be pleased to see them as well."

Bingley opens the envelope, and Darcy corroborates her friend's story, explaining that they've come directly from the printer. No waiting on messengers today!

"Look. Look. It's perfect," Bingley announces as she gives the invitation, boldly colored and yet surprisingly elegant, to John to examine.

Darcy, determined not to look at Bennet, fixes her gaze on everything else: Bingley, the manila envelope, John's grin. Then her eyes shift to the right and are arrested by the sight of the stranger. Bennet, who catches the expression on both their faces as they stare at each other, is astonished by the effect of the meeting. Both change color: One looks white, the other red. Georgia, after a moment, dips her head—a greeting Darcy barely deigns to return.

Bennet marvels at the cold exchange and wonders at its cause. He can't imagine what it could be, and he can't stop himself from wanting to know.

John admires the invitation with all due effusiveness, which further delights Bingley, and the two smile at each other in perfect accord, pleased with the result of their collaboration. Lydon's insistence on examining the invitation himself interrupts the moment, and Bennet realizes he has once again failed to make proper introductions. Before he can rectify the oversight, Bingley, seemingly unaware of what's just passed, announces they have to go.

"I'm a terrible delivery boy," she says, "dropping and running. I'm sorry I can't stay for lunch or coffee or general merriment."

"You are the opposite of a terrible delivery boy," Bennet says, laughing.

"No, *you* are the opposite of a terrible delivery boy," she says firmly, "and I seek to emulate your example. But not right now. Darcy has an appointment at one, and I've hijacked her long enough. We will see you soon. Don't work too hard—unless it's in preparation for the ball, in which case, knock yourself out."

Bingley threads her arm through Darcy's and waves good-bye as they stroll toward the door. As soon as they're gone, Bennet turns to Georgia and apologizes for failing to introduce her.

"I warned you," Lydon says gleefully, "that my brother's manners aren't always entirely appropriate."

Bennet readily concedes the point, most likely a first in their relationship, and offers to buy Georgia a cup of coffee in the café as penance. She thanks him for the invitation but regrets the timing. "I've got to get back to the office. Cases of Wite-Out don't order themselves, you know."

"Is that a dig?" Bennet asks.

"Yeah," she says.

He nods. "OK."

LYNN MESSINA

"Can I take a rain check on that coffee?"

"Absolutely," Bennet says, "and it comes with an up-grade option for dinner."

"I'm in," Georgia says, taking out her phone to enter his details. Then she snaps a quick selfie and texts it to him. "Just let me know where and when."

"Slick move," Lydon says admiringly as she walks away. "I'm totally co-opting it. In fact, I'm going to try the selfie-text right now. Later, drones."

John and Bennet barely have time to wave before Lydon disappears into the courtyard. At once surprised by their baby brother's audacity and perfectly resigned to it, Bennet and John return to the office to show Meryton the invitation. As they wend their way through the Longbourn's sweeping corridors, Bennet relates what he'd seen pass between the two women, and John, who would have defended either or both had one appeared to be wrong, is no more able to explain the behavior than his brother.

It's a mystery indeed.

CHAPTER ELEVEN

Georgia Wickham tells Bennet everything he could possibly want to know about the bobbin. Yes, the bobbin, that round object with flat ends and a tube in its center around which thread or yarn is wound.

It hardly seems like stimulating dinner conversation, and yet the way she relates the travails of her sewing class—ahem, Introduction to Construction Techniques—makes it one of the most entertaining subjects Bennet's ever discussed. She has an effortless ability, he thinks as the waiter clears their dinner plates, for rendering the commonest, dullest, most threadbare topic interesting.

"Ultimately, the bobbin is a metaphor for life," Georgia says, then holds up a hand to preempt a comment he hadn't intended to make. "I know. I know. Anything can be a metaphor for life, but hear me out. I'm right about this one." She takes a sip of red wine and dabs at the corner of her mouth with a white cloth napkin. "You see, the bobbin is a metaphor for life because it represents that commonplace thing that always does you in. We expect elaborate disasters, we prepare for them, but it's the mundane little bobbin that derails your entire final project."

Bennet laughs in appreciation of her well-articulated

and highly entertaining thesis and asks what her final project for Introduction to Construction Techniques would have been if not entirely derailed by one ill-behaved bobbin. But what he really wants to know is her history with Darcy.

He can't ask. He can't even mention her name.

Luckily, he doesn't have to because Georgia brings up the subject herself by asking how long Darcy has been in the city.

"About a month," Bennet says, and, unwilling to let the subject drop, adds, "She prefers London, I understand, even though she owns a huge mansion on Fifth Avenue."

"Yes," Georgia replies, "Pemberley is beautiful—stunning. The recent renovations, which were supposed to be merely cosmetic, hit a snag when they realized all the pipes needed to be replaced, so it's become a massive undertaking. I'm not surprised. The hot water was always a problem. Early in the morning or very late at night, it never quite reached the top floor."

Bennet can't hide his astonishment.

"I'm sure it's very shocking to discover I lived there, given the chilly nature of our meeting last week, which you had to have noticed because, well, you have eyes," she says. "But I've known Darcy and her family my whole life. Do you know her well?"

"As well as I hope to," Bennet says, wondering what the connection could be between this endearing young woman and the frosty Fitzwilliam clan. "I've been at the Netherfield a lot to help Bingley plan the ball she's throwing, so I've spent a good amount of time in her presence. I think she's very unpleasant."

"Really?" Georgia asks, her eyes widening in surprise. "Most people think she's lovely."

Bennet scoffs. "I'm surprised most people aren't put off by her pride."

"But she has all that lovely money and consequence," Georgia says, then pauses as the waiter brings dessert menus and offers coffee. They gratefully accept the latter and pass on the former. "Nobody is put off by money or consequence.

People love it. And they're intimidated by her imposing manners. She holds herself in very high esteem and the world obligingly follows suit."

After two cups of coffee are delivered with a flourish, Georgia asks, "Do you know if she plans to stay in the city for long? I expect it will be a short visit because of the plumbing situation."

"I don't know," Bennet says, "but I haven't heard anything about her leaving. I hope her plans don't affect yours."

"Absolutely not. New York is my home and I won't let Darcy drive me away," Georgia says emphatically. "*I* haven't done anything wrong. She's the one who's disgraced the memory of her mother by going against her wishes. Mrs. Fitzwilliam was the kindest woman who ever lived and the best friend I ever had. As terrible as Darcy has treated me—and it has been, I assure you, very terrible—I feel compelled to accept it out of respect for her mother."

Bennet, who truly doesn't consider himself given to gossip, finds his interest in the subject whetted to an unbearable degree. As much as he wants to know more, however, he can't bring himself to ask, and when Georgia discerns sweet hints of cantaloupe in the coffee, he nods and points to a subtle note of sunflower seed.

The conversation stays on general topics—New York, the design world, the rigors of employment.

"Don't get me wrong, I genuinely like waking up every morning and having somewhere to go," Georgia says. "If left to my own devices, I'd lounge around in my pajamas all day, binge-watching something like *Friends* and trying to decide if it holds up while I slowly sink into depression. It's just that I never thought I'd have a practical office job. All my life, I was going to be an artist. Mrs. Fitzwilliam, knowing how I felt and believing in my talent, promised to support me in that endeavor. Darcy betrayed that promise."

"What?" Bennet exclaims, truly shocked.

"When she died, Mrs. Fitzwilliam left me stock in Fitzwilliam Company, but Darcy had the will overturned so I'd get nothing. So much for painting in a garret in Paris! Instead, I had to return to school to learn a practical skill like graphic design. See? I told you the bobbin is a metaphor for life."

"I can't believe it," Bennet says, horrified. "Did you hire a lawyer to fight it?"

"With what money?" she asks. "I would have needed a team of lawyers to fight Darcy, who could have tied the case up in the courts for years and by the time I got my inheritance, it would have been barely enough to cover my legal bills. Darcy knew exactly what she was doing."

"That's awful. She deserves to be publicly disgraced. You should tell your story to Mashable or TMZ. A petty heiress would get a lot of play in the media."

Georgia shakes her head. "Sooner or later, a gossip site will get the story and expose her mercilessly, but it won't be by my hand. I owe her mother too much."

Bennet is greatly impressed with her high-minded restraint and, as he watches the candlelight flicker in her eyes, thinks she's even lovelier than before.

"But what's her motive? Why be so cruel?"

"Jealousy," she says simply. "Mrs. Fitzwilliam liked me too much. Darcy's not built for that kind of competition, especially when the other person comes out on top. It didn't help that her father died when she was eleven, only a few months after her brother was born. A new baby in the family, a battle for her mother's attention—a lot of drama unfolded. And there I was, an only child with two doting parents. I think she resented me from the beginning."

Bennet shakes his head, trying to assimilate the information. "I didn't think Darcy was as bad as that. I never liked her, sure, but she didn't seem malicious—just sort of annoyed by humanity in general. I never imagined her capable of such cruelty." He falls silent for a few moments of reflection, then continues, "That said, she did mention recently that she's very good at holding a grudge."

Georgia offers a shrug, which Bennet entirely understands. What can she possibly say on the subject?

"I just can't wrap my head around how she could treat someone like you so awfully," Bennet says. He resists the urge to add, "Someone who's beautiful, sweet and kind." Rather, he says, "Someone who'd been her friend since childhood."

"We were raised together, virtually from the cradle," Georgia explains. "My mother was the housekeeper at Pemberley, but she was more than that. She was Mrs. Fitzwilliam's friend and confidante and when my mother got sick—she had kidney cancer—she volunteered to take care of me. She did so, I think, as much out of love for my mother as for me."

"I'm shocked Darcy's pride didn't prevent the injustice. I would have honestly thought she'd be too proud to be dishonest."

"Me too," Georgia replies. "Almost everything she does can be traced back to pride. On the whole, I think it makes her a better person, but nobody's behavior is entirely consistent and, clearly, in this situation, her dislike of me is stronger than anything else."

"You really believe that? Her pride makes her better?"

Georgia shrugs. "It's the reason she's so tolerant and generous. She gives a lot of money to charity and is kind to the people who work for her, which she does out of a sense of pride in her family and a sense of what her mother deserves. She also takes pride in being a good sister, which makes her a kind and careful guardian of her brother."

"What's her brother like?"

Georgia shakes her heard. "I wish I could say friendly and outgoing because it kills me to say anything bad about a Fitzwilliam. But George is just like his sister—very, very proud. He was an adorable child, affectionate and sweet, and we got along really well. But we have no relationship now. He's a handsome man—eighteen or nineteen, and, from what I've heard, very accomplished. Since his mother's death, he's lived in London."

The waiter brings them the check, which Bennet immediately grabs. Georgia wrangles over paying her share, but he refuses to accept a dime.

"At least let me leave the tip," she says, and when he

steadfastly refuses her offers, she assures him that despite her claims to disappointment and penury, she makes a fairly decent living as a foot soldier in the Redcoat Design regiment.

He promises to let her pay the next time they go out, and as they walk to the subway, they discuss potential outings for that eventuality. Bowling is mentioned as a very strong contender, as is Coney Island. It's still a bit chilly out, but the boardwalk is always a pleasure to stroll.

As they arrive at the train, Bennet can't help bringing up Darcy one more time. "I just don't get her relationship with Bingley. How can Bingley, who's so friendly and outgoing and has an impish sense of humor, be friends with such a person? How can they stand each other? Do you know Bingley?"

"Not at all," Georgia says.

"She's lovely and charming. She must not know what Darcy is really like."

"Probably not," she concedes, "but that's because Darcy can be delightful company if she thinks it's worth her while. When she's among people she deems her equals, she's very different from when she's around those she considers beneath her. She's never not proud, but with other rich people, she's tolerant, fair, sincere, open-minded, honorable, even agreeable."

The subway rattles beneath them and Bennet realizes they can't stand there all night talking—although, actually, they could, but not on a first date. He leans down and gives her a gentle kiss, which lasts just long enough for them to realize they're blocking the entrance. Georgia laughs softly, brushes her lips against his and bids him good night as she slips through the turnstile to stand on the downtown platform for the train to Brooklyn. Bennet slides through the same turnstile but waits on the platform going the opposite way—uptown to Queens.

Georgia's train arrives first and she smiles at him through the window as the car starts to move. A few minutes later, the Queens-bound train pulls into the station, and Bennet, his head full of Georgia, climbs on. He can think of nothing but her—and what she's told him—all the way home.

CHAPTER TWELVE

On the afternoon of the Netherfield ball, Bennet and John are still talking about it—what Georgia Wickham said, what Darcy did, what Bingley knows.

John, whose astonishment and concern have not lessened in the week since he'd heard the story, can't believe that Darcy could be so unworthy of Bingley's affection. And yet it's not in his nature to question the veracity of a young woman as likable as Georgia, and the possibility that she has endured such an injustice outrages him.

"You can't keep defending both of them," Bennet says on a frustrated sigh. "You have to concede that someone did something wrong."

John, who's heard this argument at least a dozen times, says, "Something is missing from the story. I don't know what. Maybe they've both been lied to in some way. Someone with an agenda might have intentionally caused a misunderstanding. It's impossible for us to know what actually happened."

Aggravated by his brother's determination to withhold judgment, Bennet growls, "And what about this devious scoundrel with an agenda who might have intentionally caused a misunderstanding? Are you going to clear that person of wrongdoing, too, or am I allowed to think badly of him?"

John is not so easily provoked and says reasonably, "Ridiculing my opinion is not going to make me change it. I can't believe Darcy would behave so callously to a woman who her mother treated like a daughter. To deprive her not just of the money, but the decent living it would have provided, is cruel. Nobody's that mean and if they were, people would talk about it. You can't hide immorality for long."

"I can more easily believe Bingley has been duped by Darcy than Georgia made up the whole thing," Bennet says. "She gave me names, facts, dates—all without fanfare. If none of it's true, then Darcy should deny it. I'll tell you why I believe it: because I saw the way Darcy looked at Georgia at the Longbourn. There's no love lost there."

"It's complicated, and I truly don't know what to think," John admits.

"Then think what I tell you to think," Bennet says.

But it's not that easy for John, who knows only one thing: If Bingley has been misled by Darcy's true nature, then she'll be very upset when she learns the truth.

Unable to calmly contemplate Bingley's distress, he pulls up the guest list from the party, double-checks the names and forwards the document to Sasha, the event organizer Bingley's assistant hired to oversee the entire affair. Bennet, Meryton and he—as well as several other members of the Longbourn staff—are supposed to consider themselves guests at the party.

John appreciates the sentiment but knows it's not possible. When one is surrounded by donors past, present and future, one doesn't have the luxury of being something so innocuous as a party guest. As long as there are tempers to be smoothed and egos to be appeased, he'll consider himself on the clock.

That said, he'll accept with all due gratitude one of the extraordinary gift bags Sasha has assembled, leather satchels overflowing with designer jewelry, upscale perfume and small electronics. A typical Longbourn goody bag contains brochures of upcoming exhibitions, bookmarks with highlights from the collection and a pen from the gift shop. If it's been a particularly good year for fundraising or a bad year for in-house merchandise sales, the gift shop might also throw in a mug with the museum's logo.

The unprecedented glamour of the goodies—as well as their resale value on eBay and Craigslist—has almost everyone in the building jockeying for swag. John can't step outside his office without being accosted by someone looking for a hookup, and he knows Lydon is running a full-scale black market operation out of his backpack. The budding entrepreneur has yet to get his hands on any of the goods, as everything is being stored offsite, but he's confident he can squirrel enough away during the event to make a tidy profit.

John is equally confident he cannot, for the security measures that will be implemented to ensure against theft are extensive. Apparently, Lydon isn't the first impoverished intern to dream big.

As soon as John gets an email from Sasha confirming receipt of the finalized guest list, Bennet announces he has to add one more name. "Audrey Martindale, Julian Martindale's wife. She was supposed to be in Denver to meet with some clients, but that was just canceled and she'd like to come. Can we add her?"

Immediately, John hits reply to Sasha and sends the new name. "You do realize the event is in four hours? At some point, we have to stop adding people."

"Don't look at me. Bingley's the biggest offender. She added six people this morning: the entire freelance team on the *Art & Style* exhibit," Bennet says pointedly. "She can't know the truth."

"*We* don't know the truth," John says reasonably. "We only know one aspect of it. There's more to the story."

Bennet sighs. "If you're going to insist on being fair and impartial, I might as well head over to the Netherfield now to stuff the goody bags with guest memberships and exhibition brochures. I'm curious to see how the preparations are coming along."

"When I left a little before eleven last night, the crew had just finished carrying out the furniture and was about to start building the stage," John says. "Don't forget your tuxedo."

"I'm hardly likely to forget it," Bennet mumbles as he retrieves the brand-new tux from the back of the closet door. Although he's confident—or reasonably confident—that the frayed elbows on his old monkey suit would have made it through at least one more event without tearing, he graciously invested in a new one. Well, *graciously* might not be the right word because it had taken a telephone call from his mother, in which she casually let slip that John had casually let slip the deplorable state of his evening wear, to get him to the store. As much as he resented the expense, he didn't stint on quality or tailoring and walked away with one that actually fit him well in the shoulders, unlike the boxy jacket he'd been wearing since college.

Once in the taxi, Bennet calls Sasha's office to let her assistant know he's on his way to the hotel and texts Georgia to ask if she's coming the party. His contact with her has been sparse in the past week, as the last-minute details of installing the *Art & Style: Impressionism's Influence on Fashion and Modernity* exhibition have been time-consuming and many. Once, she managed to duck her boss long enough to grab coffee with him in the café, and another time she turned an errand to fetch a stapler into a twenty-minute pit stop in his office.

Although Bennet has seen her little since their night out, he has thought about her often—and not just because he's trying to get John to agree she's been horribly mistreated by Darcy. He likes her quick humor, her ready laugh, her easy sociability and her intelligent conversation, and looks forward to getting to know her better, a prospect whose chances are greatly increased by the opening of the show on Tuesday.

Traffic is light, and Bennet's cab is pulling up to the Netherfield by the time Georgia responds to his text with a series of emojis: grinning face, birthday cake, palm tree, confetti, bus, revolving hearts, breakdancing taco. Bennet, whose experience with emojis is limited to scoffing at Lydon's overemployment of them, translates this crash of festive images as a yes. It doesn't occur to him that she might not come until he enters the ballroom at the Netherfield hours later and looks in vain for her among the cluster of Redcoats gathered there.

Georgia's friend Denni, the designer who good-naturedly ran her to ground when she was sipping coffee with Bennet on a stone bench in the café, explains that her colleague had a prior commitment—a birthday party for a friend in Philadelphia. "Not that she wouldn't have blown it off in a heartbeat," she adds, "if she hadn't wanted to avoid a certain person here."

Bennet can't blame Georgia for choosing to skip a party attended by her nemesis, but he *can* blame Darcy, and when she comes over to say hello, he returns her greeting with brusque impatience. Being kind to Darcy feels like a betrayal of Georgia, and he resolves to talk to her as little as possible. Escaping conversation entirely is impossible, however, and by the time he manages to extricate himself, he's in such a bad mood that not even Bingley, who enthusiastically greets him with a piece of rugelach—"Host *and* delivery boy," she says, twinkling—can improve it. Bingley's blindness to Darcy's true nature annoys him.

But Bennet is too good-humored to remain peeved for long, and although his disappointment that Georgia didn't show is keen, he doesn't dwell on it. The party is a brilliant success, with the ballroom overflowing with people and colors—powder blue curtains, deep-purple lilies, neon yellow orchids, bright pink cocktails—and the lovely strains of the orchestra spilling onto the wraparound terrace. The hors d'oeuvres, bite-sized creations that look more like artwork than food, pass generously and frequently through the glittering crowd, and Bennet smiles when he notices Lydon firmly stationed in front of the door through which the trays travel. When he was a recent grad, he'd done the exact same thing.

Although Bennet doesn't have to work the party, he

still has to work the room, and he slowly but methodically seeks out donors. He has whiskey with a hedge fund manager on the terrace, dances the waltz with the CEO of a pet-food company and trades golfing tips with the daughter of a computer chip maker. Later, while waiting at the bar for a much-needed drink, he has the unexpected pleasure of talking about Georgia with one of her colleagues. She's universally liked, he learns, which doesn't surprise him in the least.

With a glass of Syrah and a plate of beautifully presented gourmet appetizers, Bennet finds a quiet corner from which to assess the current state of affairs. As far as his check list of important people goes, he's marked off every name, including spouses, which is a testament, he supposes, to being a guest at an event rather than part guest and part organizer. He's wondering if he should make a second round of small talk—Lila Trudeau loves badminton as well as golf—when suddenly Darcy is beside him requesting a dance.

Stunned, Bennet says yes.

The orchestra is playing a waltz, and as Bennet takes Darcy into his arms, he notices the open-jawed amazement on Meryton's face. Their neighbors on the dance floor, unaware of their track record, pay them no heed.

They dance for some time without speaking a word, and Bennet wonders if the silence will last for the entire song. So be it, he thinks, resolving not to break it. But then he realizes that forcing her to engage in meaningless chatter would be a greater punishment and makes a slight observation about the orchestra.

Darcy replies and immediately falls silent.

Bennet waits a full minute, then says, "It's your turn to say something. I talked about the orchestra so you should say something about the size of the room or the quality of the food."

"A script," she says with an approving smile. "Very well. The squid ink paella is just as delicious as I remember."

"Topical *and* a reference to an earlier conversation. Well done! That comment should keep us for a while. In a few minutes, I'll say something about the view of the George Washington Bridge from the terrace being spectacular. You might want to be prepared with a reply about traffic on the GW during rush hour. It's horrendous during rush hour—and, actually, at most hours of the day—in case you've never experienced the displeasure firsthand."

"Do you always talk while dancing?" she asks with a tilt of her head.

"Of course. As a fundraising professional, I'm obligated to interact with people. If I didn't say anything at all, it would seem odd. I've found that sometimes it's best to figure out the conversation in advance to take off the pressure to be interesting."

"Is that how you feel or how you imagine I feel?" Darcy asks.

"Both," Bennet replies archly, "because we're so much alike. We're both unsocial, taciturn and unwilling to speak unless we can say something so clever it will amaze the room and be repeated for years to come."

"That doesn't sound like you at all," she says. "I don't think it sounds like me either, but clearly I can't be trusted to judge. You seem to think it bears a striking resemblance."

"Me?" Bennet says, feigning surprise. "I would never presume to judge a donor."

Darcy doesn't answer and they're silent until the song ends, at which time Bennet fully expects to return to his quiet corner. But rather than walk away, Darcy asks if *Art & Style* is ready for its opening in three days.

"It's very close, close enough that the reviewer from the *Times* was able to get a sneak peak this afternoon," he says. "A few details still need to be worked out, but I'm sure the design team will have them finalized in plenty of time. The freelance firm the museum hired is top-notch. Bingley was kind enough to invite them tonight. I believe you know one of the designers. I'd just met her the day you dropped by the museum with Bingley, but we've become fast friends."

The effect is immediate. Darcy's features harden into

an expression of sharp dislike, but she doesn't say a word, and Bennet, bound by the demands of his profession, can't press his advantage.

After a moment, Darcy speaks and in a brusque tone says, "Georgia has an easygoing manner and is very good at *making* friends. Whether she's just as capable of *keeping* them is less certain."

"She has had the rotten luck of losing your friendship," Bennet says with emphasis, "and in a way that's likely to hurt her for years to come."

Darcy doesn't answer and seems to want to change the subject. At that moment, the music stops and the orchestra announces it will be taking a brief break. Immediately, soft music from the stereo system fills the air. Over the din of conversation, Meryton's voice rises as he assures Samuel Litchfield, the head of a Hollywood movie studio, whom he had not met above an hour ago, that Bingley's association with the museum will be long and intimate.

"Her interest is personal, you see, and I wouldn't be surprised if she and one of my most devoted employees made their association permanent very soon," Meryton crows.

Bennet winces at his employer's complete lack of discretion and cringes further when Darcy, forcibly struck by the comment, searches out Bingley and John, who are sharing a table.

Recovering herself, however, she turns to Bennet and says, "I'm sorry. I can't seem to recall what we were talking about."

"We weren't talking at all," he says. "I don't think there are two people in the room who have less to say to each other. We've tried two or three topics already and the most success we've had is with the GW Bridge. I can't imagine what we can attempt next."

"What about books?" Darcy asks, smiling gamely. "A well-read donor must be a boon to the fundraising professional."

Bennet shakes his head as they move away from the dance floor. "I'm sure everything I loved, you hated."

"Even better. We can each rabidly defend our points of view."

"Fundraising professionals don't rabidly defend anything," he explains. "We agree with donors, regardless of personal opinion."

"But I'm not a donor," she says, "so you can tell me the name of the last book you read without fear of any inappropriate stance taking."

But Bennet can't access the information in such a setting—tuxedos, kirtinis, exotic flowers, patrons of the arts—and apologizes for being too distracted. One of the things distracting him, or, rather, the largest thing, is Darcy herself and her cruelty toward Georgia. He wants to confront her directly, for hinting at the matter has not drawn forth any satisfying information, but he can't bring himself to say the words. The heir to the Fitzwilliam fortune is not a patron whose goodwill he's courting, and yet he still feels compelled to smooth feathers, not ruffle them.

So he says, "It must be nice."

Darcy's brow furrows, as if she's trying to recall a book with that title. "Excuse me?"

"It must be nice to be so confident in your opinions," Bennet says. "Remember, a few weeks ago, when you said you never let go of a grudge? I was just thinking it must be nice to know you're right. To never doubt yourself. To never worry that you might have been blinded by prejudice."

"I'm very cautious and don't form grudges easily."

"See? There's that confidence again. How can you be so sure?" Bennet asks.

Darcy tilts her head curiously. "Where's this conversation going? I feel like I'm being led somewhere but I can't see the path."

"Nowhere," Bennet answers with a shrug. "I'm just trying to get a better picture of you—for the department's files, of course."

"And how's that going?"

He shakes his head. "Fuzzy. Very fuzzy. I've heard

too many conflicting stories to get a clear sense of your character."

"I'm sure reports of me vary greatly," she says seriously, "but I'd be grateful if you left the file incomplete."

"An incomplete file?" Bennet says with an exaggerated shudder. "Oh, the horror. No, I really must continue. This might be my only chance."

"In that case, please do," she says coldly.

But Bennet doesn't continue, and when they reach the far wall, near the staircase, they part in silence, both dissatisfied with the exchange, though not to an equal degree. Darcy, whose feelings for him are strong, soon excuses his behavior and directs all her anger toward Georgia.

They haven't been separated long—Bennet's scarcely had time to procure another glass of wine—when Carl corners him near the terrace doors.

"So, Bennet, I hear you're hanging out with Georgia Wickham these days. Your brother's been asking me a dozen questions about her. I bet she didn't mention that she's the daughter of the old Pemberley housekeeper. You shouldn't trust a word the old girl says. She tells anyone who'll listen that Darcy abused her horribly, but it's bullshit. Darcy was always decent to her, and Georgia repaid her with a betrayal so awful Darcy can't bring herself to talk about it. I don't know the details, but I do know Darcy isn't to blame, and my sister, who is too kind to exclude Georgia from a blanket invitation to her design firm, was relieved that she found something else to do tonight. I'm sorry if the truth upsets you."

"What truth?" Bennet snaps. "All you've accused her of is being the daughter of Mrs. Fitzwilliam's housekeeper, and that, I assure you, she *did* tell me."

Carl looks at him with sneering pity. "Well, I tried to help you. Now you're on your own."

"Condescending snob," Bennet mutters to himself as he watches Bingley's brother storm through the terrace doors, amazed at the other man's attempt to influence him with such a paltry attack. Trying to be helpful, is he? Bennet shakes his head in disgust. The only thing Carl Bingston is, is the willfully ignorant dogsbody of Darcy Fitzwilliam.

Inhaling sharply, Bennet decides to seek out John to find out what, if anything, he's learned about Georgia from Bingley. He finds him in the living room, sitting on the sofa next to their host, and the expression of happiness on his face, the glow of pleasure and joy, removes everything else from Bennet's mind. He feels confident that Meryton's estimation of the situation is entirely accurate. Bingley's connection to the Longbourn Collection is deep and personal.

When he can pull John away—and he doesn't so much as pull John away as catch him when Bingley releases him—he asks if he's discovered anything interesting about Georgia.

"I've nothing satisfactory to report," John says. "Bingley doesn't know the whole story and is entirely ignorant of what Georgia did to offend Darcy, but she swears Darcy has done nothing wrong and is convinced Georgia is a nightmare. According to Bingley and her brother, she deserves everything she's gotten."

"So Bingley doesn't know Georgia herself?"

"Nope. Never saw her until the other day at the Longbourn."

"Did she say anything about the shares?"

"She doesn't remember the details, but she vaguely recalls something about Georgia being named in the will."

Bennet nods slowly as he digests the information. Although he finds Bingley's defense of her friend admirable—and to her credit—he's still not convinced of its merit. Bingley knows some of the story but not all of it, and what she does know, she learned from Darcy herself. Surely, such unreliable evidence isn't enough to overturn the verdict he's already arrived at.

No, he decides firmly, it's definitely not.

Bingley immediately joins them again, sliding her arm through John's as she announces she has to steal him for a few moments. "The director of grants for the Ford Foundation is asking for you by name," she says, "and I must deliver."

Although Bennet himself would not mind an introduction to the director of grants for the Ford Foundation, he nods easily and watches them disappear into the crowd. Then he returns to the ballroom, where Julian Martindale and his wife are sampling toro from the sushi bar. They're both delighted with the affair—and not just because the tuna belly is the best Audrey has ever had, though that does weigh heavily with her, most definitely more than the kirtinis, which are also excellent—and Julian announces that Venture Marts is one hundred percent on board with the Bauhaus exhibit.

"My team has been impressed with your organization and clear-sightedness," Julian says, taking a break from eating to shake hands. "We'll set up an appointment next week to nail down the numbers."

"That's wonderful news. I promise you, this exhibition is a great fit for Venture," Bennet says as a little cash register in his head goes *ka-ching*. It's rare for one of their shows to be solidly funded so far in advance.

After staying long enough to confirm that the toro is indeed remarkable, Bennet leaves the couple to their enthusiastic sushi consumption. Aside from a few hiccups—*I'm looking at you, Mr. Carl Bingston*—the evening is going well. Important new contacts have been established, vital existing ones have been reinforced, and significant commitments have been made. And as if that's not enough good stuff for one night, his brother is well and truly on his way to falling in love with a wonderful woman. It's as plain as the besotted grin on his face.

It's so obvious to him, he's startled to discover his younger brother, who he finds near the check-in table a half hour later, can't see it.

"If John wants to snag an heiress," Lydon says thoughtfully, "he really needs to step up his game. You know, invest more in the situation. He's playing it too casual, like he can take it or leave it, and that doesn't fly with women."

Bennet doesn't know which part of this statement to

address first, and deciding Lydon will never believe their brother isn't trying to *snag an heiress,* devotes himself to the second half. "John's totally invested in the situation. If he were any more invested, his eyes would be shaped like cartoon hearts."

Lydon shakes his head doubtfully. "I don't know. He seems pretty chill to me."

"That's because you're too busy trying to figure out how to sneak loot from the gift bags without anyone noticing," Bennet says with a glance at the long table covered end to end with leather satchels. "Trust me, it's obvious how John feels and I'm sure Bingley knows it."

Even if Lydon wants to argue his point further, he's too busy affecting outrage over the unfair charge of swag theft to bother. "How dare you, sir! I'm not trying to sneak loot, as you so coarsely put it. I'm helping out the fine men and women who are manning the check-in table. It's hard work, and we deserve your respect."

Bennet isn't fooled, but he's amused by the amount of heartfelt indignation his lazy brother is able to muster. "Hard work, huh?"

"Hard work," Lydon repeats firmly. "Some of these people checking in don't even know their own name. One guy said Sinjin, but it was clearly St. John."

"It's English," Bennet explains.

"Yeah, I know it's English. *Yo hablo los Ingles,*" Lydon says with an eye roll.

"I mean, it's British."

Lydon wrinkles his brow as he digests this information.

"I hope you weren't rude," Bennet adds.

"It isn't rude to correct a mispronunciation," Lydon says defensively. "In fact, it's rude *not* to."

Bennet shakes his head and, wondering how much offense his brother has given during the course of the evening, asks him to leave check-ins to the staff Sasha hired to oversee them. Then he suggests Lydon go mingle and enjoy the party. Even as the words come out of his mouth, he knows it's a bad idea and yet his options are limited. He can't let his brother steal from the bags, and he can't have him thrown out of the party.

"Hey, they need me here," Lydon protests, "and my intentions are pure."

Sighing, Bennet pulls a pristine white box with a Fitbit logo from Lydon's pocket and points to the stairs leading up to the ballroom. "Go."

Smart enough to cut his losses, Lydon smiles winningly at his brother and shrugs as if to say, You can't blame a guy for trying. Then he saunters up the stairs to find a new challenge.

"Thank you, Mom," Bennet mutters as he looks at the table and wonders which one is missing a Fitbit. It could be all of them or none of them, depending on how much time Lydon had and his method for filching swag.

Defeated, Bennet hands the box to a member of the check-in crew and apologizes for not knowing where it belongs just as another guest arrives—a tall, heavy-looking man of about twenty-five who announces himself to be Collin Parsons. His name can't be located on any of the lists on five clipboards, even though the staff checks under *C* and *P* and even *B* for the first letter of his middle name, which, he admits, he didn't supply when he replied to the invitation.

As Collin Parsons waits for someone to straighten out the misunderstanding, his air is grave and stately, and his manners are very formal. His attire, though elegant and pristine, is striking, with its elaborately tied cravat, high collar and sage-and-salmon-striped waistcoat.

Unable to find his name or to decide who should eject him from the foyer, the check-in team calls Sasha, who promptly turns up to handle the situation. With smooth efficiency, she discovers Mr. Parsons to be a relation of Darcy's and kindly requests that he wait another few minutes while she confirms that information.

He graciously agrees.

Bennet also waits. Although he knows it's none of his business, he can't turn his eyes away.

Two minutes later, Sasha, convinced of his lineage, waves the gentleman through, and Bennet follows him up the stairs. Spotting Darcy at once, Collin snags several orchids from a vase, wraps them in a light-blue linen napkin and boldly strides up to her with the flowers on offer.

Fascinated, Bennet stays a few steps behind and watches the exchange.

Collin prefaces his speech with a solemn bow, but before he can launch into his purpose, Darcy says with curious weariness, "I'm not marrying you."

"I am not now to learn," Collin replies, with a formal wave of the hand, "that it is usual with young ladies to reject the address of the man whom they secretly mean to accept, when he first applies for their favor?"

Darcy eyes him with unrestrained wonder and tells him in a cool tone not to be a fool.

Undiscouraged, Collin continues in the stiff, affected voice he has adopted for this proposal, which bears no resemblance to the more-relaxed tone he'd used downstairs. "As I must conclude that you are not serious in your rejection of me, I shall choose to attribute it to your wish of increasing my love by suspense, according to the usual practice of elegant females."

She scoffs, but Collin blithely ignores her contempt.

"I know it to be the established custom of your sex to reject a man on the first application," he says, "and perhaps you have now said as much to encourage my suit as would be consistent with the true delicacy of the female character."

"Collin," Darcy says warningly.

Now the gentleman shrugs and laughs, and the stiff pomposity with which he made his proposal vanishes as quickly as it appeared.

"My apologies," he says easily, "but I'd be very grateful if you'd reconsider. You're the only woman I can bear to face every morning over breakfast as long as I don't have to face you at night over the pillows."

Darcy shakes her head. "If you'd just tell Aunt Catherine you're gay, she'd stop trying to marry you off."

"You adorably naïve child," he says with a fond smile. "It's precisely because I am gay that the dear old battle-ax is so determined. She wants me married with children like any properly repressed homosexual of 1952. Our aunt has very old-fashioned notions. She wants you to get hitched, too. An unmarried woman of a certain age is a scandal."

As much as Bennet wants to hear Darcy's response to this provoking comment, he can't shirk his duties and when Meryton calls his name, he immediately answers the summons.

His curiosity about Collin Parsons, however, is appeased a half hour later when John introduces him as Darcy's cousin by marriage. He's the son of Catherine de Bourgh's late husband's sister, which clears up the legality of his proposed union, if not the moral and ethical concerns.

"He wants to volunteer at the Longbourn," John explains.

Using the pretentious tone with which he proposed to Darcy, Collin says, "It is the particular advice and recommendation of the very noble lady whom I have the honor of calling patroness—and, yes, that *is* sarcasm you hear in my voice—that I find some useful occupation. Since the family is appallingly rich, she doesn't mean *work* work but rather some genteel distraction that will make me appear to be a useful member of society while actually requiring very little effort."

Amused by how easily the gentleman pivots from full-bore pomposity to down-to-earth friendliness and back again, Bennet asks, "Your patroness?"

"My aunt, Lady Catherine de Bourgh. She isn't actually of the British aristocracy, but she carries herself with *such* nobility that it's impossible to think of her in any other way. I've even observed to her that she seems born to be a duchess, and that the most elevated rank, instead of giving her consequence, would be adorned by her. These are the kind of little things which please her ladyship, and it is a sort of attention which I conceive myself peculiarly bound to pay."

Now Bennet smiles. "That sounds like a lot of work."

Returning again to his normal, conversational tone, Collin says, "Not at all. The old bat doesn't appreciate anything but herself. But she administers my trust fund, so I do what she tells me to do. You will let me come into the office, won't you, and do office-y stuff like—I don't know—order cappuccinos for the boardroom?"

"We don't have a boardroom at the Longbourn," Bennet says, "only one slightly rundown conference room that we fight over like cats and dogs, and the cappuccino budget was diverted years ago to pay for new door handles in the bathroom. But if that doesn't discourage you, we'd be glad to have an extra pair of hands."

"It sounds fantastically shabby. Sign me up. When Lady Catherine ordered me to donate my time to a high-minded cultural institution, she meant the Met or the philharmonic. My working at a little nothing place on the outskirts of Queens will drive her crazy. No offense intended, of course," he hastens to add.

Bennet assures him none is taken. "We're happy to be a weapon in your ongoing war. Can you swing by on Monday?"

Collin nods and salutes as if addressing a superior officer. "Yes, sir. I shall be there at noon sharp. And I promise you'll regret this only a little."

Knowing he can't possibly regret anything more than agreeing to take on Lydon, Bennet tells him he's not worried.

It's on the tip of Bennet's tongue to ask Collin about Georgia Wickham. As a member of the family, he's more likely to be informed of the details than Bingley. But he can't bring himself to be that forthright, not with someone he's just met. Perhaps after he's worked in the office for a few weeks, Bennet will feel comfortable asking a few leading questions.

Now, however, he thanks Collin for his willingness to serve and requests that he pass along his gratitude to his patroness.

Collin's eyes twinkle. "We're going to get along so well. Would you mind greatly if I continue most perseveringly by your side to ensure the rest of the evening brings you little amusement?"

To Bennet's relief, Collin is joking and after a few minutes, he excuses himself to say hello to a friend he spots loitering by the bar. It's easier to spot loitering friends now because the crowd has started to thin.

The Longbourn party are the last of all the company to depart, and thanks to a maneuver by Mr. Meryton, they have to wait for their car service a quarter of an hour after everyone else is gone. Fifteen minutes is just enough time to see how heartily some members of the family wish them gone. Hurst and Carl, who open their mouths only to complain about how tired they are, repulse every attempt Meryton makes at conversation. Meryton, whose triumph can be measured in actual dollars, is incapable of resting on his laurels and continues to pitch the museum to the exhausted company.

Bennet wishes them gone, too, and suggests more than once that they wait in the lobby. Bingley, however, insists they're perfectly fine exactly where they are. What she means, of course, is that *she* is perfectly fine exactly where she is—only inches from John, whose head is close to hers in conversation.

Finally, Meryton's phone chirps, alerting them that their car has arrived. Rising to leave, Meryton says with disconcerting firmness that he hopes to see the whole group soon at the Longbourn.

"Particularly you, Ms. Bingston," he says. "You must come by whenever you want. We'll have an informal dinner in the trustees' dining room. Please don't feel as though you have to wait for an invitation."

Bingley, who's flying out to London in the morning—no, Bennet thinks with a glance at his phone, in six hours—promises to call as soon as she gets back.

"It'll be a short trip," she says, with a sidelong glance at John. The besotted look he gives her in return speaks volumes.

Bennet darts a glance at Lydon to see if he caught the exchange, but his younger brother is in the middle of violent yawn. "Lord, how tired I am," he exclaims.

Meryton is perfectly satisfied and leaves the hotel daydreaming happily of John's future as the fabulously wealthy Mr. Charlotte Bingston. He concedes the necessity of a prenup and calculates how long it will take the lawyers to hammer out a settlement. And the wedding, too. Planning something that immense can't be done overnight, but the template for the party has already been established, and it would be folly itself to move all that furniture back into the Netherfield ballroom only to have to move it out again a few months later.

Three months, he thinks as the car drops him off first at his little house less than a mile from the Longbourn, before everything is set.

Four tops.

CHAPTER THIRTEEN

Bennet starts to measure time in units of Bingley.

Every day that passes without word from her is another Bingston. Today, the first official day of summer, although the weather has been unbearably hot for two weeks, marks four dozen Bingstons.

A month ago, he would have bet everything he had—his apartment, his first edition of *David Copperfield,* his right arm—that they wouldn't reach this milestone. And yet here they are: 48 days without any contact from Bingley.

It doesn't make sense. The look on her face when they'd left the Netherfield after the ball had said, *I'm all in.*

And now she's out, without a word of explanation. A few texts to John, a giddy email describing a misunderstanding with a flight attendant on the way out ("And then I said, 'But I named the *frog* Templeton!'") and one brief telephone call had dwindled into resounding silence. The cursory email John sent, ostensibly addressing Gold Circle Diamond Society matters but really a desperate plea for connection, was answered by her assistant, Mitzy.

No, it doesn't make any sense at all.

But it does make sense, Bennet thinks as he climbs the stairs to their office. It makes perfect sense because clearly snobbery has prevailed over sentiment, with Carl somehow convincing Bingley once and for all to sever her ties with a suitor whose lineage doesn't befit her pedigree and whose career—professional beggar!—ill-suits his pride.

Bennet doesn't have proof, but he knows he's right. He can feel it in his bones.

John won't talk about it. As Lydon says, he's a very cool customer and sometimes even seems surprised that he once knew someone named Bingley. "Who?" he'll ask when Bennet brings up her name. "Oh, yeah, right."

When Bennet backed him into a corner—at mark 28 Bingstons—John irritably announced that he's not so naïve as to mistake flirtation for infatuation.

But he *is* naïve, Bennet thinks with frustration, for his brother can't conceive of a person such as Carl, who would ruin his sister's happiness merely to satisfy his own vanity. No, it's far easier for him to believe Bingley never felt anything at all, and he steadfastly refuses to try to get in touch with her again. He can't imagine anything more mortifying than playing the jilted lover or accosting her with his emotions. It's beneath his professional dignity. When Bennet suggests he fly to London, he turns white and then red and then excuses himself from the room.

That was 13 Bingstons ago.

Meryton, of course, is entirely oblivious to the anguish unfolding directly in front of him and continues to discuss Bingley daily. If he's not lamenting her departure, he's speculating about her return. Sometimes, when things are quiet, he'll step into their office and fondly recall a small detail about the Netherfield ball, some aspect of the event so minor and negligible—"The silver serving platters were so well polished I could see my reflection"—that it doesn't need to be mentioned at all.

It's during these moments when John's composure slips and Bennet glimpses his brother's suffering. It bothers him to distraction that there's nothing he can do to alleviate it. Not even fulfilling his own fantasy of meeting Carl in a dark alley and beating him senseless can improve the situation.

Of course, if John would just *call* Bingley....

Given that it's been almost fourteen days—a full fort-night of Bingstons—since Bennet last told John to get in touch with her, he resolves to bring it up again. All John can do is blanch and blush and leave.

But Bennet doesn't mention Bingley now because the office is full. Lydon and Collin, stuffing envelopes at his desk, have exiled him to a folding chair in the corner. He thinks about going down to the café to work for an hour or seeing if the conference room is empty for once, but he doesn't want to upset the delicate balance of productivity. The intern and volunteer are for once crushing their as-signment, folding, stuffing, licking and stamping as if they've known how to do menial office tasks all along.

John notices it, too, and darts a puzzled glance at him, as if to say, What's going on?

Bennet shrugs and continues entering new contacts into the data management software.

After an unprecedented stretch of twenty-five minutes of silence, Collin says, "I'm happy—nay, eager—to serve the cause any way I can, but if you really want a return on your investment, you should send me into the field to charm rich old biddies. They love me."

John doesn't look up from his computer as he says, "The number one rule of development is, don't call them rich old biddies."

In the middle of folding a flier, Lydon looks up and says the proper term is *loaded old crones*. Then he snickers at his own joke.

"The trick," Collin explains, "is to pretend they're all Lady Catherine. Puff up their consequence with obsequious blather and they're putty in your hands."

Although Bennet doesn't doubt that Collin's upbringing gives him privileged access to the privileged, he's equally sure he lacks the tact and temperament for wooing donors. After a few calls on their behalf, Collin would give so much offense to his aunt's old biddy friends that Bennet can easily imagine all of them being tossed out of the Longbourn on their ears.

"You're doing a great job with the mailing," Bennet says.

Collin adds a stamp to an envelope, realizes he's placed it in the wrong corner, and unable to remove it smoothly, throws both into the trash. "You show great wisdom in not trusting me, but you should at least let me have a crack at my aunt. She's the linchpin. Get her and the rest of the DAR will fall over themselves to cut you a check."

Bennet shrugs noncommittally, as if he's actually considering the suggestion. In fact, the decision is not his to make; his purview is corporate giving. John's in charge of individual gifts and Meryton is in charge of the museum. Still, Bennet doubts it's a good idea to approach Lady Catherine, the one relative of Darcy's who is, by all reports, even more insufferable than she is.

Although Bennet has directed the vast majority of his anger over Bingley's abandonment at her brother Carl, he has yet to acquit her best friend of wrongdoing. He knows Darcy is in some way complicit; he just hasn't figured out the extent of her involvement. Several times he's been on the verge of asking Collin what he knows, but given how unhelpful he was with the Wickham matter—merely shrugging and saying nobody in the family likes to talk about that ugliness—he's resisted the urge. The young man is either too discreet to discuss private family matters or too oblivious to provide useful information. Either way, he's not a source to be tapped.

When Meryton enters the office a few minutes later, he's surprised to see so many people working industriously in the small space and he pauses momentarily to take it all in before returning to his original purpose: preening over a contact he made at the Netherfield ball.

"I just had the most delightful conversation with Mrs. Everett Pokelberg, whose name you most likely know from the board of the Whitney, where she was a huge force behind moving the museum to the Meatpacking District."

"Very rich old biddy," Collin says under his breath.

"She was thoroughly charmed by us at the party," Meryton continues. "Actually, in our conversation, she said she was charmed by me, but of course I would never take full credit for anything. She's very interested in learning more about the Longbourn, and I'm going to her apartment on Park Avenue next week to discuss it further. As you know, her husband, Mr. Pokelberg, is a dry-cleaning magnate and jumped fourteen slots on the Billionaires Index in March after the introduction of a new line of earth-friendly chemicals. I'm sure she'll be good for a donation in the mid five figures. Or," he gasps as the numbers spiral dizzyingly in his head, "maybe even the low sixes."

Lydon, who needs very little provocation to cease working, stands up and shakes Meryton's hand with more enthusiasm than the moment requires. "Great work, sir. Really great. Maybe she'll even go as high as the mid six figures. You have to dream big, sir. You taught me that."

At this praise, Meryton swings from preening to basking. "Yes, well, sure," he says, his eyes glowing brightly. "But if I am an excellent teacher, it's only because you have proven to be an adept student."

Adept is one word for it, Bennet thinks cynically.

"I must dash off a note to Bingley, alerting her to the connection and thanking her for her help," Meryton says. Then he shakes his head decisively. "No, I'll wait until she returns to New York and tell her in person."

"Bingley's not returning to New York," Collin says as he puts a stamp—in the right place this time (huzzah!)—on another envelope.

"What?" Meryton asks.

"Bingley's not coming back," Collin says again. "She's staying in Europe."

Meryton shakes his head. "I don't understand."

"She bumped into an old boyfriend at a party in London, a college friend of Carl's, I believe, and he's invited her to his chateau in the Alps for July. They're all going: Carl, Hurst, Lucy and Bingley. Maybe Darcy, too. I'm not entirely clear on the details."

Although Collin has spelled out the young heiress's

intentions in clear, simple language, Meryton is unable to process it. "That's all right. Bingley will supply all the details when she returns."

Unaccustomed to Meryton's particular brand of self-delusion, Collin tries again to make him understand the situation, but the executive director remains impervious to the truth. After all, Bingley is the chair of the Diamond Circle Patrons Committee and she has a very special relationship with the museum—wink, wink, John—and has promised to throw another event over the summer. Something more intimate. A lunch, he believes.

Collin darts a baffled look at Bennet, then turns back to Meryton to make a third attempt, but the little man runs into his office rather than be forced to accept an unbearable truth.

While Collin marvels over Meryton's willful incomprehension—"Did that actually just happen?"—Bennet watches his brother struggle to keep his emotions in check. John blinks wildly, taking several deep breaths, and Bennet can only imagine how painful it is to hear the words.

It's one thing to know what you know and another thing to *know* it.

Lydon laughs at some quip Collin makes and then says, "Hey, Bennet, you were dumped by your hottie, too, right?"

For once, Bennet is grateful for his youngest brother's thoughtlessness because it keeps the focus off John. "Well, I'm not sure *dumped* is the right word. We only went out a few times and most of our dates were just coffee in the Longbourn café. It was hardly a thing. Still, whatever the thing was, it's over. I believe she's seeing a banker now."

"Dissed for the financial sector," Lydon says with an empathetic shake of the head. "You know that move was all about the Benjamins. It's the guys with the money who get the girls."

Bennet wants to protest his brother's cynical interpretation of events, but part of him knows it's true. A drudge in a provincial museum's development department is never going to make as much money as a senior vice president at Goldman Sachs, and while he wouldn't expect that to factor into the dating decisions of most modern women, he understands how it would for Georgia. Having been deprived of her dream one way, she's determined to get it another. If that means marrying a man rich enough to let her paint all day, then so be it. He doesn't blame her.

"I'm the guy with the money," Collin says, "and I dearly hope I don't get any of the girls."

"More for me," Lydon says with a grin. He looks down at the stack of envelopes filling the cardboard box as if seeing it for the first time, and struck by how much work they've already done, asks Collin if he wants to take a coffee break.

They're gone in seconds, zipping out the door so quickly the fliers actually flutter in their wake, and Bennet waits a beat before saying to John, who's been typing furiously for several minutes, "Let's get a drink."

John doesn't break stride as he says, "Maybe later."

Bennet sighs and watches him doggedly evade eye contact for entire minutes. Then he gets up and reads the screen over his brother's shoulder. It's a Word document filled with the same sentence repeated over and over: *The quick brown fox jumped over the lazy dog.*

John stops typing, but he keeps his eyes determinedly ahead. "I will not pine," he says with quiet dignity. "I'll forget her and before long neither one of us will be able to recall what the big deal was."

His brother knows this is patently false. John will pine and repine and even on occasion supine glumly on his bed in the silence of his apartment. And Bennet can do nothing about it.

"Let's get a drink," he says again.

Wearily, John gestures to his computer as if to imply he can't interrupt his work, but he recognizes the futility of pointing to a screen filled with paragraph after paragraph of the same half dozen words and agrees to go.

Two hours later, when Meryton returns to ask when Bingley will be back in town, he's surprised to find the office empty.

CHAPTER FOURTEEN

Having scotched Collin's proposal to woo his aunt on the museum's behalf in late June, Bennet finds himself agreeing to court her himself in mid-July.

He's not entirely sure why he fell in with the plan, other than it's hot in the city and John is in Cape Cod and Lydon's constant complaints about the heat are getting on his nerves. Plus, Collin is persistent. He doesn't so much as issue invitations as carpet bomb them. After an extended campaign, Bennet surrenders—yes, a weekend in the Hamptons would be a wonderful way to get away from the city and, sure, while he's out there he may as well try to convince a wealthy patron of the arts to consider the Longbourn as an institution worthy of her attention.

In the moment, the logic had been irrefutable.

Now, as Collin leads him down the path to his country house, Bennet isn't so sure the weekend is such a good idea, for it seems foolhardy indeed to believe that the woman who owns this sprawling seaside estate would welcome him with anything other than contempt.

"The formal gardens, set out in such perfect symmetry that not a rose dare bloom on the east walk without a bud on the west walk demonstrating equal boldness, were designed by Frederick Law Olmstead's partner's great-great-grandson," Collin explains with withering pomposity. "The fields to the left, which extend for several acres, are pleasantly dotted with trees. There's a clump of fifteen oaks, a clump of twelve walnuts, a clump of ten pines and a clever assortment of honeysuckle, forsythia and rhododendron."

The walk from the road to the house is short, but Collin's commentary, delivered with a minuteness that leaves beauty entirely behind, is long on details as he points out every view.

"Of all the views my garden or the country—no, the nation—can boast, none can be compared with the prospect of Rosings," Collin continues in his self-important drawl as he gestures grandly to the stately home across the large field. "A handsome modern building, Rosings is well situated on rising ground. To its right, you'll note the Atlantic Ocean, which Lady Catherine has positioned to perfectly align with the southern views from her second-floor bedroom window."

Bennet chuckles. "Is the sunset her doing as well?"

Switching to his regular conversational tone, Collin says, "She'd be the first to give herself credit for it."

Finally, they arrive at his house and Collin reaches into his pocket for the keys. "And this is the Parsonage," he says, unlocking the door. He then leads Bennet to the parlor, and welcoming his guest to his humble abode, offers refreshments.

"How does a beer sound?" he asks, disappearing around a bend.

"Perfect," Bennet calls.

A moment later, Collin returns with two bottles from a microbrewery in Montauk and a bowl of pretzels. "Sit down. Make yourself comfortable," he says as he puts the beers on the coffee table. "I trust I don't have to point out the neatness of the entrance?"

"As long as I don't have to admire every article of furniture in the room," Bennet says with a smile.

"Gawd, no, we'll get plenty of that later at my aunt's."

"But it *is* a great house," he adds, looking around with sincere admiration. It's rather small but well built and convenient.

"It is, and I'm very grateful to have it. On special days, my aunt drives by in her silver Rolls," he says, shifting effortlessly into his tone of excessive formality. "It's a particular honor to rush to the window to observe her progression."

Collin opens a window to let in the ocean breeze, and Bennet, listening to the breaking surf of the Atlantic, realizes he's very happy to be there. All week, he'd been thinking of this trip only in terms of Lady Catherine—that is, an unpleasant work assignment he felt ethically, if not morally, obligated to accept. But now, as he takes a long sip of his beer, which is icy and crisp, he relishes the prospect of the weekend itself: the sun, the beach, the fresh air, the peace, the solitude.

"Thank you for inviting me," he says.

"My pleasure," Collin says as he sits in an oversize armchair. "I love flaunting my boyfriends in front of my aunt."

"I'm not your boyfriend."

Collin's grin is as wide as it is mischievous. "Lady Catherine doesn't know that."

"I thought the point of the weekend was for me to pitch the Longbourn to your aunt," Bennet says.

"That's *your* point," Collin says. "I'm here to administer my monthly dose of annoyance."

It occurs to Bennet that their goals for the weekend are at cross-purposes, but he'd never be so churlish as to point that out. Furthermore, he doubts that Mrs. de Bourgh's homophobia will be the deciding strike against the Longbourn.

Sadly, the Longbourn will be the deciding strike against the Longbourn.

They finish their beers in companionable silence, then Collin leads him upstairs to his room, hitting all the essentials along the way: bathroom, thermostat, linens.

"Towels are on the dresser," Collin says, "and extra blankets are in the closet. I'll leave you to get settled in. We've been summoned to the manor at eight for cocktails. We have to dress for dinner but don't stress over your clothing selection. Just wear your best thing. My aunt won't think less of you for being simply dressed. She likes to have the distinction of rank preserved."

Bennet packed a lightweight gray suit for just such an occasion, and he takes a brief, absurd moment to wonder if dressing too well for dinner will be held against him.

The weather is lovely, so they have a pleasant walk across the field. Collin talks a little bit about his childhood and what it was like to grow up amid such luxurious surroundings, punctuating his tale by enumerating the windows in the front of the house and relating what the glazing had originally cost Sir Lewis de Bourgh.

"It goes without saying, I trust," Collin says as they ascend the steps to the hall, "that old Uncle Lew wasn't of the peerage either."

The butler promptly shows them into the living room, and though they're precisely on time, Lady Catherine takes them to task for being late.

"That's my fault, darling," Collin says in a tone somewhere between the high pomposity of his mockery and the easy informality of his conversation. "I was pointing out the fine proportion and delicately carved ornaments in the entrance hall and lost track of time in my rapture."

Although this comment strikes Bennet as over the top, for who could utter the word *rapture* without at least a hint of ridicule, Collin's aunt seems gratified by his excessive admiration and gives her nephew a most gracious smile.

After he introduces Bennet and the formalities are observed, they're instructed to sit on the sofa in expectation of their other guests. While they wait, cocktails are not so much served as assigned, with their hostess deciding unilaterally what would suit them best, which is how Bennet winds up with a vodka tonic despite his dislike of clear liquor.

Lady Catherine, who is a tall, large woman, with strongly marked features, allocates a glass of champagne for herself, which strikes Bennet as unfair and yet somehow entirely fair. Her air, he discovers, is not conciliating, nor is her manner of receiving guests designed to make them feel comfortable. What Collin said is true: She likes to have the distinctions of rank preserved. From the moment Bennet enters the room, he knows he's a vodka tonic and will always be a vodka tonic. Collin, for all his filial devotion and duty, is only a whiskey and soda.

Fascinated, Bennet leans back comfortably on the cushion and enjoys what he immediately thinks of as the "Lady Catherine Show," for there's little to be done in her presence but listen to her talk, which she does without intermission until dinner is served, delivering her opinion on every subject in so decisive a manner it proves that she's not used to having her judgment contradicted.

Poor Collin! How familiarly and minutely she delves into his personal life, offering a great deal of advice as to the management of every minor detail. She finds no particular too small for her notice and she counsels him on where to stand on the train platform (at the western end of the green painted line), which train to take (5:43 p.m. on Sunday evening or the 6:31 on Monday morning) and how to store his train ticket in his wallet (in the front pocket with the corner tilting upward). Exhausting the matter of the Long Island Rail Road, though having meditated on the subject for an impressive sixteen minutes, she's devoted more time to it in a single cocktail hour than the chairman of the MTA does in an entire week, she applies herself to meat preparation efforts. The subject is dear to her heart, and she provides a twelve-minute off-the-cuff tutorial on the proper procedure for handling poultry to avoid an outbreak of salmonella whilst cooking on one's Alfresco LX2 stainless-steel grill.

It's unclear whether she knows her nephew is a vegetarian, but it's entirely apparent she considers such a state to be as injudicious a lifestyle choice as refusing to date members of the opposite sex.

Despite the onslaught—or, perhaps, because of it—Collin remains upbeat, good-naturedly acquiescing to every directive and even raising the level of detail as if trying to outdo her. When she tells him to pull milk at the grocery store from the row farthest from the front to ensure the most agreeable expiration date, he asks her the best technique for rearranging the milk cartons. To no one's surprise she's already considered this problem and suggests what she calls the sales clerk method, in which you ask a sales clerk to do it for you. Many of her solutions employ the clever contrivance of using other people, and Bennet, processing the depths of her highhandedness, realizes he'll never be able to think of her in any terms other than the ones Collin has already established. Title or no title, she'll always be Lady Catherine to him.

In the intervals of her discourse with Collin, she addresses a variety of questions to Bennet, of whom she knows nothing. She asks him how many brothers he has, whether they're older or younger than himself, whether any of them are married, whether they're gainfully employed, whether they're handsome, where they've been educated, what kind of car his father drives and what his mother's maiden name had been.

Although Bennet concedes the validity of some of the questions, for asking about one's siblings is a conversational standard, even in Michigan, he finds the majority of her queries nosy and it requires considerable effort on his part to calmly reply that Dad drives a Prius. He's more inclined to tell her it's none of her damn business.

Bearing no particular allegiance to fossil fuels, Lady Catherine applauds the efficiency of a hybrid while questioning his parents' need for economy. She's speculating on their profligate spending habits—"You did say the house had *three* full baths, did you not?"—when the door opens to admit the missing dinner guests.

Darcy enters followed by her cousin, a blond woman of about thirty years with long, tanned limbs and a grateful smile. Bennet, not anticipating this development, rises slowly to his feet and examines Darcy critically, noting she looks just as she had in the city.

Bennet is unsure what he wants to say to her—naturally, he wants to challenge her on the matter of Bingley, but he knows to confront her directly in her aunt's drawing room would be a gross faux pas—and is spared the necessity of talking by Lady Catherine, who immediately admonishes her new guests on the lateness of their arrival.

Having failed to take her advice on the superiority of the railroad over the expressway, the two women are now obliged to listen to a recitation of the many ghastly traffic jams through which their aunt has had to suffer. Although egregiously abused by Suffolk County roads in particular, she doesn't limit her account by geographic relevance, and relates, in vivid detail, intolerable gridlock in Marseille caused by a visiting dignitary from Rome who may or may not have been the pope.

Collin leans over to Bennet and says softly, "Isn't she fabulous?"

Bennet isn't quite sure *fabulous* is the right adjective to describe Catherine de Bourgh, for she is more pedant than orator, but he understands her appeal for Collin. There is something rather epic in her ostentatious display of trivialities.

When her nieces have been suitably chastised, Lady Catherine announces that dinner has been held long enough and begins to worry that their poor decision-making skills have adversely affected the béarnaise sauce, a concern that wasn't on her radar during the whole of her seventeen-minute lecture.

By and by, the party is shown to the dining room, where Catherine oversees the placement of her guests, assuring that Bennet finally has the pleasure of meeting Darcy's cousin Celia Fitzwilliam. They enter into conversation directly, and he likes her right away. She's easy to talk to and has a nice, open manner.

Darcy is quiet during dinner, adding only a slight observation on the house and garden to one of Collin's comments.

The dinner is exceedingly lavish, with a generous assortment of plates of food presented by somber servants. Collin, seated at his aunt's elbow, praises everything with delighted alacrity. Although fewer than half the dishes are available to him because of dietary restrictions, he commends each one in a manner of such exaggerated obsequiousness Bennet wonders how his aunt can bear it. But Lady Catherine seems gratified by his excessive admiration and smiles most graciously, especially when any dish proves to be a novelty to him.

A servant is centering a cheeseboard on the table when

Catherine turns her attention to Bennet and resumes her earlier interrogation, delving further into the careers of his father and mother and trying to ascertain the skills and talents of him and his brothers.

"Do you play, Mr. Bethle?"

"Play what?" he asks.

"The piano," she says, as if explaining the obvious. "Do you play the piano? And do you sing?"

"A little," he says.

"Later we shall be happy to hear you play. Our instrument is a capital one. Do your brothers play and sing?"

"One of them does."

"Why did you not all learn? Your parents should have made sure you all learned. The Miss Webbs all have well-rounded educations, and their father's income isn't as good as yours."

Bennet isn't sure how his father's income was calculated, nor how it was inserted into the conversation, but he's positive it's no business of Lady Catherine's. Darcy, he notes, seems to agree—she looks a little embarrassed by her aunt's ill breeding.

Before he can address the comment, Collins says, "The Webbs are Aunt's neighbors in Vail. Do you not know them?" His eyes are wide with feigned curiosity. Obviously, he knows the answer.

Lady Catherine makes a moue of disgust at this condescending explanation and continues her interrogation. "Do you draw?"

"No, not at all."

"What, none of you?"

"Not one," he says without appearing the least bit repentant for this grave oversight in his education.

"That's very strange. Did your tutor have no talent?"

"We never had a tutor."

"No tutor! How was that possible?"

"We went to school."

"You mean public school?" she asks, as if simultaneously

intrigued and appalled by the concept. "Were there no sufficient private schools in your area? Surely, your father could
afford the investment—or didn't he think you were worth it?"

At this second mention of his family's financial status,
Bennet imagines a head-to-head battle between the brazen
society matron and Mr. Meryton, a hotly contested show-
down to see who can make the most inappropriate observations about money, wealth and power. Amused by these
thoughts, he says calmly, "Despite the disadvantages of my
upbringing, I've managed to cultivate a deep and abiding
appreciation for art and I now work in an art museum to
ensure that others can as well."

"Art museums serve a function," Lady Catherine says
cautiously. "At which one do you work?"

"The Longbourn."

"I've never heard of it."

Bennet nods. "It's the collection of wealthy industrialist Cyrus Longbourn. The museum was established by a
trust when he died in 1913."

"I've never heard of him either."

"Oh, but you have, darling," Collin says with a grin.
"I've been volunteering there for months. I'm sure I mentioned it."

She considers her nephew silently for several moments,
then fixes her gaze on Bennet. "That monstrosity in Queens?"

"Yes," he says with satisfaction, "that monstrosity in
Queens."

"And what do you do at this monstrosity?"

"I work in the development department."

Although this answer displeases her, it actually gives
her a great deal of joy, providing her with an opportunity to
offer advice on the behavior and performance of institutional development projects, with which she has an intimate
familiarity. Suffering through an endless string of proposals,
pitches and propositions has allowed her to cultivate an
opinion on every stage of a fundraising campaign down to
the selection of the font for the prospectus, and she generously bestows the wisdom of her experience on Bennet.

Then she says, "I'm on the board of the Metropolitan Museum of Art."

"I'm aware of that."

"What sort of art does this monstrosity—what do you call it?"

"The Longbourn," he supplies.

"What kind of art does the Longbourn exhibit?"

"Mostly Impressionism," he says. "We have one of the best collections of Impressionists in the world."

Catherine scoffs. "I don't believe in Impressionism."

"My aunt is a fan of representational art," Darcy says.

Bennet is surprised—she's barely acknowledged his presence before now. She and her cousin have both been fairly quiet during the meal, and he wonders if their silence is for his benefit or their aunt's.

"Paintings should bear a close resemblance to what they portray," Lady Catherine explains. "A seaside should be represented as a seaside, with all its features clearly delineated and immediately recognizable. Dots are for Dalmatians and children with chicken pox. *Aristotle with a Bust of Homer* by Rembrandt, *The Death of Socrates* by David, *Madonna and Child* by Duccio—these are masterful and precise and create within the bosom of the observer precisely the appropriate feelings. *That* is art."

Speaking diplomatically, Bennet says, "Without question, those are all great works of art, and, though I'd hesitate to suggest that there's a particular way in which art is supposed to make one feel, they do indeed evoke a particular sensation. My definition of art, however, is more expansive. I think there's a mastery in capturing the transient effect of sunlight on a rambling brook or wind blowing across a plain. Perhaps you should reconsider your opinion on Impressionism. The Met has an outstanding collection."

"Upon my word," Catherine says, "you give your opinion very freely for a man in your position."

"What position is that?" he asks with more than a hint of disingenuousness.

"Beggar at the feast. Are you not here to cultivate my patronage?"

"I'm not, ma'am, no," he says simply, aware that it's the truth. He never actually believed Lady Catherine de Bourgh would take to him or the Longbourn. "I'm here because my friend Collin invited me to get away from the city for the weekend. If you'd like to have your patronage cultivated, please make an appointment with my brother John. He's in charge of individual giving."

Lady Catherine seems quite astonished at not receiving the deference due her status, and Bennet suspects he's the first person who's ever dared to trifle with so much dignified impertinence.

Delighted with the exchange, Collin gives him a thumbs up, a not-so-subtle gesture his aunt observes and immediately criticizes—not for the rudeness of its implication but for the inferiority of its execution: One should not overrotate the distal phalange.

"Like this, Aunt Catherine?" Celia asks with a cheeky grin, as she also gives Bennet her approval.

Darcy remains silent, but Bennet thinks he detects a lightening of her countenance.

After the cheese course, the party returns to the drawing room for coffee, and while Catherine is engrossed in conversation with Darcy and Collin answers texts, Celia sits down next to Bennet. They talk of the Hamptons and New York, of traveling and staying home, of new books and bands with so much spirit and flow they draw the attention of Catherine and Darcy. Darcy's eyes had frequently turned toward them with a look of curiosity; that her aunt, after a while, shared the feeling is not in doubt, for she doesn't scruple to interrupt.

"What's that you're saying, Celia?" she calls out. "What is it you're talking about? What are you telling Mr. Bethle? Let me hear what it is."

Unable to avoid a reply, her niece says, "We're talking about music."

"Music! Then do speak louder. It's one of my favorite

subjects. I must participate in the conversation if you're talking about music. There are few people on the East Coast, I suppose, who enjoy music more than I do or have a better natural taste. If I'd ever studied, I should have been a great proficient. And so would my children, if I'd had any. They would have performed delightfully. How does George get on, Darcy?"

Darcy, speaking with affectionate praise of her brother's proficiency, announces that he finished at the London conservatory in June and will start Juilliard in the fall.

"I'm glad to hear he's doing so well," Lady Catherine says, "and do tell him for me that he can't expect to excel if he doesn't practice a great deal."

"I assure you, ma'am," Darcy says, "he doesn't need such advice. He's had the importance of practice drilled into him since the age of four, when he was discovered to have a great natural talent for music."

"So much the better. It can't be done too much," she says, "and when I talk to him next, I'll reinforce the message. I often tell young people that no excellence can be acquired without constant practice. That goes for you, Mr. Bethle, and your playing, as well. I haven't forgotten you said you played a little. Perhaps now would be a good time to start improving?"

Imagining there's very little Lady Catherine forgets, Bennet thanks her for her interest and suggests he should first perhaps practice in private. It's been years since he last played, and although he's confident he can cobble together something recognizable, he's not sure his audience would enjoy it. Celia dismisses his refusal as mere modesty and insists that he play.

"If I were being modest," he says, sitting down at the instrument, "I would have said I don't play. This is pure recklessness, and I'm sure you'll live to regret it."

Celia scoffs again and pulls a chair closer to the piano.

Bennet starts with scales to familiarize himself with the instrument and is relieved to discover he still has the basics down pat. A few moments later, he launches into "Fur

Elise," the bane and balm of all beginning piano players. Lady Catherine listens to half of the song and then talks, as before, to her other niece until the latter excuses herself. Moving with her usual deliberation toward the piano, Darcy stations herself next to Bennet.

He sees what she's doing, and at the first convenient pause, turns to her with an arch smile and says, "You're trying to throw me off by staring at me while I play. But I will not be unnerved, even if your brother is training to be a professional and I went to public school. I'm stubborn and don't intimidate easily."

Darcy rests her elbow on the piano. "It won't work."

"What?" Bennet asks, amused.

"Provoking me into an argument. I'm on to your game now."

"What game?"

"You like to say things you don't mean just to get a rise out of people."

Bennet laughs at this description of himself and says, "How am I going to make a good impression on your cousin if you go around revealing my true character? You should be careful or I might retaliate. Then your cousin will truly be shocked."

"I'm not afraid of you," Darcy says, smiling.

"Do tell," Celia says. "I should love nothing more than to be shocked by Darcy's behavior."

"Very well," Bennet says, "but prepare yourself for something truly dreadful. The first time I met Darcy was at the Longbourn's gala fundraiser, where she coldly rebuked every offer to dance."

"Well, saying no is a woman's prerogative," Celia points out thoughtfully.

He nods. "True, and I would deny no woman her prerogatives. But if you could just imagine the scene: a dozen adoring young men girding their nerve to request the honor of a single dance with your beautiful cousin and she rejecting them all with an abrupt shake of her head like a Roman emperor in the Colosseum turning his thumb down—perfectly rotated, of course."

"I didn't know any of them," Darcy explains.

"Right, and nobody can ever be introduced at a party," Bennet says. "Well, Celia, what shall I play next? 'Chopsticks'? Or maybe you prefer 'Chopsticks.' Which would be less grating to your nerves? My fingers await your orders."

"Perhaps I could have handled it better," Darcy says, "but I'm not good with strangers."

"Should we ask your cousin the reason for this?" Bennet says, still addressing Celia. "Should we ask her why a sophisticated woman with a first-class education and every advantage of birth is unable to interact with strangers?"

"I know the answer to that one," Celia says. "It's because she doesn't try."

"Conversing easily with strangers is a talent I don't possess," Darcy says. "I know other people excel at it, but I do not."

"I know other people can play this piano better than I—I've heard them," Bennet says reasonably. "But I also know it's not the instrument's fault that I'm so terrible; it's my own for not practicing."

Darcy smiles and says, "You're perfectly right. Neither one of us performs for strangers."

Before he can respond, Lady Catherine interrupts to ask what they're talking about now. Bennet immediately launches into an alarmingly enthusiastic rendition of "Chopsticks." Her ladyship approaches, and after listening for a few minutes, makes copious remarks on the quality of his performance, mixing with them many instructions on execution and taste. Bennet receives them with all the forbearance he has, and when he can no longer suffer it politely, indicates with a speaking glance to Collin that it's time to go.

His host readily agrees and makes an extravagant goodbye to his aunt, who expects nothing less.

CHAPTER FIFTEEN

Collin leaves Bennet a basket of muffins, three sections of the *New York Times* and a note apologizing for the sparse selection in muffins and newspaper sections. Undaunted, he makes himself comfortable in the kitchen with a steaming mug of rich coffee and a generously buttered muffin. The newspaper turns out to be three weeks old, but the article on teacher evaluations in city schools is interesting. The debate over high-stakes testing has yet to be resolved.

All in all, he's perfectly satisfied with his morning.

The sun is beating down with its usual ferocity, but the oppressive heat of July is tempered by the ocean breeze blowing gently through the window. He thinks about what he'll do first—take a walk, lounge on the beach, go for a swim—while wondering if he'll ever move from this chair.

Certainly not while there are muffins, butter and coffee.

A ring at the door startles him, and he reluctantly gets up to answer it. To his very great surprise, Darcy—and Darcy only—enters.

She seems astonished, too, on finding him alone and apologizes for the intrusion by explaining she'd thought Collin and Celia were there.

"Nope, just me," Bennet replies, holding the door

awkwardly for a moment before deciding to invite her in for coffee and muffins.

Darcy passes on the muffins because she's already had a full breakfast, but she accepts the coffee and follows him into the kitchen, where they both sit at the little white table. Bennet asks after her aunt and, assured of her continued good health, says he enjoyed dinner very much.

The statement isn't exactly true, but nor is it entirely false: The dinner was a compelling anthropological study, and he's grateful he got to observe the de Bourghs in their natural habitat.

"I'm sure my aunt enjoyed having you," Darcy says.

Bennet nods, takes a sip of his coffee and wonders if they'll now descend into total silence. Searching for a topic, he recalls the last time they had met and decides there's no reason not to appease his curiosity on the subject of her hasty departure.

"You all left the Netherfield very suddenly in April," he says.

"Yes," Darcy says.

The one-word answer is hardly satisfying. "Bingley must have been surprised to see you in London. She herself left only the day before. How is she?"

"Very well."

Another helpful response! "Will she return to New York soon?"

"She hasn't said anything one way or the other, but I think it's unlikely she'll be back in the foreseeable future. She has many friends and obligations in Europe. I think she'll stay there."

"As she's not returning to New York, I suppose she's effectively resigned as chair of the Golden Diamond Circle Advisory Board?" he asks. "It would be nice if she could inform John of her intentions so someone else can fill the position."

If Darcy is aware of the subtext, she does not let on. "I'm sure she will."

As it's been almost three months since Bingley last

contacted John, he knows Darcy is wrong. Feeling a renewed spurt of anger at the people who broke his brother's heart, he resolves not to speak further. He's afraid he might say something he'll regret. Instead, he leaves the trouble of finding a subject to Darcy.

After a pause, she takes the hint. "Collin appears to be working out well at the Longbourn."

"He actually is," Bennet says with some surprise. "I had my concerns at first because he seems to view it as a great lark."

"Collin views everything as a great lark," she says. "It's part of his charm."

"He's quite productive when he puts his mind to it. He's shown an unexpected talent for stuffing envelopes," he says, ruthlessly smothering the urge to call him a great proficient, "but his stamp placement is a work in progress."

"He was always a very industrious castle builder when we came down here as children, taking great care about the placement of a turret or a window."

"If his sand castles had windows, then he was very industrious indeed," Bennet observes. "Any sand castle I've ever built was lucky to get a guard tower, and even that inevitably got knocked down by one brother or another."

Darcy draws her chair a little toward him and says, "I'm glad Collin invited you out."

Bennet looks surprised, and Darcy seems to experience some change of feeling. She draws back her chair, takes the newspaper from the table, and, glancing over it, says in a colder voice, "Do you like the Hamptons?"

A short conversation on the subject of the beach community ensues, on either side calm and concise, and is promptly ended by the entrance of Collin and Celia.

"Hello, hello," Celia says cheerfully, brandishing a racket. "Gorgeous day for tennis. I'm raring to go. Who's next? Collin's wiped."

Collin throws himself on the couch and drops his own tennis racket onto the floor. "Collin's bored," he corrects her. "I'm always up for a friendly game, but you play as if it's war. You don't have to crush me like an advancing army, you heartless colonel."

"That *was* a friendly game," Celia insists with a laugh. "What do you say, Darcy? You play twice a week, right? Let's swat a few over the net."

Darcy declines with a firm shake of her head. "I'm going down to the beach to read before it gets too hot."

Celia turns to Bennet. "What about you? In the mood to get your butt kicked?"

He smiles. "Curious thing. I'm never in the mood to get my butt kicked."

"Oh, come on. I'll spot you thirty-love," she says in a wheedling tone, and when that fails to move him, she adds, "I'll play left-handed."

Unable to resist the desperation, Bennet agrees. "But play properly. I don't need your pity."

"Yes, you do," Collin calls from the living room.

Celia claps her hands and then grabs a bottle of cold water from the fridge and hands it to Bennet. "You're going to need that. It gets hot on the court. Also, a racket. You can borrow Collin's. Also, sunscreen. Have you put it on yet? I have some if you need." She considers him silently for a moment, tipping her head to the right as she thinks. "You know what, you better change, too. Light colors or you'll overheat too soon. Did you bring a white T-shirt?"

Collin laughs. "She's fattening you up for the slaughter, son. It's going to be a rout. You might as well surrender your troops now and save yourself the shin splints."

"Don't listen to him, Bennet," Celia says. "A fine strapping lad like yourself? You'll hold your own. Now hurry up and change."

Amused, Bennet follows the colonel's orders and runs upstairs, where he puts on a white concert tee and tan cotton shorts. On the matter of holding his own, he's not entirely convinced he won't humiliate himself. He played squash all through college and is decent with racket sports, but if Celia is as good as Collin says, then he should indeed prepare to get his butt kicked.

The tennis court is on the northern edge of the property, behind the garage and to the left of the swimming pool, amid a copse of evergreens. It's a truly lovely spot, and he can easily imagine Collin effusively relating the age and needle count of each tree.

Colonel Fitzwilliam is every bit as punishing as Collin had said, and even though Bennet manages to hold his own during the first set, he goes down in flames in the second. Ultimately, it comes down to stamina. He simply doesn't have the endurance to run around the court at top speed for an extended period in the oppressive heat, and that's precisely what's called for when playing Celia. She returns a ball to his dead zone every single time.

"You're pretty good," Celia says as they sit on the bench toweling off. She tosses him one of the bottles of water. "I was afraid you'd offer no challenge at all, but you've got great form and a strong serve. Did you play a lot growing up?"

He takes a long swill of the water and shakes his head. "Never. There was a lot of football during my formative years."

"How very manly," she observes with a light in her eye.

"Well, you know, the middle classes," he says with an ironic shrug. "But I went to college in the South and mastering a racket sport was a distribution requirement."

"Ah, a great liberal arts education. Nice."

"I also learned how to throw clay on a potter's wheel, another specialized life skill that will no doubt assist me in my rise up the corporate ladder."

She squints at him in the sun. "But you work in a museum."

"True. I've seemed to have missed my opportunity to make obscene amounts of money. Perhaps it's not too late for me to start a hedge fund."

"I plan to marry obscene amounts of money," Celia

announces without a speck of self-consciousness, "so do let me know how that works out."

Bennet gives her a sidelong glance. "You seem able-bodied. Is there any reason why you can't join the twenty-first century and earn your own fortune?"

"Omigod, *so* many reasons," she says, smiling. "Just thinking about them makes me exhausted, which should give you a hint as to my work ethic. I'm from the poor branch of the family—and, yes, I realize *poor* is a relative term, so don't lecture me on self-denial and dependence—and running with Darcy has accustomed me to a certain lifestyle that would be difficult to sustain on your typical nine-to-five salary. Also, I'm not wage-slave material. I want the freedom to do what I want when I want. At the moment, I'm at Darcy's disposal. She arranges things as she pleases and I say thank you."

"I don't think I've ever met anyone who enjoys the power of doing what she likes when she likes more than Darcy."

"She likes to have her own way very much," Celia agrees, "but so do we all. It's only that she has the means to make it happen because she's rich and we're not, an oversight I intend to rectify through an advantageous marriage. The Fitzwilliam name is very marketable. It was my grandfather, by the way, if you're wondering how my branch of the family contrived to make itself poor. He cashed out of Fitzwilliam Company in 1954 to open a hula hoop factory, which did very well for a while and then went bust."

"And what's the going price of a Fitzwilliam? Being the granddaughter of a hula hoop tycoon must adversely affect your value—I suppose you can't expect above fifteen million."

Celia answers him in the same teasing tone, and the subject drops. Breaking the silence, which he fears might seem judgmental, Bennet compliments her tennis again and asks if she plays often and how frequently she gets out to the Hamptons and if she'd like to chair a social committee for the Longbourn. Their conversation flows just as easily as it had the night before.

Celia pretends to consider the social committee position seriously and asks a series of questions about her duties and responsibilities, ultimately deciding that it seems like far too much work for her to handle.

"The problem is Bingley," Bennet announces. "We shouldn't take her as your model. She was far more hands-on than any other heiress I've worked with. Let's use Geraldine Livers instead. All she did was give us a dozen names to invite. She didn't even come to the event."

"Bingley?" Celia says. "As in Charlie Bingston?"

"Yes, do you know her?"

"I do. She's a great friend of Darcy's."

"Oh, yes," Bennet says drily. "Darcy is a wonderful friend to Bingley and takes excellent care of her."

"Care of her," Celia repeats thoughtfully. "Yes, I really believe Darcy *does* take care of her when it's necessary. During the ride down, she told me something that makes me think Bingley owes her big time."

"Oh?" Bennet asks.

"I'm only guessing it was Bingley; Darcy didn't use names. But she was patting herself on the back for having saved a friend from making a terrible mistake with a man. As I said, she was vague on the details, and the only reason I suspect Bingley is it's exactly the sort of scrape she'd get into. Just last year, she ran away to Mexico with a grifter who could perform some pretty neat magic tricks, though I don't suppose you can call a grown woman using her own funds to travel 'running away.' But she does tend to jump in with both feet before considering the consequences."

"Did Darcy tell you why the man was such a terrible mistake?"

"Oh, you know, not quite up to snuff."

"How'd she break it off?"

Celia shrugs. "She didn't say. She only told me what I've told you."

Bennet says nothing, and too indignant to sit still, stands up and paces the court. Celia asks him why he's suddenly so worked up. Then she tosses the tennis ball in the air and effortlessly catches it. "Wanna go another round?"

He shakes his head and says he's thinking about the situation with Bingley. "Why is it Darcy's decision whom Bingley loves? What gives her the right to dictate what should make her friend happy? Who made it her business?" he says angrily, then, realizing his response must seem over the top, adds, "But we don't know the details so we really can't judge. The couple probably didn't feel very strongly about each other anyway."

"A natural conclusion," she says, "but it takes something away from my cousin's triumph."

Celia's kidding, but the comment so accurately sums up Darcy that Bennet doesn't trust himself to speak and abruptly changes the subject. They talk of inconsequential things as they gather their stuff and return to the Parsonage. There, Celia commends him again on his performance—"We just need to tweak your serve"—and says she'll see him later.

After she leaves, Bennet sits on the couch with a cold glass of water and thinks about what he's just learned. That Darcy had taken steps to separate Bingley and John, he'd never doubted, but he had always assumed it was at Carl's instigation. Now he knows it's Darcy and Darcy alone who's responsible for his brother's heartache. It's Darcy who ruined his hopes of happiness.

"Not quite up to snuff," Celia had said. And no doubt John's snuff is inadequate, with his middle-class upbringing and his museum job and his—what had Lady Catherine called it last night—beggar-at-the-feast position. She was referring to his career as a fundraiser, but also to a deeper level of unworthiness. To people like Catherine de Bourgh and her niece, the Bethle brothers will always be supplicants, straining for attention they do not deserve. They should accept their place.

Bennet knows his understanding of the situation is accurate because to John himself there can't be any objection. His brother has everything to recommend him: He's kind, funny, smart, polite, independent and handsome. Darcy might cringe at the thought of the Longbourn's obscurity or Meryton's coarseness, but those things are too tangentially related to John to have weighed with Darcy. No, Darcy's pride simply could not handle the idea of her friend marrying a man of no consequence from an insignificant town in lowly Michigan.

Angered beyond all reasonable thought, Bennet changes into a pair of nylon shorts and goes for a long, grueling run in the midday sun. The heat and the effort bring on a headache that grows steadily worse the longer he runs, and by the time he returns to the Parsonage, he's ready to fall down on his bed and never rise again.

Collin calls hello from the kitchen and says his aunt has invited them for lunch.

"Can I take a pass?" Bennet asks, leaning against the wall as he wipes the sweat from his neck. "I think I pushed it a little too much today: tennis and the run. I've got a headache."

"Lady Catherine will be rather displeased at your staying here," Collins says, "but at the same time, she has more than two dozen recommendations for avoiding and treating headaches, so she'll be delighted too. Prepare yourself to be bombarded with elixirs and poultices, which she's sure to send over with a servant."

"I can't wait," Bennet says and, deciding to get a jump on the parcel of treatments soon to arrive at his door, runs upstairs to take a shower.

CHAPTER SIXTEEN

Bennet realizes that scouring John's Facebook page and rereading his vacation texts for hints of romantic suffering isn't going to help lessen his anger at Darcy. The majority of the messages are short, containing only information relevant to the topic at hand, and while he can discern no pervasive sadness in the missives, neither can he find a sweeping happiness. They're most revealing in what they lack, which is any mention of female company. Although it's summer and the sight of John in a bathing suit attracts the opposite sex like flies, he hasn't met a single woman in Cape Cod.

Disgusted again at how easily Darcy inflicted misery on his brother, Bennet drops the phone on the couch and goes into the kitchen to find something to eat. It's been many hours and many miles since the bran muffin.

He's opening a jar of peanut butter when the doorbell sounds, and expecting Lady Catherine's butler with a boxful of remedies, he opens the door.

To his utter amazement, he finds Darcy standing on the step. Slowly he opens the door to let her in. In a hurried manner, she immediately begins to ask about his headache, attributing her visit to concern about his health. He answers her with icy politeness. She sits down for a few moments, then gets up and walks around the room. Bennet is surprised but doesn't say a word. After a silence of several minutes, Darcy comes toward him in an agitated manner.

"I can't do it," she mutters. "I've tried and I've tried, but I can't hold in my feelings any longer. I admire you, Bennet. I admire you and love you."

Bennet's astonishment is beyond anything he's ever experienced before. He stares, unable to even understand what she's saying. Her words are like nonsensical syllables strung together in a children's song.

Considering his stunned silence to be sufficient encouragement, Darcy launches into a declaration of all that she feels and has felt for several months. She speaks well—of his wit, of his intelligence, of his willingness to state his opinion freely without concern for consequences—and she speaks long, detailing the slow evolution of her feelings, the way her interest was sparked by the glint of humor in his eye and held by his audacity.

Only Darcy doesn't stop there. Oh, no, she continues to talk and talk, and the insults begin to pile up: His father is an ambulance chaser; his uncle is a huckster; his boss is the most cringe-inducing human being she's ever had the misfortune to meet.

"In many respects, I realize it's unfair to hold you accountable for the behavior of others. It's not your fault Mr. Meryton is an idiotic man who offends and appalls with his gauche displays," she says reasonably. "But it's also disingenuous to argue that we are unaffected by the people who surrounded us. We're all judged by the company we keep, and although I never expected to keep such low company, it can't be avoided. The heart wants what the heart wants. You're not the brilliant match everyone expects of me. Indeed, you're not the brilliant match I expect of myself. The nephew of a used-car salesman! He might as well be hawking snake oil."

With every word she utters, Bennet feels his compassion melting away until it dissolves completely into a fit of anger. Even as his resentment grows, he resolves to remain calm and let her down easy when she finishes her speech. She concludes by citing the fact that she's speaking now, despite all her oaths to say nothing, as proof of her affection, and by expressing her hope that they can spend time together in a couple-like fashion. Maybe dinner at a restaurant in East Hampton? Lobster, perhaps, if he has no objection to shellfish?

Darcy *speaks* of apprehension and anxiety, but her manner reflects no uncertainty. Such confidence only angers Bennet further, and when she finally stops, his shoulders stiffen and he says, "I'm sure there's a proper protocol for how one should behave in a situation like this, but I don't know it. I should probably express a sense of obligation for the sentiments avowed and thank you for your feelings. But I won't do that because I'm not thankful. Neither one of us wanted this, you clearly no more than I. I'm sorry if my response hurts you, I really am, but I'm confident the pain will quickly go away. Considering how reluctantly you've succumbed to your feelings, I'm sure you'll overcome them easily enough."

Darcy, leaning against the mantelpiece with her eyes fixed on his face, is at once surprised and resentful. Her face becomes pale with anger—turmoil is visible in every feature. Struggling for the appearance of composure, she doesn't open her lips until she's certain she has attained it.

After a pause, she says in a voice of forced calm, "You're very angry. Can I ask why you've decided to be so mean in your rejection?"

"You can," he says, "but only if I can ask why, with every intent on offending and insulting me, you decided to tell me that you liked me against your will and better judgment? That's justification enough for my own callousness. But I have other reasons, and you know it. Even if I didn't already dislike you, do you honestly think I'd give the time of day to the woman who has made my brother miserable?"

As he says these words, Darcy changes color. She listens without attempting to interrupt.

"I have every reason to think the worst of you. There isn't a single thing you can say to justify what you did to Bingley and John. Despite their growing feelings for each other, you broke them up to ensure nothing came of it. Can you deny it?"

Bennet pauses, and watching her, realizes with no small indignation that she isn't the least bit remorseful. She even smiles at him with affected incredulity.

"Can you deny it?" he asks again.

With an assumed calm that requires some effort, she replies, "I don't want to deny that I did everything in my power to separate my friend from your brother or that I'm glad I succeeded. I should have done myself the same favor."

Bennet pretends not to hear the insult and says, "It's not only the way you callously and calculatingly broke my brother's heart that makes me dislike you so much. I learned all about you months ago from Georgia Wickham. What favor were you doing for a friend on that occasion?"

Now she's less tranquil and, as her flush deepens, she says, "You're very interested in her life."

"I am," he concedes, "as anyone would be who has heard her terrible story."

"Her terrible story!" Darcy jeers with contempt. "Oh, yes, her *story* is very terrible indeed!"

"It's all your fault," Bennet says scathingly. "You deprived her of the inheritance left to her by your own mother, and now you mock her misery."

"And this," Darcy says as she walks with quick steps across the room, "is what you think of me! Thank you for explaining it so fully. Clearly, I'm an awful person." She stops pacing and turns to look at him. "But perhaps you wouldn't have minded my faults so much if I hadn't insulted you by explaining honestly the evolution of my feelings. This entire exchange might have been avoided if I'd simply flattered your ego by saying I eagerly welcomed the attraction I felt. I'm sorry your feelings were hurt, but can you honestly blame me for having reservations about a relationship with someone whose station in life is so beneath my own? Your education, your family, your career are not what I envision for myself."

Bennet feels himself grow even more angry—an impressive feat considering how livid he already is—and it takes everything he has to speak calmly. "You're wrong if you believe that the way you declared your feelings has anything to do with my reaction. All it did was let me off the hook. If you had behaved more like a decent human being, I'd have felt bad about refusing you."

He sees her start at this, but she says nothing, so he continues, "You could not have made this offer in any possible way that would have tempted me to accept it."

Again, her astonishment is obvious, and she looks at him with incredulity mingled with mortification. He goes on: "From the very beginning, from the very first moment I met you, I've been appalled by your arrogance, your conceit, your behavior, and your selfish disdain for the feelings of others. Those traits formed the foundation of my dislike, which succeeding events have only made stronger."

"That's enough," Darcy says. "I understand your feelings and am now embarrassed by my own. Forgive me for taking up so much of your time and accept my best wishes for your health and happiness."

With these words, she quickly leaves the house, and Bennet hears her pull the door forcefully behind her.

As soon as she's gone, the enormity of the episode strikes him and he finds himself replaying it moment by moment. The more he thinks about it, the more stunned he becomes. To have received such a proposal from Darcy—to discover she's been in love with him for months, so much so as to wish to establish a relationship, which she had prevented her friend from doing—is incredible. It *is* gratifying, he realizes, to have inspired such strong affection without meaning to do so. But the satisfaction he feels at the compliment is fleeting, immediately supplanted by disgust for everything else: her ridiculous pride, her shameless acknowledgment of what she did to John, her inexcusable satisfaction in claiming it and her mocking cruelty toward Georgia.

Agitated by these reflections, Bennet dashes upstairs to change into his running clothes again and hits the beach at full force, even though the sun is still directly overhead and the peanut butter sandwich he'd intended to eat for lunch is lying half made on the kitchen counter. In the upheaval of Darcy's visit, he forgets all about it.

CHAPTER SEVENTEEN

Bennet wakes at the first light of dawn still marveling over the events of the previous day, and unable to fall back to sleep, decides to go for an early-morning jog. After yesterday's regime of exhausting exercise, he barely has the energy for another run and yet he has too much energy. He needs to do something to burn off the agitation.

By the time he returns to the Parsonage, the sun has fully risen, but his host is still asleep and Bennet makes himself comfortable at the kitchen table with a plate of scrambled eggs and buttered toast. He sips his coffee; answers texts from his mother, Lydon, John and an old college friend who'll be in the city the following week; and logs into his email. Naturally, there are a half a dozen new messages from Meryton, each one with its subject line using more capital letters and followed by more exclamation points than the last. In person Meryton is very easy to distinguish from a teenage girl, but over email the difference grows disconcertingly vague.

The majority of new messages are from his boss, and the rest are from various associates: Hannah in special events, Evan in the registrar's office, Alexis in curatorial, Darcy Fitzwilliam, Julian Martindale from—

Immediately, his eyes track back up to the previous line and he confirms he read it correctly. Darcy had indeed sent him an email earlier that morning.

As curious as he is apprehensive, he clicks on the message and begins to read.

Don't worry. I have no intention of pestering you further with my feelings. I think it's best that we both forget yesterday as soon as possible. The only reason I'm writing now is to address the charges laid at my door, which, I'm afraid, I simply can't let stand. I spent the entire night trying to let it go, but my character compels me to try to exonerate myself where possible.

Regarding the matter of your brother and Bingley—yes, I noticed right away that Bingley was very taken with your brother and enjoyed flirting with him. I didn't think anything of it until the night of the ball, because I've seen Bingley not only flirt with dozens of handsome men but fall in love with them too. It's what she does. Then, on the night of the ball, I heard your boss, Mr. Meryton, say with satisfaction that John had succeeded so well in charming Bingley that he expected them to announce their engagement soon. From that moment, I observed my friend very carefully and noticed that what she felt for John was different from her light flirtations in the past. I could see that her emotions were truly engaged this time. I also watched your brother closely for indications of how he felt. He was as cheerful and engaging as ever but treated Bingley no differently than he treated any of the other women in the room. It seemed to me that he was in work mode, which required him to be equally charming to all female donors. Naturally, you know your brother better than I, and if you insist my actions caused him pain, then it must be true, in which case your anger with me is entirely understandable. But I'm compelled to say that even the most acute observer would've failed to perceive the depth of his feelings, so well were they hidden. My objections to the marriage were not just those I mentioned yesterday, though they, of course, stand. My biggest concern was that Bingley had fallen for a man who would marry her for her money regardless of how he felt about her personally. I'm sure that makes you angry to hear, but I won't apologize for drawing the only conclusion available to me at the time. The data seemed conclusive, especially in light of the comments Mr. Meryton made as well as things your own younger brother said.

At this point, I felt obligated to act, especially after I discovered that Bingley's brothers had the same concern. After a brief discussion, we decided we had to move quickly, so we followed Bingley to London, where I pointed out with all necessary frankness the many ways your brother was an unsuitable match for her. My opinion would not have mattered to Bingley had I not also been able to convince her of your brother's indifference, which came as a great disappointment because she'd believed her feelings to be reciprocated. Over the years, Bingley has piled up many romantic disasters and, no longer trusting herself, has come to rely on my judgment. To convince her that she had misread the situation required very little effort, and she naturally agreed she shouldn't return to New York for a while.

That's the extent of my participation in the matter, but do let me point out that your brother did not try to contact Bingley. He made no attempt to explain either in writing or in person how he felt about her, nor did he question her sudden lack of interest. This calm acceptance of her behavior only reaffirmed for all of us his lack of interest. In light of this evidence, I can't apologize for my actions because they appeared to be correct.

With respect to the other, more weighty accusation of having deprived Georgia Wickham of the inheritance left to her by my mother, all I can do is tell you it's absolutely not true. Georgia is the daughter of the wonderful woman who oversaw the running of Pemberley for my family. She grew up in the house with me, and my mother, caring for her greatly, happily supported her education, paying for private school in the city and footing the expense of Rhode Island School of Design. It was necessary because Mrs. Wickham, whose husband had a gambling problem, would never have been able to pay for either. My mother was not only very fond of Georgia, whose company she enjoyed, but believed strongly in her talent and thought she would be a great artist one day. I would agree about her talent, but it has been many years since I found her company enjoyable. Being in school with her allowed me to see a side to her that my mother never did, and I found her vicious, vindictive, scheming and mean.

My mother died five years ago, and as fond as ever of Georgia, she left her 1,000 shares in Fitzwilliam, intending for her to use the dividends from the stocks to subsidize her career as an artist. The income would be modest but sufficient. Georgia's own mother died soon after, and immediately after the funeral, Georgia told me that she'd rather have a lump sum than the stocks themselves and requested that I buy them from her at a generous price. She had a plan, she explained, to go to Paris to study and paint, and while I doubted her intention to follow through on it, I was perfectly happy to agree to her wishes. I gave her $400,000 dollars and considered our association at an end. She did go to Paris, as she'd planned, but rather than study, she burned through the money. Three years later, broke and in debt, she got in touch with me to request the return of her shares, which, she argued, I'd swindled her out of by taking advantage of her grief over her mother's death. Surely, she said, I couldn't ignore my dear mother's wishes. You can hardly blame me for not complying with this request or for denying it the dozens of times she reiterated it. My refusal infuriated her, and I don't doubt she disparaged me to anyone who would listen. Eventually, she gave up and disappeared. I didn't know where she went or what she did for money and I didn't care. I was just relieved not to have to deal with her. Then, last summer, she resurfaced in the most awful way possible.

As you know, I have a brother George. Since he's ten years younger than me, I was made his guardian. George is a very gifted pianist and has just finished his studies at a prestigious conservatory in London. Last July, he went to Ramsgate to spend the summer with a friend's family. The Younges are lovely people but hardly sophisticated, and when Georgia made a great show of "bumping" into her old friend George, they happily welcomed her into their home. Through this contrivance, Georgia grew very close to my brother, who, naturally, remembered her from his childhood as the funny, kind girl who would take him to the park or to Serendipity for ice cream. Georgia managed to convince him not only that he was in love with her but also that the only way they could be together would be to elope, because I'd never approve of the relationship. Given that George was only seventeen at the time, I would not have approved of any serious relationship with anyone, let alone marriage. Still, George was set on it, but then I happened to drop by Ramsgate the morning of their intended flight, and George, wracked with guilt, confessed everything to me. Georgia at once made herself scarce, and the Younges were mortified by what they let happen right under their noses. Make no mistake: Georgia's goal was to get her hands on my brother's fortune, which is equal to my own, but I'm sure revenging herself on me was also a strong motivation. Her revenge would have been complete indeed.

This is, I swear to you, the truth about my association with Georgia Wickham, but if you still need corroboration, you can ask Celia, who, as one of the executors of my mother's will, knows every detail of the sordid story. She'll be happy to confirm what I've told you. That said, I hope you will take me at my word and acquit me of any cruelty toward her. I'm not surprised you believed her—you had no reason not to. I apologize for not explaining all of this yesterday, but my thoughts were in too much of a jumble to be articulated clearly.

I appreciate your taking the time to read this letter.

Sincerely,

Darcy Fitzwilliam

CHAPTER EIGHTEEN

Bennet is not swayed. Indeed, he's entirely unmoved by the claim that John appeared to be wholly indifferent to Bingley at the Netherfield ball. Clearly, the interfering friend had seen only what she'd wanted to see, and, having her wishes obligingly fulfilled, felt justified in her actions. She all but called his brother a gigolo, a description that incites Bennet to fury, and expressed no regret at all for that. Her tone wasn't penitent but arrogant. It was all pride and insolence.

But when the subject switches to Georgia Wickham, to a truly horrifying account of immorality and greed, Bennet no longer knows what to think. His instinct is to reject every detail, and as he reads through the seemingly endless block of text, he mutters under his breath a series of denials: "This is ridiculous!" "This can't be true!" "She's lying!" When he's finished reading the message, he turns off his phone and puts it at the other end of the table, determined not to think about it anymore.

And yet, thirty seconds later, he's reaching across the table and flicking on the device to read the passage about Georgia again. Determined to consider the information dispassionately, he examines the meaning of every sentence. Darcy's account of Georgia's relationship with the Fitzwilliams matches Georgia's own account perfectly, including the kindness of Darcy's mother. But as soon as the women get to the will, their stories diverge wildly. With Georgia's words still fresh in his mind, Bennet is inclined to accept her version of events—he doesn't want to believe he can be so easily deceived. Also weighing in Georgia's column is Darcy herself, whose intolerant air makes her version of anything harder to accept.

But it's possible, Bennet thinks as he reads and rereads the email, that I might be a little prejudiced against the horrible woman.

Keeping that bias sharply in mind, he considers the facts once more, this time resolving to be truly dispassionate. The first thing he acknowledges is that he doesn't know anything about Georgia that she herself hasn't told him. She is, without question, a great person to be around—funny and thoughtful and gracious—but charm does not equal character. He need look no further than his brother Lydon for proof of that. Next, he thinks about how quick she was to trust him with her story. They'd met only the week before, were still more like strangers than friends and yet she'd confided her tale of woe without any provocation. At that time, she professed having no fear of seeing Darcy but just a week later, she left the city rather than attend the ball. And, now that he thinks about it, what was up with her swearing him to secrecy over the whole miserable affair and then blabbing it to anyone who would listen *after* Darcy had returned to London? Even Hannah in special events, whose connection to Georgia must be remarkably slight, was told the whole of it during an elevator ride to the third floor. She had *said* that respect for Mrs. Fitzwilliam would keep her from exposing her daughter.

Just as Georgia is losing points, checks are stacking up in the Darcy column. To start with, there's the fact of her cousin Celia, who, Bennet doesn't doubt, is willing and capable of backing up the whole story. Darcy wouldn't have offered her as proof if she weren't able to give it. Another point in her favor is Bingley, who, when questioned by John, had long ago asserted her friend's blamelessness in the affair. Lastly, there's

Darcy herself. As proud and obnoxious as she is, she's always behaved with rigid morality. Her friends respect and admire her, and surely, if she had done the terrible thing of which she's accused, they would know about it and judge her accordingly. Her love for her brother can't be disputed, as even Georgia admitted she was an affectionate sister.

All the evidence is there, even Georgia's dropping him for a well-to-do fund manager, and as Bennet examines it, he realizes he's been blind, partial, prejudiced, absurd. His discernment—ah, yes, his highly developed ability to discern on which he prides himself—has been appallingly lacking, and he's mortified to recall the confidence of his former opinions. How easily he'd been misled by simple vanity, for Georgia had flattered his and Darcy had offended it. That, apparently, was all it took to make up his mind.

Grasping the depth of his folly, Bennet rereads Darcy's explanation of her treatment of John and this time begins to concede the validity in her observation that John appeared indifferent to Bingley. Lydon himself had said something similar at the ball. John's feelings, though fervent, were not on display. And how could they be? Bennet thinks defensively. His brother is a consummate professional who'd never let his personal feelings affect his work, certainly not to the extent where he would make a declaration to a patron of the Longbourn. There's nothing more indecorous than pestering one's benefactor with one's emotions.

With this in mind, Bennet can understand the root of Darcy's concern for her friend. He knows how Meryton in his giddy excitement over funding can come across like an eager fisherman about to reel in a huge catch and realizes the proprietary air he'd already established over Bingley's fortune would be unsettling to Darcy, if not wholly offensive. Lydon, too, with his firm commitment to the path of least resistance, had made John's interest in Bingley seem largely mercenary.

The irony of all this isn't lost on Bennet, and he smiles thinly as he imagines the distress with which Meryton would greet the information that he's primarily responsible for losing all of Bingley's lovely money. But the amusement doesn't last long, and Bennet feels only sad about all that has happened.

Although he isn't fit for conversation, he greets Collin cheerfully when he eventually appears in the kitchen and enthusiastically falls in with his plans for the day, which includes sunbathing on the beach—with a book or without, depending on one's preferences—and a swim in the ocean followed by another swim in Lady Catherine's pool to wash off the sand and salt.

"No tennis, thank gawd," Collin says as he opens the fridge to poke around for viable breakfast options. "Celia and Darcy were on the first train out this morning, to my aunt's both horror and delight. Horror because they left so soon after arriving but delight because they took the correct train for Sunday morning travel."

Bennet smiles at the dilemma such a conflict of emotions must have created for Lady Catherine and nods as Collin outlines their beach-going options, for, with his host, it's never a simple matter of finding an unoccupied swath of sand and dropping one's towel.

Collin shudders in distaste at the mention of a towel. "We have beach chairs and sand chairs and reclining chairs and lawn chairs and chairs with umbrellas and chairs that look like Adirondack chairs but fold down almost to nothing. We have every kind of chair you can think of, except an electric chair, though if Lady Catherine had been able to persuade the governor, we'd have one of those, too. And of course we have a wide variety of towels, which we'll bring to the beach, but there must be a larger barrier between my butt and the sand than a strip of multicolored terry cloth."

Bennet readily agrees to the irrefutable inadequacy of the cotton towel, though he's never really found the item wanting before, and, gratified, Collin begins cataloging all the factors that go into finding the right spot on the beach. One must avoid children and smokers, of course, but also aggressive users of coconut-scented sunblock.

The list goes on, and as attentive as Bennet seems, his mind is miles away.

CHAPTER NINETEEN

Bennet almost tells John the truth about Bingley the moment he sees him Monday morning. Even before he enters the office, he hears the relentless clack-clack-clack of the keyboard and knows his brother is already there, furiously typing some email or updating a spreadsheet. He opens the door, crosses the threshold and strides to his desk, but as his desk is directly across from his brother's, separated by no more than three feet, it's nearly the same thing as walking to John. He looks at his brother, his blond hair streaked with sun from two weeks at the beach and his bright blue eyes focused intently on what he's writing, and decides he has every right to know the truth. He opens his mouth to speak.

And promptly shuts it again as he realizes how little he's thought about the consequences of such an action. Yes, it's Bennet's deepest hope that once John comprehends what has happened, he'll nobly rise to the occasion and finally hop on that plane to London. Or, failing that, send a goddamn email.

But Bennet is sensible enough to concede that what he wants his brother to do and what his brother will do are two entirely different things. Before he says anything, he needs to consider that fact and figure out if the new information will make things worse for him.

159

John adds an emphatic period to the end of the sentence he's writing and glances up at his brother. "The traveler returns!"

Bennet shrugs off his messenger bag and drops it next to his desk. Then he slides into his chair and boots up his computer. "Traveler hell. I just went out to the Hamptons for a couple of days. You've been gone for two weeks. How was the Cape?"

"A little soggy, very lobster-y. I learned how to stand-up paddle board," John says with a gleam in his eye.

As expected, his brother winces. "Oh, no."

"It gets worse. I can do yoga on the paddle board. That's right, on the water, my friend."

"What about our pact to avoid any and all hipster activities?" Bennet asks, then gasps as something truly horrifying occurs to him. "Dear God, next you'll tell me you did it all while wearing a fedora!"

John laughs. "Please, I still have some soul left. I promise you, I will remain fedora-free and continue to resist growing a bushy beard, even though that's what our people do now."

"Our people?" he asks with curiosity and suspicion.

"Fellow Queens dwellers."

With rents continuing to soar in Brooklyn, parts of Queens have indeed become ridiculously trendy as well as pricey. "Yeah, well, those accomplishments aside, I'm not sure I'll be able to forgive the stand-up paddle board yoga."

"You'll get over it as soon as you see how cool it is. We can do it on the Hudson at Pier 40. I've already investigated. But enough about me. How was the Hamptons?" John asks.

"Entirely devoid of paddle boards," he says for starters and then launches into a description of the Parsonage and Rosings and the beautiful sand dunes and coastline stretching for miles.

"And Lady Catherine? Is she all that Collin promised?"

Bennet grins as he recalls the imposing matron with

her grand empire and micromanaging ways. "She's what human resource managers around the world call a detail-oriented self-starter. She has a carefully considered opinion on every conceivable topic and a strong disapproval of anything that seems the least bit modern. If she approved of stand-up paddle boarding, she'd still be horrified to see you do it in a bathing suit."

"She sounds awesome," John says. "I'm sorry I didn't meet her. Do you think Collin will manage to get her here one day?"

His brother glances meaningfully at the tiny office, with its practical furniture and worn carpet, and says, "I sincerely hope not. This room offers so much opportunity for improvement—and telling people how to improve is her most favorite thing in the world—it might make her head explode. But we don't have to worry about that just yet because Collin is spending the rest of the summer out there. He said he'd check back in some time after Labor Day."

John nods, says he'll miss their volunteer's entertaining if not very productive presence and asks what one does for fun in the Hamptons.

Bennet pauses, then decides it's better to admit everything than to try to hide some things. "I played tennis with Collin's cousin Celia, although *played* rather overstates the case, as my game never rose to that level. Celia is also cousins with Darcy, who was there as well. She and I"—Bennet lowers his voice to make sure Meryton, if he's in his office, won't hear a thing—"had an interesting conversation. Despite all evidence to the contrary, she has developed feelings for me and proposed a dating situation so we could get to know each other better."

John raises his eyebrows. "A dating situation?"

"Yeah," he says with a shrug. "I don't know what else to call it." Determined to preserve some of Darcy's dignity, as it's only the gentlemanly thing to do, Bennet gives his brother just the broadest outline of the conversation, saying merely that he rebuffed her advances in the strongest possible terms.

Immediately, John is full of sympathy for the proud woman who put herself on the line by forthrightly stating her feelings. Bennet, already defensive, for he now knows how badly he mangled it, assures his brother that even as she was making the declaration, she was still trying to talk herself out of it.

Although Bennet's tone indicates amusement, recalling the way Darcy chose to make her proposal continues to infuriate him two days later. That indignation, however, is immediately eased by the memory of how coldly and unfairly he'd condemned and upbraided her. Now the anger turns inward as compassion for Darcy kicks in. She was not only disappointed by his refusal but blindsided by it as well.

Ever since Bennet read the email, his emotions have been swinging from anger to pity and from pity to anger, and because he can't get a handle on how he feels, he has yet to respond. He knows it's wrong to remain silent. An email as detailed and honest as the one Darcy sent deserves to be acknowledged. But how? That's what he can't figure out. A brief note thanking her for the information seems almost as bad as saying nothing, and he can't imagine what he'd write in a longer message. Each hour that passes, the likelihood of his responding grows less and his guilt grows more.

Ultimately, all he knows is, he doesn't want to see her again.

To take the focus off his own faults, Bennet relates with surprising detail the information about Georgia contained in Darcy's email. Even faced with this devastating truth, John strives for even-handedness and posits that they're still missing some vital piece of information that would clear both women of all wrongdoing.

"No," Bennet says firmly. "You'll never be able to exonerate them both. Be decisive: Pick a horse and lay down your money. I choose Darcy."

Although John's reluctance is keenly felt, he eventually decides against Georgia. "But it's difficult to accept. Georgia is so likable."

"I know. And Darcy is not."

"I never thought Darcy quite so unlikable as you did."

Bennet knows this is true because his brother has never found anyone to be entirely unlikable. If he knew how Darcy had intentionally removed Bingley from New York to save her from his evil clutches, he'd immediately argue that his clutches, while in no way wholly evil, do have an element of evilness about them.

"So the question is, do we tell people the truth about Georgia?"

John is taken aback by the query. "Tell what people?"

"The people here," he says. "You know how the Longbourn is—it's like a small, rural village. Gossip spreads like wildfire and everyone talks about the same four things. The building is buzzing with Darcy's awfulness. Shouldn't they know the truth?"

His brother is unconvinced of the necessity. "Exposing Georgia to gossip and ridicule doesn't serve any practical purpose, does it?"

"No," Bennet concedes, "it doesn't, and Darcy would not want me to say anything about her brother. Darcy is so unliked around here, I don't think anyone would actually believe me. I guess I'll just let the matter rest. Georgia will be gone soon enough—Redcoat is putting the finishing touches on the redesign of the Smithson. That's their last project with us."

"I'm sure she regrets her actions, and the fact that she's taken a steady job indicates she's turned over a new leaf," John says sensibly. "We shouldn't ruin that for her."

Having talked it through with John, Bennet feels much better about the Georgia situation and returns the conversation to the matter of stand-up paddle boarding, a concept he still can't wrap his head around. John defends it stridently, gleaming with smug confidence, because he knows his brother will enjoy it just as much as he does.

They've only just settled down to work when Meryton arrives, eager to hear all the details of Bennet's visit with Mrs. de Bourgh, of whom he has great expectations. Despite his young employee's insistence that the grand dame would never give her time, much less her money, to a backwater institution that features nonrepresentational art, Meryton refuses to have his high hopes dashed and disappears into his office to compose a follow-up letter for Bennet to send with a box of moderately priced gifts from the museum store.

Bennet rolls his eyes in his boss's general direction but doesn't make the added point that Lady Catherine would never donate time or money to any institution that employs him, so strongly does she disapprove of his freethinking ways. He holds his tongue because he doesn't have time for an extended lecture on the importance of toadying favor with rich New York patrons.

Two hours later, Lydon strolls in, and he checks his swagger when he sees his two brothers back in the office. "Hey, homies, good to see you safely returned from parts unknown."

John wrinkles his brow. "I was in Cape Cod and Bennet was in the Hamptons. The parts don't get much more known that that."

Although already apprised of their whereabouts, Lydon acts as if it's the first time he's heard it and attributes his possible forgetfulness—he's still not willing to concede prior knowledge—to his very busy couple of days. Since he's clearly itching to share some interesting information, John asks him what he's been up to.

Bennet would never have been so obliging.

"Oh, you know, nothing much," he says with aggressive casualness, "just hanging with movie stars and world leaders."

Naturally, Bennet is intrigued by this remarkable tidbit, but he knows better than to gratify Lydon with a follow-up question. John isn't as circumspect. "What?" he asks, his eyes popping in surprise.

"It was the craziest thing. Friday night, I went out with the Redcoat crew for happy hour. We hit one of the bars on Continental, the one with the big blue question mark over the door. It's pretty divey, very low-key. We're hanging and having a good time, and then the door opens and in walks Johnny Rumba. He's filming a movie down the block in some empty warehouse—a comedy called *Mr. Chamberlayne* about a military officer who has to dress up as a French chambermaid to catch a killer—and swung by for a drink. He's got his boys with him, a pretty big entourage, both in size and number, which is hardly surprising because, hey, international action star! One of the Redcoats, Pen Harrington, is fearless. This guy, he marches right up to Johnny, past all the huge dudes surrounding him, plops himself down at the table and asks Johnny what he's drinking. And Johnny goes for it, impressed, I guess, by the bluster, and before you know it, Georgia, Forster, Pen and I are pounding beers with him, and Georgia is telling him all about the Longbourn, you know, the turrets and the balconies, and he has to see it. So we all come back here but it's late now so it's all locked up. Johnny says he's got to take off, he has a party he has to go to, and Georgia says, 'Aw, can't we come, too?' and Johnny's like, 'Sure,' so we all climb into his limo—a sweeeeet ride, let me tell you—and wind up in Brighton Beach at a birthday party for a Russian oligarch who owns half of Siberia. Total open bar and celebrities everywhere. It was fresh. And that was just Friday."

Indeed, that *was* just Friday. Lydon still has a whole weekend to relate and, assisted by selfies, tweets and Pen Harrington's Tumblr, he does so in minute detail. Bennet listens as little as he can, but there's no escaping the frequent mentions of Georgia's name.

"We're going back to Brighton Beach tonight," Lydon adds when he finishes describing the pool party at Soho House the night before. "The oligarch's daughter's BFF likes Forster and invited all of us to dinner at her uncle's restaurant. Georgia's coming, too, Bennet, and—you probably don't know this—she's no longer seeing that investment banker. He was relocated to Liverpool, which is hardly a bustling financial capital, so clearly his reassignment was a demotion of sorts. I'm glad Georgia is done with him because she can do so much better."

165

Bennet thinks it's the other way around: The investment banker can do better.

Lydon encourages his brothers to come to Brighton. "The sea air will do you good," he insists, having already forgotten that they've both just returned from visits to the ocean. "Lots of vodka and bellinis. It'll be a blast."

Bennet declines the invitation for several reasons, not in the least because he doesn't want to see Georgia again. He can't wait for her and her colleagues to be gone from the museum.

But it turns out to be a long two weeks, with Georgia somehow showing up everywhere Bennet turns. She's in the café having coffee or in the lobby waiting for a delivery or in the development department's office chatting with Lydon. Although his manner is cool toward her, she flirts outrageously, seemingly determined to restore their relationship to its previous footing. She makes repeated references to earlier exchanges, dropping the word *bobbin* in conversation as if it's a top-secret code rife with suggestion and twinkling brightly as she laughs. Bennet isn't charmed by such idle and aggressive flirtation and can't decide whose vanity she's trying to appease: his or hers.

Finally, the last day arrives, and Georgia, having coffee with Pen Harrington in the café, calls to Bennet to join them as soon as he enters the courtyard. He demurs with a shake of his head, which she finds insupportable and reproaches him for being elusive. "I've barely gotten to talk to you in weeks," she says as she joins him in line. He orders a large black coffee; she gets an Earl Grey tea. "I haven't heard a word about your visit to the Hamptons. How'd it go?"

Bennet takes the cup from the barista and walks over to the side counter to get a sugar packet. Annoyed with Georgia's refusal to take a hint, he says, "Better than expected. The weather was excellent and the beach is beautiful. Darcy was there with her cousin Celia. Do you know Celia?"

Georgia looks surprised, displeased and alarmed, but after a moment's hesitation, she smiles fondly and replies that she used to see her often. "She's very nice."

"Yes," Bennet agrees, stirring his coffee, "she's very nice. Friendly and enthusiastic with a killer serve. She's an excellent tennis player."

"Did you see much of her off the court?"

"A fair amount."

"She's very different from her cousin."

"Yes, very different. But it turns out Darcy improves on acquaintance."

Georgia is unable to suppress her surprise. "Really! Has she suddenly become friendly? Is she now being kind to strangers and small children? I'll never believe," she continues in a lower and more serious tone, "that she's actually become nice."

"Oh, no," Bennet says. "She's the same person she always was."

The look on Georgia's face is priceless. She clearly can't decide whether she can trust the meaning of his words. Her eyes grow apprehensive and anxious when Bennet adds, "When I said she improves on acquaintance, I didn't mean *she* actually improves. I just meant that knowing her better makes her behavior more understandable."

Georgia doesn't like this because the implication is clear, and her cheeks darken noticeably. But ever the canny soldier, she takes a moment to regroup, then shakes off her embarrassment and launches an attack from another direction. "Well, I don't have to tell you how impressed I am that Darcy has at least learned how to assume the *appearance* of basic decency. I suspect, however, that what you were seeing is what I call the Aunt Catherine Effect. She's always been intimidated by her aunt and tends to behave much better when she's around."

Bennet can't repress a smile at this, but he answers with only a slight inclination of his head. He knows she wants to engage him on the old subject of her grievances, and he's in no mood to indulge her. Instead, he tosses the sugar wrapper into the trash, tips his coffee cup in her direction and saunters off. She lets him go, as determined as he is, he imagines, to avoid another meeting.

CHAPTER TWENTY

Bennet is googling Bingley when his aunt and uncle arrive. Keeping cybertabs on her is something he's been doing for six weeks now. At regular intervals, usually first thing in the morning, though sometimes not until after lunch, he'll type her name in to see what new information is available. On Monday, she surfaced at a movie premiere in Cannes in the company of a dashing Frenchman called LeAillard—that's it: just the one word all across. The guy won the Tour de France two years ago and now offers commentary on biking events on several European sports channels. He has jet-black hair and light gray eyes that are often hidden behind chic sunglasses. A brief item on Tattler identified them as "just friends," but Bennet knows enough to be suspicious of that benign description, and he's certainly not going to tell John the truth about Bingley while there's a jet-black-haired biking champion on the scene.

For more than a month, Bennet's been looking for the moment to tell his brother the whole story, but every time it seems as if Bingley is free and unencumbered, another photo of her smiling next to a handsome man pops up. The more he googles, the more convinced he becomes that Bingley was always just a pipe dream. The universe she lives in—the private planes, the staff of servants, the dashing from high-profile event to high-profile event—is so far removed from John's that the two of them would never have seriously made a go of it. As soon as they hooked up, they'd have realized their incompatibility. A flirtation doesn't require compromise or the slow dissolution of one's dignity.

With these thoughts most forcefully in mind, he resolves once and for all not to tell John the truth about Bingley. As firm as his conviction is now, he knows in the morning he'll google her again.

Luckily, his aunt and uncle's appearance means he doesn't have to think about it anymore that night.

"We're late," his Aunt Emily says as she knocks gently on the office door, which is open.

Bennet immediately stands up to greet them. "Did you get lost?"

His aunt shakes her head. "Our business ran long. You know how your uncle likes to chat."

Although the Gardiners flew into New York that morning to take a cruise to the Bahamas that leaves the next day, his uncle is constitutionally incapable of taking a vacation and arranged a full afternoon of meetings.

"I'm a used-car salesman," Edward explains. "Occupational hazard."

Laughing, Bennet gives him a warm hug. "You haven't been on a lot in a dozen years."

His uncle scoffs at the notion of leaving the lot behind. "Once a used-car salesman, always a used-car salesman."

Aunt Em glances around the room thoughtfully. "So this is where you work. It's not what I was expecting."

"More glamorous, eh?" Bennet asks with an amused grin. He puts his computer to sleep and takes his phone off the charger.

"More cozy," she replies tactfully.

Bennet points to the wooden chair to the left of the door. "That's Lydon's office. It doesn't look like much because, well, it isn't much, but it hardly matters because he's never here."

Uncle Edward notices Lydon isn't there now, nor John. "Aren't your brothers joining us for dinner?"

"John's at a patrons' event he couldn't wiggle out of, though, I assure you, he tried his hardest. He should be free around ten, so he'll try to meet us for a drink at your hotel later." Bennet tosses his phone into the front pocket of his messenger bag. "And Lydon's in Brighton."

"England?" Aunt Em asks.

"Beach," Bennet clarifies. "He went to the birthday party for the daughter of some Russian oligarch last night. No," he says before his aunt can even open her mouth, "don't ask. He's still out there. Apparently, it takes forty-eight hours to fête the daughter of a Russian oligarch, rather than the usual two to three. So you're stuck with just me tonight. I hope that's not a problem."

"Are you kidding?" his aunt says. "A one-on-one inquisition is my favorite conversation."

Uncle Edward laughs. "You think she's kidding, but let's just see if she lets me get a word in edgewise."

Delighted with the pair, whom he doesn't get to see nearly as much as he'd like, he says, "I can't wait. Let me just make sure I've gotten everything. Phone, keys, wallet. Yep." He looks out the windows and, noting how bright it still is, suggests a quick tour of the museum before they head out. "Our reservation isn't until eight, so we have plenty of time."

Bennet's throwing his messenger bag over his shoulder when Hannah strides into the office asking for one of John's packets for individual donors. "You know the one I mean, right? It's got lots of little pamphlets explaining all the levels of individual giving and a copy of the latest magazine?" she asks, her eyes sliding over to the Gardiners as if she's just noticed them standing there. "I'm interrupting. I'm sorry."

Bennet assures her it's all right and introduces her to his aunt and uncle.

"You're from Chicago, right?" Hannah says. "I'm sure John mentioned it. You're taking a cruise from New York."

Emily grins widely. "We leave tomorrow for the Bahamas. We're very excited. We've never been on a cruise before, and, of course, it's a treat to see our nephews."

"I know you have dinner plans, so I'll just take that packet and get out of your way."

Sliding open one of John's desk drawers, Bennet says, "Why are you sending it out? Special events doesn't usually deal with individual gifts."

"No, we don't," Hannah says with a grimace. "Meryton said he called your office and you didn't pick up. He wants it to go out tonight. He had a real bee in his bonnet about it. Some new scheme he's cooked up to reconnect with a former donor who somehow managed to slither off the hook."

"I'm sorry you got stuck with it," he says sincerely but doesn't volunteer to take over the task. He knows a dodged bullet when it whizzes over his head.

She shrugs. "It's no big deal. I'll have to skip the gym, but Meryton signed off on a car because it's a huge inconvenience for me to go to the Upper East Side. So there's that."

Bennet finds the packet in the drawer, pulls it out and hands it to Hannah. "Who's it for?"

Hannah flips through the pages to make sure everything she needs is there and then looks up. "Darcy Fitzwilliam."

Bennet's heart hitches—there's no other way to explain the way it stops for the briefest pause before resuming its regular beat. "Cool," he says.

His aunt, however, is not nearly as nonchalant. "*The* Darcy Fitzwilliam?" she gasps, her eyes as round as saucers. "Of Pemberley? The mansion on Fifth Avenue? *That's* where you're dropping off the package?"

"Yes," Hannah says, her lips twitching.

"Let us do it," Aunt Em says suddenly and with surprising forcefulness.

Hannah looks from Emily Gardiner to Bennet, unsure how to respond to such a request.

Seeing the hesitation, Emily says, "Please let us do it.

You can go to the gym like you planned. Take the car. We'll grab a cab." Now she turns to her nephew. "Please, Bennet, it would be such a treat."

"But Hannah's only dropping it off," he says, confused by his aunt's interest. "She's not staying for tea."

"I know," she says, "but even a chance to glance into the foyer of such a mansion would be a privilege. Pemberley is supposed to be magnificent. The Discovery Channel did a whole show on it last year. All I want is a glimpse."

His uncle adds his support. "A glimpse won't hurt anything."

At a loss, Bennet looks at Hannah, who shrugs. "Far be it for me to deprive a pair of vacationing Chicagoans of such an ardently desired treat. I'll put this in the envelope with my letter asking her to pass the information on to Charlotte Bingston and meet you down in the lobby in five minutes."

Thrilled by the unexpected turn of events, Emily claps and, noticing her nephew's distinct lack of enthusiasm, says, "My love, don't you want to see a place you've heard so much about?"

Bennet knows it's unlikely he'll see Darcy—even if she has returned from Europe, she's hardly likely to answer the door of the huge house herself—but he still thinks he has no business going to Pemberley. "One famous mansion is very much like another," he says cynically, "fine carpets, silk curtains, et cetera."

But he can't deny his aunt the overwhelming joy of peering over the shoulder of the butler at Pemberley and agrees to the scheme. Confident that he won't bump into Darcy, he admits silently that he's curious to see the house where she grew up. Without further comment, Bennet closes the office door and leads his relatives to the lobby to wait for Hannah. A few minutes later she appears with an envelope beautifully addressed in extravagant script and after a brief argument over who should take the car waiting in front—"You take it," "No, you take it"—they bundle into the elegant black car to drive into the city.

To Pemberley we go, Bennet thinks.

CHAPTER TWENTY-ONE

As determined as Bennet is not to gawk, his jaw drops a fraction of an inch as he stares at the large, handsome stone edifice that Darcy calls home. He's seen the building before—has certainly walked by it on his way to the Central Park Zoo or up to the Met—but passing an imposing structure owned by a stranger and standing before one owned by a woman who once tried to court you are two entirely different things. Suddenly, the elegant but impersonal building seems oddly familiar.

His aunt and uncle are effusive in their praise, and they stand on the sidewalk discussing the architecture for several minutes, marveling at how dignified and at home the building seems in its setting. Unlike other Gilded Age mansions, Pemberley's not overwhelmed with crenellations and battlements, chimneys and rotundas. Its simple beauty wasn't made outrageously elaborate by the awkward and unfortunate taste of a new millionaire trying to establish his eminence. The stately home was built only a few years after Vanderbilt House but aped none of its pretensions.

While Bennet debates with his aunt who should have the honor of knocking, a pleasure they both equally believes belongs to the other, Uncle Edward presses the button to the left of the door. Everyone falls silent as they listen to the lovely ring of the chimes. After a moment, the door opens and a trim woman in a tailored gray suit and neat gray chignon opens the door. She's holding a clipboard and glances up at the trio with piercing blue eyes.

"Inspector or insurer?" she asks, stepping aside to let them in.

The abrupt question, snappishly stated, as if they've already wasted too much of her time, disconcerts Bennet, and he hesitates on the threshold. His aunt, however, takes full advantage of the invitation and strides boldly into the house. Uncle Edward eagerly follows.

"Neither," Bennet says, stepping cautiously into the entry hall, a large, gracious room with golden marble and towering vases filled with brightly colored gladioli. "We have a delivery for Ms. Fitzwilliam."

"Deliveries on the table," she announces briskly. "Where do I sign?"

"I don't—"

Her phone chirps, and she cuts him off with her hand before answering the call. "Ms. Reynolds." Silence for a few seconds. "No, I'm her executive assistant. You talk to me."

Bennet waits and feels silly for waiting. He doesn't need a signature, so there's no reason to linger.

Ms. Reynolds holds up a finger, indicating he should give her a minute. The doorbell rings and she marches to the door, which she opens while barking "Excuse me!" into the phone. On the step stands a wiry man with thick black glasses and a harried expression. She looks him up and down. "Inspector or insurer?" she demands.

The table for deliveries is a small console already piled high with envelopes, and Bennet carefully places his package on the top of the neat stack. He listens patiently as the new arrival complains at length about traffic on the FDR.

Only, Bennet isn't really patient. He's agitated by the grandeur all around him, by the lavish display of wealth and privilege that are Darcy's daily life, and every passing second is a fresh temptation to see just a little bit more. He cranes his neck to get a better view of the hallway; he tilts his head to get a better look at the staircase.

"A parking lot," the man says, still angry and anxious from the ordeal. "Like a fucking parking lot. Nothing moved for almost an hour. It was probably that goddamn U.N. Some foreign dignitary wants to go to lunch so they shut down the entire east side for his fucking motorcade."

While the man rants and Bennet gapes, his aunt shrewdly sizes up the situation. In the scowling visage of Ms. Reynolds, she sees the opportunity of a lifetime, and when yet another person presents herself at the door, Emily Gardiner seizes the moment. Without a word to her husband or nephew, without even a glance indicating her intentions, she darts across the large entry hall, dashes down the long corridor and disappears around the bend.

Bennet is stunned. Unable to believe his eyes, he stares at the empty space, trying to convince himself he did not just see his sane and otherwise trustworthy aunt sneak into the house of one of the richest women in New York City. It's so shocking, it takes his breath away, and he turns to his uncle to make sure he saw it, too. But his uncle is no longer there. No, his other formerly sane relative is making his own hurried sprint across the floor.

Cursing silently, Bennet glances at Ms. Reynolds, confirms her attention is elsewhere and runs after them. He finds them a few seconds later in an elegant sitting room next to the kitchen, giggling like schoolchildren.

"What in God's name were you thinking?" he asks, his voice a low hush. For all he knows, there are dozens of people in the house—assistants, servants, pipe inspectors, *Fitzwilliams!* He can't conceive of anything more embarrassing than to be caught wandering around the halls of Pemberley.

Struggling for composure, his aunt chokes out a partially coherent explanation about the house calling to her. It was as if Pemberley *wanted* her to come in. "I'm sorry," she says, noticing how upset her nephew is. "I really am."

But she's not. There isn't a speck of sincerity in her apology, and, unrepentant, she walks over to the fireplace to examine a cluster of photographs. She picks one up to inspect it more closely.

Aghast, Bennet runs over and orders her to put it down. "Fingerprints!"

Aunt Emily laughs lightly, kisses her nephew on the cheek and calls him a darling boy. But she doesn't put down the photo. Bennet, torn between fear and frustration, takes the picture from her grasp and returns it to the mantel. Only then does he realize the subject is Darcy. It's a snapshot of her as a teenager standing beside—can it be?—Georgia. Fascinated, he stares at the much-younger Darcy, already beautiful at sixteen or so, with a mischievous grin on her face. He knows that look. He saw it months ago at the Longbourn gala. Something Carl said had provoked it.

He replaces the photo and picks up another—Darcy with a gangly boy, all arms and legs, in front of a piano. That must be her brother George.

Transfixed by the images of Darcy, by the unexpected glimpse into her life, he loses track of time and space, and it's only when his aunt taps him on the shoulder that he remembers where he is.

"Let's go upstairs," she says, tempting him like the devil.

It's on the tip of his tongue to insist they sneak out with the same stealth with which they'd snuck in, but he can't muster the words. Instead, he follows his aunt and uncle up the sleek staircase to the second floor.

He's horrified and mortified by his weakness, but make no mistake: He wants this as much as his aunt does. Probably more.

The stairs lead them to the dining room, a large, well-proportioned room, beautifully decorated. Bennet peruses it thoughtfully while his aunt recalls facts from the documentary she saw. She cites names, dates and manufacturers. His uncle gleefully responds, admiring everything and marveling at his wife's memory. Bennet wanders over to the window and takes in the view of the sea lion pool in the central courtyard of the zoo.

They pass into other rooms, and Bennet is surprised to discover how much he likes Darcy's taste—it's neither fussy nor gaudy. The furniture is elegant, with none of the self-conscious splendor of the furnishings at Rosings.

As he tours the house, Bennet finds it impossible to remained unmoved. He can't look at the beautiful living room and not picture himself comfortably ensconced in the armchair by the window with a book on his lap. He imagines his aunt's uncontained giddiness at being invited to Pemberley as a guest—*his* guest.

And that, he realizes, is the dash of cold water he needs to return to his senses. He can fantasize about playing gracious host all he wants, but in reality, he would never have been able to invite his family to Pemberley: Darcy's detailed account of his inferiority made it clear she'd never let him forget the disparity of their situations. He'd have always been the supplicant, asking permission and seeking approval and never feeling quite as comfortable in that armchair as he'd like.

Although he wants to linger, he follows the Gardiners up the grand staircase and enters a large game room with comfortable couches, several large screens and a variety of game consoles. He tries to imagine Darcy playing *Call of Duty,* which, he notes, is among the games piled neatly on the shelves, and decides this room must be used primarily by her brother. Since George just finished studying music at a conservatory in London, he imagines the room, which seems recently redone, must be a welcome home gift.

Next, they visit the picture gallery, a sweeping hallway lined with ancestral paintings, and Bennet, standing before the portrait of Darcy, is arrested by the striking resemblance, especially in the smile, which he recalls sometimes seeing on her face when she looks at him. At this moment, as Bennet stares at her picture, he feels an unprecedented friendliness toward Darcy, an unexpected sense of camaraderie, and he wonders if her declaration could have been quite as offensive as he remembers.

Bennet is reluctant to delve deeply into this strange sensation and is saved from unwelcome contemplation by a stern voice demanding, "Veranda or dwell?"

At once, he looks up to see Ms. Reynolds standing in the doorway, clipboard in hand. He opens his mouth to speak but nothing comes out. He has no glib explanation prepared.

Luckily for him, his aunt is undaunted and she immediately rushes over to the woman to beg her pardon. She's apologizing for their brazen intrusion, but Ms. Reynolds thinks she's asking for clarification.

"Which magazine are you from: *Veranda* or *Dwell?*" she explains impatiently, her eyebrows drawn in a fierce scowl. "Both are scheduled for a site visit to see the renovations."

Faced with two unfamiliar publications, his aunt does the only logical thing—invents a third option. In a matter of minutes, she introduces herself as the senior lifestyle editor at *Real Simple,* promotes herself to creative director and establishes the gallery as the must-have venue for their December fashion story on faux-fur coats.

Consulting her clipboard, Ms. Reynolds insists she has no appointment scheduled with *Real Simple.*

Bennet's aunt affects amazement at this news—"No appointment? But that's impossible!"—and throws him under the bus, recruiting him as her administrative assistant one moment and firing him the next.

Ms. Reynolds nods approvingly, Uncle Edward guffaws, and Bennet decides to come clean before his aunt hires a film crew for a fake photo shoot. "We're trespassers," he announces without hedging. "We came to drop off an envelope for Ms. Fitzwilliam and found ourselves unable to resist looking around. It was most definitely wrong, quite possibly illegal and wholly insane. I have no excuse except to say we were overcome by the magnificence of the house. We're very sorry for invading your privacy and apologize for the intrusion."

Bennet expects to be led away in handcuffs. He can't imagine this impatient woman, this curt creature who doesn't have time for full sentences, calmly accepting the inefficiency of intruders. Having to eject random strangers from the premises—what a galling waste of time!

Waiting for her to respond, he swears he can hear the sound of approaching police sirens.

But Ms. Reynolds doesn't call the 19th precinct. Instead, she shrugs.

Shrugs—as if it's no big deal.

"It happens all the time," she says. "Not a week goes by where I don't find a tradesman wandering around the halls supposedly looking for the bathroom. I once discovered the attorney general in the conservatory watering the gardenias. She said they looked thirsty."

"The conservatory," Aunt Emily says thoughtfully. "I don't recall seeing a conservatory."

Before his shameless relation can request a rectification of that oversight, Bennet jumps in with another apology. "We appreciate your understanding, but I'm sure your employer isn't as nonchalant about uninvited guests in her home."

Ms. Reynolds blinks at him in momentary confusion. "You mean Darcy? She'd never get worked up over something so minor. She's remarkably easygoing. That's one of the things that makes her such a pleasure to work for."

Bennet is so astonished by this statement, he feels like a character in a cartoon doing an elaborate double take. At the very least, he wants to comically clean out his ear with an oversize Q-tip and say, "What's that again?"

His aunts smiles. "I'm happy to hear it. We'd hate to get you in trouble."

"There's no reason to worry on that score," Ms. Reynolds assures them. "I've known Darcy for years—I worked with her mom before her death—and have never had a cross word from her. She's a delight."

Bennet's sense of unreality deepens, and he grows convinced he's entered an alternative universe. Somehow, by stepping into the house, they stepped into another dimension, one in which the bad-tempered and rude Darcy Fitzwilliam is considered a delight.

Honestly, no other explanation makes sense.

"That's nice," Uncle Edward says. "You never know what to think about the people you read about in the tabloids. They seem so friendly and kind and then they throw their cell phone at the bellhop."

"Darcy is the real deal," Ms. Reynolds says, "a genuinely kind person. She's a wonderful employer, so even-keeled and good-natured. I genuinely don't think anyone who works for her would say a word against her. And she's a great landlord. Very responsive and reliable. She has a reputation for being proud, but I don't see it. I suspect it's because she doesn't rattle on like other young women."

The conversation turns to Darcy's mother, with Aunt Emily spouting vaguely remembered facts about her from the Pemberley documentary, and Ms. Reynolds, clearly pleased by the compliment, chats happily about her old employer. For ten precious minutes, minutes during which she can be crossing items off her check list, she talks about Ms. Fitzwilliam's work with the poor—work, she insists, her daughter is carrying on.

Bennet is as grateful for the information as he is agitated by it. This portrayal of Darcy as a lovely person, as a generous employer and a decent landlord, unsettles him in a way he can hardly understand. That these revelations come from an underling makes them twice as meaningful, for he knows how difficult it is to earn the respect of one's employees. Keeping their goodwill is nearly impossible. If Ms. Reynolds's assessment of Darcy is correct, then his own estimation of her is wildly off base.

It's a disconcerting discovery, for he'd been so sure—so very sure—he had her all figured out.

Now he's sure of nothing.

He recalls the scene at the Parsonage, the harsh way he rejected her, and feels a fresh bout of shame. He'd had no concept at the time of the compliment she'd paid him with her interest and affection.

Lost in these thoughts, Bennet's startled to hear Ms.

Reynolds announce that she's kicking them out. It's late, she's tired and the insurance adjuster never showed. "I'm going to leave him a strongly worded message and head home."

They return to the entry hall and thank Ms. Reynolds again and again for her patience and understanding. Bennet can still scarcely believe they're walking away without rap sheets. By rights, they should be heading down to the police station to be charged with trespassing.

On the stone path in front of the house, Bennet turns back to look at Pemberley again. His uncle and aunt also stop, and while the former is conjecturing as to the date of the building, the owner of it herself suddenly comes forward from the street, where a livery driver is just then pulling away.

Darcy is so close, only a few feet away, there's nowhere to hide, and yet Bennet looks around quickly for a hedge to dive behind. Knowing such a plan is unfeasible—even if there were foliage to offer cover—he looks at her and their eyes meet instantly, the cheeks of each spreading with the deepest blush. She starts, and for a moment seems immovable with surprise, but quickly recovering, speaks to Bennet. If she's not perfectly composed at finding him at her home, she is, at least, perfectly polite.

Mortified to be there, on her doorstep, after so coldly rebuffing her offer of affection, Bennet answers her courteous enquiries after his family. Amazed at how different her manner is from their last meeting, he finds his discomfort growing with each sentence. The few minutes in which they stand there talking are some of the most awkward of his life. Darcy doesn't seem much more at ease. Her tone has none of its usual calm, and she asks about John and Lydon so often and in such a rush, it's clear she's very distracted.

At length, she runs out of conversation—it does not even occur to her to ask about Bennet's companions—and after standing a few moments without saying a word, suddenly recollects herself, says good-bye and disappears into her house.

The Gardiners, who watch the entire exchange in silent amazement, immediately launch into questions, but Bennet is too engrossed in his own feelings to hear them. Instead, he strides silently to the sidewalk, chastising himself for behaving so stupidly. How could he have agreed to come there? To show up on Darcy's doorstep—it was madness! Did she think he'd arranged the meeting on purpose? Did she believe he had intentionally thrown himself in her path? The idea is unbearable!

If only they'd taken their leave of Ms. Reynolds a little more quickly. Sixty seconds fewer and they would have been clear of the walk by the time Darcy's car pulled up. But no, they had to express their gratitude one more time. As if six thank-yous weren't enough! They had to linger over the seventh. He cringes again and again over the perverseness of the meeting. And her behavior, so strikingly different—what could it mean? That she talked to him at all is amazing but to talk so kindly, to ask about his brothers! Bennet has never known Darcy to be so pleasant or to speak so nicely. What a contrast to her last address at the Parsonage, when she'd pulled the door coldly behind her. Bennet has no idea what to think or how to account for it.

He wants to leave the area as quickly as possible—run to the corner and down Fifth Avenue and all the way to the restaurant in Soho—but the Gardiners are too fascinated by what they've just witnessed to hurry. They meander in astonishment, wondering how their nephew could have failed to mention he knows Darcy Fitzwilliam personally. They walk so slowly that they're barely at the corner of Sixty-fifth Street when Darcy catches up to them. Bennet, however surprised, is at least more prepared for a conversation than before and resolves to speak calmly. He begins by admiring the beauty of Pemberley, but he hasn't gotten beyond the words *elegant* and *charming* before it occurs to him that maybe Darcy wasn't trying to catch up to them and he abruptly stops talking.

But of course she'd been seeking them out—she's hardly likely to be running to the corner store for milk—and she breaks the silence that follows by introducing herself to his aunt and uncle. Bennet doesn't know what to make of such unprecedented friendliness, but he expects Darcy to be somewhat horrified when she realizes she's meeting the relatives to whom she had objected so stridently. That she's surprised by the connection is evident, for Edward Gardiner has neither the look nor the manner of the usual used-car salesman, which perhaps says more about the popular perception of used-car salesmen than about him. Regardless, Darcy's smile remains firmly in place and, far from running away from the disgraceful pair, she enters into conversation with them.

The conversation soon turns to Pemberley and their impromptu and unsanctioned tour of the mansion, which, true to Ms. Reynolds's prediction, Darcy doesn't seem to mind in the least. Indeed, she doesn't mind so much that she actually invites them back to see the conservatory when his aunt reveals that they somehow missed that room. Both Gardiners are excited by the gracious offer and express their gratitude with much sincerity. Bennet says nothing. He's too astonished and confused by the change in Darcy to do anything but wonder at its cause. It can't be for *his* sake that she's so friendly and outgoing. His criticisms in the Hamptons can't have led to such a radical change. It's not possible, is it, that she still has feelings for him?

Unsettled by these thoughts, Bennet remains silent as Darcy chats with his aunt and uncle on the corner of Fifth Avenue and Sixty-fifth Street. But when Aunt Em agrees to go back to Pemberley—*back,* as if the first visit weren't extraordinary enough!—Bennet's forced to mention their dinner reservation at eight in Soho.

At once, Darcy suggests they dine at Pemberley. "It's already 7:45, so it's unlikely you would make it all the way downtown in time."

It's a rather flimsy excuse—and not only because one typically has a fifteen-minute window in which to make a reservation—but Bennet takes its slightness as more evidence Darcy has changed. After a pause, he agrees, although his relatives have already voiced their enthusiastic approval of the plan, and they all walk the short block back to the house, his aunt threading her arm through her nephew's as she gives him a look of wonder.

After a comprehensive tour of the conservatory and the kitchen, as well, for Emily Gardiner has never been able to resist a well-laid-out island, the small party settles in the front parlor. Somehow Bennet finds himself sitting in an armchair by the window. It is, in fact, the exact same chair he'd imagined himself sitting in earlier, and as Darcy converses with the Gardiners, he's disconcerted to realize he doesn't feel like a supplicant at all.

Darcy hands him a glass of red wine—a Syrah, which indicates she has remembered his preference from months before—and sits down on the ottoman adjacent to his chair. After a moment's hesitation, Bennet leans forward to make it very clear that their intention had been only to deliver an envelope. "We didn't mean to intrude and I never imagined my aunt would insist on giving herself a self-guided tour. We were just dropping off a packet from Meryton," he adds with an apologetic smile.

But at the mention of his boss's name, Bennet's thoughts are instantly driven back to the time when it had last been mentioned between them, and judging by Darcy's complexion, her mind is similarly engaged.

Finding the silence excessively awkward, Bennet tries to think of a subject that offers no potential embarrassment to either and comes up blank. At last, he recalls the room with all the game consoles and asks if it's her brother's. She concedes that she had it designed with him in mind but has a weak spot for *Minecraft*.

"Sometimes when I can't sleep, I'll come down at three in the morning and play for a few hours. I like to build things I've seen," she says. "Right now I'm working on a scale replica of Mount Rushmore."

Bennet laughs and says he re-created Citi Field down to the benches in the dugout. "But my phone crashed and I lost everything and didn't have the heart to rebuild. So I gave up."

Darcy smiles at him and Bennet feels a strange sense of connection. It's not merely that they're having their first relaxed and comfortable conversation; it's also the discovery that they have something in common. Despite all their differences, here's a shared experience.

Before Bennet can figure out what this means or why he's unsettled by it, Darcy's brother appears in the doorway. "Reynolds says we have guests for dinner. Did I forget something?"

Darcy assures her brother of the gathering's impromptu nature and stands up to make the introductions. George Fitzwilliam is taller than Bennet, and though little more than eighteen, he cuts an impressive figure, with broad shoulders and a narrow waist. His features are not as handsome as his sister's, as they lack a certain pleasing symmetry, but his face is strong and his manners are good humored and unassuming. Almost immediately, Bennet decides he likes him because he's not shy about teasing Darcy about her ambitions for his future, which are considerable. She clearly expects a lot from him—single greatest classical pianist is mentioned several times—but rather than let her outsize expectations intimidate him, he lobs them right back at her, stating he expects her to cure world hunger by the end of the decade. Darcy effortlessly takes this treatment in stride, a fact that doesn't amaze him as much now as it would have only a few hours ago.

With three younger brothers, Bennet converses easily with George about his experience at the conservatory and his aspirations—actual, not fantastical—as a musician. He doesn't look at Darcy often, but whenever he does catch a glimpse, he sees an expression of polite interest and her tone of voice has none of the hauteur or disdain that had previously given it inflection. Watching her court the good opinion of his aunt and uncle, two people of whom she had openly professed disdain only six weeks before, is a revelation. Never, not even in the company of her good friends at the Netherfield or her dignified relations at Rosings, has he seen her so gracious and outgoing, so down-to-earth or approachable, as now. Bennet can't imagine what she stands to gain from this display of such engaging behavior.

Dinner is announced and Darcy leads them into the dining room, with its large picture window overlooking Fifth Avenue. The meal is lovely and elegant but without the buttoned-up severity Bennet would expect from a refined feast served by two liveried servants. As soon as his salad is placed in front of him, George takes out his phone and Instagrams the elaborate mélange of peas, prosciutto and butter lettuce leaves. Darcy rolls her eyes but doesn't say anything. As a close friend of Bingley's, she's accustomed to such self-conscious treatment of food.

"So what do you do?" George asks Mr. Gardiner as the dessert plates are being cleared.

Prior to this question, the conversation had centered on travel and music and whether George should become a Yankees or Mets fan and how one can survive a two-week cruise without gaining two hundred pounds. Now, as the focus shifts to his uncle's profession—a profession that Darcy once scorned as hucksterish—Bennet tenses his shoulders in expectation of an awkward or even unpleasant exchange.

"I'm a used-car salesmen," Uncle Edward says.

"He owns about two dozen auto malls in Illinois and Indiana," Bennet quickly adds, as if quantity would somehow make up for quality.

"I've always loved the term *auto mall*," Darcy says. "I imagine animated little cars shopping for hubcaps and windshield wipers."

Bennet is astonished by the whimsy of her comment, and he stares at her with his mouth half-open as his aunt suggests a tattoo parlor for detailing.

"And a fitting room, naturally, so they can change their oil in private," Darcy says.

George proposes a jewelry store for hood ornaments and Bennet's uncle says he has one of those. "Only the owners, not the cars, pick them out. The vast majority of our customers are humans, though we have gotten the odd Mustang or two."

Darcy laughs, and the uncomfortable exchange Bennet fears never materializes. The conversation jumps easily from car dealerships to road tests to driving lessons, and he listens in surprise as George tells an anecdote of Darcy's failed attempt to teach him how to drive.

"I'm talking full-on crash position, like on an airplane that's about to go down," he says, giggling as he re-creates the pose.

"He's exaggerating," Darcy says. "It was more like a catcher's stance—you know, hunched over. My head never actually touched my knees."

"But you were still in the parking lot, right?" Bennet asks.

"An entirely empty parking lot," George says. "Not another car in sight."

Bennet looks at Darcy and shakes his head sadly. "I taught three younger brothers to drive, so you know I've been there, but you have to at least get out of the parking lot before you can legitimately fear for your life."

Darcy looks at him and smiles. "You have your threshold. I have mine."

It's well after eleven by the time they leave, and before Bennet opens the door to the taxi to escort the Gardiners to their hotel, he leans in and gives Darcy a kiss on the cheek. It's an automatic gesture, something one does at the end of a pleasant evening when one is feeling genial toward one's host, but he becomes keenly aware of the impropriety as soon as his lips meet the warmth of her flesh. He straightens awkwardly and stiffly offers his hand to George for a departing handshake, even though he has already performed that courtesy.

As soon as the cab pulls away from the curb, his aunt turns to Bennet and demands a full explanation of what just happened. She understands the general outline—dinner with Darcy Fitzwilliam—but she can't wrap her head around the fact that Bennet knows her. How could he not mention that they're such good friends?

Naturally, the only thing for Bennet to do is to insist he and Darcy are not good friends, but his aunt and uncle won't hear a word of it. Rather, they parse the evening for evidence of Darcy's affection, for this is the conclusion they've come to: The only way to account for such attentions from such a quarter is to assume a partiality for their nephew.

LYNN MESSINA

His aunt practically sings it, so pleased is she by the development. Well aware that his denials will only make it worse, he suffers in silent dignity for the rest of the ride to the hotel, which, luckily, isn't very long. He climbs out of the car to walk them to their room, but the Gardiners contend it's far too late for such courtesies and insist on paying for his taxi back to Queens. Too exhausted to argue, he accepts the twenty-dollar bill his uncle slips him and promises to see them in the morning for breakfast before they ship out.

The cab ride home is long but not long enough for Bennet to figure out his feelings for Darcy, and he lies awake for hours trying to make sense of them. He certainly doesn't hate her. No, hatred had vanished some time ago, and, recalling it, he's embarrassed that his dislike had ever risen to such a strident level. Although he's been reluctant to acknowledge Darcy's good qualities, he sees them clearly now, especially in the wake of Ms. Reynolds's testimony, and feels considerable respect for her. But more than that, more than respect and esteem, he feels grateful—grateful that she doesn't seem to hold the past against him. Nobody would blame her if she did, for his behavior at the Parsonage had been petulant and acrimonious and unjust. And yet rather than bear a grudge, which is something even she owns she does very well, Darcy treated him with friendliness and familiarity, going out of her way to make his aunt and uncle comfortable. If Bennet thinks about it too much, and, indeed, it's impossible for him not to, the only conclusion he can reach is the one the Gardiners did in the taxi hours ago: Darcy cares for him. It's a wholly improbable proposition, and yet her welcoming treatment of him and his family this evening was even more unlikely. If the supposition is true, if Darcy's feelings toward him remain unchanged, then it's up to him to decide what happens next. Does he want to encourage her affection? Is there a future in it for them or merely more heartbreak?

Bennet doesn't know, and by the time his exhausted mind stops puzzling over the question long enough to let him fall asleep, it's almost time to get up.

CHAPTER TWENTY-TWO

Bennet doesn't expect to get the worst news of his life via text. Like everyone, he expects to be woken by a ringing telephone at 4 o'clock in the morning. The message, conveyed before noon by John using far fewer characters than such a weighty matter necessitates—as if *now*'s the time to start worrying about data overages—strikes Bennet at first as a joke. In the cab on his way back to the Longbourn after leaving his aunt and uncle at their ship, he shakes his head over his brother's perverse sense of humor.

Then he recalls that his brother doesn't have a perverse sense of humor and reads the message again: Lydon in possession of FBI.

Because the most obvious interpretation of the text is also the least plausible, Bennet wonders three things: 1) What does *FBI* stand for? 2) Why does Lydon have it? 3) Why does John think this is remarkable?

Operating on only three hours' sleep, Bennet's not at his sharpest. It's barely 11 o'clock, and he feels as if he's already put in a full day: meeting his aunt and uncle for breakfast before escorting them to the cruise terminal at West Fifty-second street, helping them settle into their quarters and waving them off. John, who was only able to carve enough time

189

out of his schedule to meet them for coffee, had gone back to the office while Bennet took the Gardiners to the dock. Standing on a pier with his arm raised for twenty minutes had hardly invigorated him, and as Bennet yawns widely in the cab, he's not surprised he can't decipher John's message.

Before the truth finally penetrates his dulled brain, he actually googles *FBI* to find out how the kids are using the acronym these days.

But once he realizes that the text means exactly what it says—Lydon is in the possession of the FBI—he loses all feeling in his fingers and the phone drops to the floor. He stares at it, a bright blue rectangle against the dark-gray backdrop of the cab's worn mat, and tries to imagine what Lydon could have done to be arrested by the FBI.

Has he been arrested? What does *in possession* actually mean?

Bennet picks up his phone and dials John, but the call goes straight to voicemail. He leaves a message telling him to call him back as soon as possible, hangs up and immediately dials his number again. He does this over and over as the taxi travels down Continental Avenue.

He's still calling when he arrives at the Longbourn, and he's so angry, frustrated and panicked, he doesn't notice Meryton standing in the lobby waiting for him until he almost knocks the man over. He offers an absentminded apology and then realizes that his boss might know something. He opens his mouth to ask, but Meryton is already firing him.

Firing him?

"Obviously, I know you're not directly involved, as you're far too upstanding and ethical a person to even consider theft," Meryton explains, his eyes focused somewhere to the right of Bennet's shoulder, "but the connection is too pronounced to ignore and, naturally, you'll be tarred with the same brush as your brother. In the face of such a scandal, the Longbourn needs to be seen as acting swiftly and conclusively. I'm sure you understand."

Bennet doesn't understand anything, and he asks

Meryton to stop talking for just a moment so he can gather his thoughts. But the executive director can't be halted.

"Although this disgrace is deeply devastating for me personally, I have to put concern for myself aside and think of the Longbourn. Henry's grandchildren are already using this debacle as proof of their grandfather's incompetence."

Before Bennet can scream in frustration, his phone rings and he barks, "John!" into the receiver without looking at the display. Meryton, ravaged by the shame delivered unto him by this appalling and as yet unexplained episode, doesn't notice him walk away.

"What the fuck is going on?" Bennet asks, his heart racing in dread now that the moment of truth has arrived.

"Lydon and Georgia Wickham stole $450,000 dollars from the museum by hacking into the bank accounts. Lydon gave her access to Meryton's computer and the passwords. The FBI traced them to London and apprehended them there. Apparently, they flew out Wednesday night rather than going to the oligarch's daughter's party. I'm at the FBI downtown trying to get more information, but they won't tell me anything."

Bennet wants to ask how Lydon could be so fucking stupid, but he already knows the answer and doesn't waste his breath. "Stay there," he says. "I'm coming right now."

He slides his phone back into his pocket, flicks a glance at Meryton, who's now reprimanding the brochure rack for pressuring him into hiring a third Bethle, and walks toward the door. Before he can reach for the handle, the door opens and Darcy enters. It's a testament to the urgency he feels that her sudden appearance barely registers. He doesn't pause to wonder why she's there or to speculate as to what her presence might mean.

Bennet's pale face and agitated manner make Darcy start, and before she can recover herself enough to speak, he hastily says, "I'm sorry but I have to go. I have to go now. I've got to get a cab."

"Oh, my God. What's wrong?" she asks fervently, then

recollecting herself, adds calmly, "My car is here. It can take you wherever you need to go. I have nothing planned. I was only here to ask you for a tour of *Art & Style*."

Bennet hesitates for the briefest moment before accepting the ride and follows Darcy out to the black car, which is idling in the driveway. He instructs the driver to take them to Federal Plaza on Broadway and Worth, then leans back in the leather seat and closes his eyes. Fucking stupid Lydon.

Seeing how miserably ill he looks, Darcy asks if he'd like an Advil and a bottle of water. "You look as if your head is throbbing."

"No, thank you," he replies, forcing himself to open his eyes and look at her. "I'm fine. I just got some really terrible news, and I'm still trying to process it."

Bennet falls silent, and Darcy, knowing better than to intrude on private grief, waits in wretched suspense for him to explain. As the car heads into the Midtown Tunnel, he says, "There's no point in trying to hide it, because it'll probably be on the news tonight. Lydon stole $450,000 from the Longbourn."

Darcy is astonished. "What?"

"With the help of Georgia Wickham, Lydon stole almost half a million dollars from the museum. It had to have been her idea," Bennet adds, his tone growing more agitated as he considers it. "Lydon is lazy, but he's not conniving. That trait is all Georgia, and I knew it. I knew it, but I didn't say anything to Lydon. If I'd warned him, this never would have happened."

"I'm very sorry," Darcy says, "sorry and shocked. But it's certain, absolutely certain?"

"Oh, yes, the FBI is very certain," he says and laughs without humor. "They were traced to London and arrested there. I don't know what happens next. Extradition, I suppose. John is at the FBI's office waiting for news."

"What's been done? Have you hired a lawyer?"

Bennet admits that hiring legal counsel hadn't occurred to him yet, and he doesn't know what difference it will make. "The case is hopeless. If only Lydon weren't so fucking stupid."

Darcy shakes her head in silent agreement.

"If only *I* hadn't been so fucking stupid," Bennet continues. "I know how impressionable Lydon is. I should have tried to steer him away from her the very first time he mentioned her name. I knew they were hanging out and did nothing."

Darcy doesn't answer. She turns her eyes toward the window and looks out at the passing landscape with a gloomy air.

Now, in the calm of the car, Bennet has the clarity of mind to think about Darcy's strange appearance. He doesn't know if her interest in the *Art & Style* exhibition is genuine or merely an excuse to come see him. He ponders the plausibility of both explanations for several minutes—the show *did* get a rave review from Holland Cotter in the *Times*—before conceding the irrelevance of the answer. In light of this—how did Meryton put it?—deeply devastating personal disgrace, Darcy can't even bring herself to look at him. Whatever relationship they might have had is impossible now. Everything is impossible now. He doesn't hold her decision against her, for he knows it's the only one she can make. The Bethle brothers might have been borderline respectable before, but now they're mired in scandal and shame. Tarred by the same brush, as Meryton said.

Bennet cannot find any humor in the situation, but he does concede with bitter irony that Lydon's transgression has made his own feelings startlingly clear, for now that he knows he doesn't have a chance with Darcy, he desperately wants one.

Eventually, they arrive at 26 Federal Plaza, and Bennet calmly, politely and sincerely thanks Darcy for all her help. He knows it's the last time he'll see her, and as much as he wants to linger, he's too smart to waste time on futile gestures. John is waiting in the FBI's office and might, for all he knows, have new information. At the very least they should see about hiring a lawyer for Lydon. And their parents. Someone has to call them.

Not it, Bennet thinks glumly as he walks across the plaza, but he knows the mess they're in won't be resolved with something so easy as a childish refrain.

CHAPTER TWENTY-THREE

John and Bennet settle in for the long wait for information, and the wait is very long indeed. Elsewhere in the world, gigabytes of data travel at the speed of light, but in the FBI's office news dribbles in so slowly it might as well be arriving by mail coach. It takes three days for them to even discover where Lydon's being held, and for those first seventy-two hours they imagine him in some CIA black site trussed up like a turkey.

Although the investigation into the theft clears Bennet and John of all wrongdoing, the lead agent still treats them with suspicion, as if they've somehow been wily enough to escape detection. The other agents treat them with boredom and answer their questions with a dull monotony as if responding a child's repeated query of why, why, why.

As angry as Bennet is with the unjust treatment, he doesn't have the luxury of righteous indignation. Lydon is guilty of the charges. Regardless of his frame of mind when he entered into Georgia's scheme or the sufficiency of his understanding of it, he committed the crime. The only reasonable target of Bennet's outrage is Lydon; he doesn't rail against Georgia because you can't fault a snake for being a snake.

That the scheme was Georgia's Bennet doesn't doubt.

Of course he's haunted by the glimmer of awe in Lydon's eyes as he examined the department's budget reports, and intellectually, he knows it's possible: A boy who lies easily to his parents would not scruple to rob his employer. But the grandness of the plot, the decision to steal hundreds of thousands of dollars, exonerates him from the worse crime. As Meryton likes to lament about the other two Bethle boys, Lydon lacks vision. He would pocket spare change from the petty cash box without a second thought, but it would never occur to him to take the till.

Following Darcy's advice, though of course he or John would have thought of it soon enough, they hire a lawyer to represent Lydon, and this capable woman immediately gathers more information than they. It's she who discovers Lydon has been transported from a holding cell at a police station to the FBI's London headquarters. With Eleanor Kramer on the case, Bennet and John know there's no point in their showing up at Federal Plaza every morning to wait for news, and yet they can't seem to help themselves. Being near the source is better than being cooped up in their small apartments or, worse, trying to go about their business as if everything is normal.

Anyway, they don't have business to go about. What are they going to do while their brother is being extradited for grand theft larceny? Job hunt?

Well, actually, they *do* need to job hunt because excellent lawyers don't come cheap. The considerable retainer has seriously strained their bank accounts, and they refuse to apply to their parents for help. They consider Lydon's fall into criminality and disgrace to be their fault. It happened on their watch, and they did nothing to warn him of Georgia's depravity. Only double-teamed fast-talking has managed to convince the elder Bethles to remain in Michigan. Why hop a plane to wait in the FBI office for hours on end?

Although most of their days are given over to pacing and glaring angrily in the general direction of Special Agent Tompkins's office, Bennet always devotes an hour or two every morning to scouring the Web for any new and infuriating gossip.

"I don't know why you do that," John says as crushes an empty coffee cup and tosses it into the trash. In a moment, he will make another run. Caffeine and nerves seem to be the only things sustaining him. "You're just going to make yourself angry."

Bennet shrugs. "I'm already angry."

"Angrier, then."

"Impossible," he says, clicking on a Gawker item and reading.

John watches him silently for a few minutes, then says, "These reporters don't know what they're talking about."

"Really? This one calls Lydon 'a charming wastrel who's never done an honest day's work in his life,' so he knows something," he says.

His brother walks to the other end of the drab waiting room and looks out the window at the passing traffic.

"He also calls you a gifted fundraiser," Bennet adds, "so he's got good sources. I wonder who at the Longbourn is talking to him. Actually, it's probably more useful to wonder who's not. Oh—now he goes on to imply that you're the mastermind behind the plot, as it's impossible for a low-level drudge like Lydon to have access to such privileged information. Little does he know Meryton keeps a Post-it stuck to his computer with all his passwords."

"Is there a quote from Jackson?" John asks, despite himself. He doesn't want to care what the press are saying, and yet it's impossible not to obsess about the stories being told about him and his family. Information about Georgia has come out, too, with colleagues who seemed to be her good friends describing her as irresponsible, unreliable and vindictive. Apparently, she borrowed from her fellow designers all the time to pay for clubs, cabs and drinks—debts she failed to settle by dipping into her illegally acquired largesse, a move that turned out to be far from deft.

Bennet smiles without humor. "Of course. What would an article about the great Longbourn scandal be without a quote from Henry's oldest grandson? 'You have to ask yourself, why would three brothers work in the same department at the same institution? The answer is very clear: for total infiltration. But that's beside the point now. This scandal proves what I and my family have been saying for years—Cyrus Longbourn's dream has become untenable in the modern age.'"

John sighs, saddened that Lydon's thoughtlessness—or, as Bennet would say, his fucking stupidity—hasn't just brought down the Bethle family but the 100-year-old institution as well. "At least he didn't call for proposals from real estate developers like he did in yesterday's *Times*."

As dire as the situation is, Bennet has just enough humor left to appreciate Jackson Longbourn's audacity. Delivered the opportunity of a lifetime, he's wasting no time in capitalizing on it. He wouldn't be surprised if this time next year Longbourn Estates broke ground in Forest Hills.

"Here's another juicy passage," Bennet says with bitter relish. "'Bennet Bethle, the second oldest of the so-called Bethle Gang, is reputed to be a communist, having recently been overheard at a fundraiser extolling the virtues of good design for the masses. Some industry insiders wonder if it's this desire to redistribute wealth that led him to allegedly participate in such a nefarious crime.' I don't mind being called a communist, but it really bugs me that the reporter didn't call out the Bauhaus exhibition by name. This article has gotten a lot of page views. The show could use the publicity."

John's only response is to announce another Starbucks run and to take requests. Bennet absently shakes his head, and Ida, the pretty redheaded receptionist whose good opinion John has been cultivating all week, asks for a soy latte. So far, this cultivation has yielded few benefits, but this morning, their seventh in a row, she greeted them with a smile and actually said hello. Perhaps soon she'd feed them information.

Despite the severity of the situation, John's essential faith in the goodness of humanity remains intact, though much tattered. Like Bennet, he blames Georgia—she *must* be the villain—and yet part of him rebels at the idea of total condemnation. There has to be some undiscovered piece of information that would mitigate the crime. Even with all the evidence, he persists in wondering if all this—the beige FBI waiting room, the Gawker articles, the caffeine—might still be a misunderstanding.

"Hurry back," Bennet says as his brother presses the elevator button. "I've got Buzzfeed's listicle on the fourteen best museum heists burning a hole in my browser."

As soon as John is gone, Bennet throws the phone onto the chair cushion in disgust and walks across the room with nervous energy. It's as if one of the Bethle brothers must always be pacing in unrestrained agitation at any given moment. While he takes his turn striding uselessly from the window to the elevator bank and back again, his thoughts drift to Darcy. His thoughts have drifted to her often during this seemingly endless vigil, and he can't help but feel that the pressure weighing on his chest, a heavy dread that never leaves him, would be a little less oppressive had he never met her. It would have spared him, he thinks, at least one or two sleepless nights.

When John returns, he drinks his coffee and talks to Ida first about the road work out front, which seems entrenched, and then about her career in the FBI. It's interesting enough and Bennet listens to bits and pieces of it as he passes. Eventually, he goes for a coffee run himself, and John takes up the relentless pacing of the floor.

And so the day passes, just like every other day they've spent there, until 4:47 p.m., when Special Agent Tompkins emerges from behind the glass doors to the left of Ida's desk and asks to speak with them in his office. His office— the inner sanctum! Bennet feels relief and dread and excited anticipation that the next moment won't be exactly the same as the last and the one before that.

Special Agent David Tompkins's office is at once sparse and messy. His walls have no art except for a poster of the Leaning Tower of Pisa with the words *Don't fall* along the bottom. Every surface, however, is covered with folders, books, magazines and printouts. Following his lead, John and Bennet sit down on the other side of a dark brown desk, and though the chairs are comfortable, they begin to fidget. It's hard for both of them to be seated at the same time.

"I'm pleased to report that the charges against Lydon Bethle have been dropped," Tompkins says.

Neither brother responds immediately. They stare at the agent from the FBI and wonder if he's suddenly talking in tongues.

Bennet tries first. "Some of the charges?"

"No," Tompkins says. "All of the charges."

John leans forward. "But there will be new charges?"

Tompkins shakes his head. "There will be no new charges. Your brother has been cleared of all wrongdoing."

The agent's words couldn't have been any clearer, and yet Bennet and John can't understand how Lydon has come through such an infamous episode unscathed. Is this a delusion brought on by anxiety and boredom? Bennet surreptitiously pinches himself on the wrist and feels the sting. Not a delusion, then.

But Tompkins's next statement, perhaps the most absurdly implausible one ever made on the planet Earth, even more so than the moon landing was faked, convinces him he must in fact be in the middle of a dream. "The United States government is very grateful to Mr. Bethle for his assistance in catching a clever and dangerous criminal."

Bennet can't form words. He's simply incapable of putting together a coherent thought. As baffled as he is, John manages to say, "It is?"

Tompkins nods. "For the past five weeks, your brother's been part of a covert operation to entrap Ms. Wickham, who we've suspected of various financial crimes for some time. With Mr. Bethle's help, we have enough evidence to put her away for a very long time."

Both brothers know this is impossible, but John knows it a little less resolutely than Bennet, and as Tompkins relates some particulars of the operation, he gloms onto the details that sound the most likely. Lydon is secretive, prone to intrigue and loves a good lark.

"The money's been restored to the Longbourn, with the FBI's apologies for any inconvenience suffered," Tompkins says. "Mr. Bethle will be free to go as soon as we put the paperwork through. Your lawyer has been alerted and is already working on it. The process should take only a day at the most, and then he'll be transported back to the States. The FBI thanks you for your patience."

"*All* the money?" Bennet asks suspiciously, as he struggles to process what Tompkins is saying. He knows something is missing from the equation, for his brother, though certainly not evil, is definitely not heroic.

"Every cent," the agent says.

Bennet can't conceive how this is possible. Last-minute tickets to London aren't free, and two villains clever enough to hack into private accounts wouldn't have made the rookie mistake of charging the flight to their credit cards.

John stands up. Everything has been resolved in the best way possible, and he sees no reason to nitpick over how many pennies were recovered. Bennet, he knows, is inclined to stay and go over the accounting until the math makes sense. The thing his brother doesn't understand is that nothing about this episode will ever make total sense. It will defy sense until the day all three of them die, hopefully as free citizens and not guests of the United States government.

"We'll get out of your way and let you get back to work," John says, holding out his hand. "We appreciate the time and effort you've put into this."

Bennet stands up, as well, and thanks Tompkins for his time and shakes his hand and follows John into the waiting area, where Ida is pleased for them. After seven days and thirteen lattes, she's invested in their drama and genuinely relieved at its outcome. Bennet presses the button for the elevator while John jots down his email for Ida. He's relieved, too, by the outcome of their drama—of course he is!—but he doesn't have his brother's willful sanguinity. Happy resolution or not, the damage has been done. Their lives won't simply pick up where they left off as if the incident were merely a technical glitch. They'll never recover what's been lost. He's thinking of his job, his standing, his reputation, yes, but also of Darcy. He wishes now that he hadn't, in the extreme agitation of the moment, told her about his brother's crime, because his own ready acceptance of it gives the original story more credence. He provided just enough information to make her leery of any version that shows Lydon to advantage and reveal the outrageousness of his heroics as the sordid lie it is.

And that's it in a nutshell, Bennet thinks as he waits for the elevator. The whole affair is just a little too sordid, even with the whitewashing that's sure to come in Gawker, Buzzfeed, et al, and he can't imagine Darcy, who somehow overcame her scruples once, would be able to do so again with this further provocation. Her estimation of his family and his own upbringing, education and profession might be outdated, but it aligns with the values of the rarefied world she lives in. Carl Bingston's scorn and Lady Catherine's condemnation are not trifles to be so easily dismissed, not for someone for whom breeding and pedigree still matter.

A relationship between them would have been nothing more than a grand experiment designed to fail, and yet he feels the ineffable sadness of so much opportunity lost. It turns out Darcy's temperament, her intelligence and humor—so opposite of his own—would have suited him perfectly, and if she'd taught him to take life a little more seriously, he would most certainly have taught her how to take it a little less.

What a triumph for her, he thinks without humor. What only two months ago he'd proudly spurned, he now finds himself ardently desiring.

The elevator finally arrives, and as he and John step into the car, they establish the course of action for their immediate future: find a bar, get a drink and call their parents. But shortly, while Bennet imagines downing three glasses of scotch in as many minutes, John suggests they reverse the order and call their folks first.

CHAPTER TWENTY-FOUR

The negotiations begin at once. As soon as the FBI issues a release clearing Lydon of all wrongdoing and detailing his assistance in apprehending a notorious criminal, Meryton asks Bennet and John to come back. But even John, whose mortification is not nearly as acute as his brother's, feels there's something untoward about returning to an institution that had summarily fired him little more than a week before. Never one to accept a polite refusal, Meryton immediately sweetens the deal by offering an additional week of vacation and an extra ten percent discount at the Longbourn gift shop. When they decline that as well, he ups the ante with yet more vacation time—provided it's taken at Christmas— and twenty percent off at the in-house café during the non-peak hours of 10 to 11 and 3:30 to 5:30. Now John weakens, not because the lure of cheap coffee is too much to resist but because Meryton wants them back so badly he's managed to finagle a discount long-denied to the Longbourn staff. Many managers have tried to wheedle special dispensation for their employees; all have failed.

Although Bennet is equally cognizant of the compliment Meryton has paid them with the café discount, the humiliation of being fired in the lobby, of not being trusted enough to enter his own office, is too intense and he declines. He encourages John, however, to return without him, but his brother refuses to consider it.

Meryton's next gambit is a five percent pay raise, an earnest apology for mishandling the situation and unrestricted access to office supplies, including Post-its and highlighters. Bennet, as moved by the extravagance of Meryton's generosity as he is the sincerity of his apology, calls up his former boss and painstakingly explains why he simply doesn't feel comfortable returning. It is, he believes, a good, clear, precise explanation, one that Meryton purports to not only understand but respect, and yet ten minutes later he calls back to throw in three free mugs and Arbor Day off.

Sighing, Bennet launches into another detailed explanation, using different words to say the same thing, but Meryton sighs even more loudly and begs him not to make him beg.

"You must consider this from my perspective," Meryton says. "I made the best decision I could based on the information I had. I hear what you're saying about the lobby. I understand you feel a particular humiliation in not being let up to your office to clear out your desk, but think about what I did give you: enough trust to let you into the building. I could've dispensed with your services on the walk in front of the museum, which, for the record, the employee handbook explicitly states is standard operating procedure in the case of a federal investigation, but I decided that was a little too shabby for someone who has worked with me for so many years. See? I *did* treat you with respect. Furthermore, I didn't hover over you in the lobby. I gave you space to process your emotions and didn't worry for above a few seconds—fifteen, really, at the most—that you might try to steal hundreds of dollars from the registers."

Here Bennet is compelled to point out that very little cash is kept at the admissions desk because most visitors use their credit card, and although Meryton finds it curious that Bennet has thought about how much money the admissions desk has at any given moment, he doesn't remark on it.

Instead, he says, "These points must count in my favor, as well as the fact that I've been a kind and generous employer for almost a decade."

Bennet considers this statement, which is true but cuts both ways—he's been an honest, reliable and nonthieving employee for almost a decade—and finds himself growing angry again.

Sensing the direction of Bennet's thoughts, Meryton digs deeper. "I gave you a job when nobody else would. I took a chance on an untried kid."

Amused by the blatant revision of history, Bennet laughs, and hearing it, Meryton makes a squeaky gargling sound before his tone takes on a strong wheedling inflection. "You must come back. You and John. You simply must return to your former jobs. Your refusal puts the Longbourn in an untenable position. Yes, we had to move swiftly to ensure the security of our donors' money, but that was when Lydon was a thief and a villain. Now that he's a hero, our dismissal appears harsh, rash and needlessly severe. Gothamist called our response draconian—they're questioning the morality of an institution that holds an entire family responsible for the actions of a single member. We can't have the media questioning the morality of our institution. We've been the backbone of this neighborhood for generations. Please," he says, sounding almost on the verge of tears. "Please. I promised Henry that you and John would be happy to come back. Please, please, *please* don't make me disappoint that kindly old man."

Bennet is stubborn, but he's not cruel, and in the face of such desperation, he can do nothing but agree. He accepts the last deal on the table—extra vacation, raise, discounts, free mugs—and switches out Arbor Day for Flag Day because the weather's much better in June than April.

John, who would never have returned without Bennet, is relieved by the restoration of the status quo and shows up bright and early the next morning to pick up where he left off. Aside from the few personal effects Meryton had mailed to his apartment, his desk is eerily untouched. His bottom drawer, which he'd been looking through when Meryton broke the news about Lydon, is still open.

Bennet is not as eager as his brother and he arrives at the Longbourn several minutes after ten-thirty, then stops at the café to order four coffees with his new discount. Only one is for himself; he drops two off in special events, lingering just long enough to explain his munificence and to annoy Meryton by arriving a little before eleven. He gives the last coffee to John.

Although being back at the Longbourn isn't as awful as Bennet expects, it's not without its weirdness. Colleague after colleague drops by the office to assure him and John they never for a moment doubted their innocence. Smiling politely, he gets through every uncomfortable encounter and by the end of the week, everything has returned to normal. His aunt and uncle's cruise arrives back in New York, and John and he have dinner with them near their hotel.

He hears nothing from Darcy. He doesn't really expect her to get in touch, and yet as he leaves the Gardiners at the Sheraton, he realizes that a tiny sliver of him had been convinced she'd call out of the blue to invite them all to dinner. The expectation was patently absurd, of course—even if Darcy hadn't been appalled by his family's public disgrace, she still wouldn't have known when his aunt and uncle's ship would arrive back in New York Harbor.

Lydon returns on the same day the Gardiners leave, having decided to extend his stay in London by a few days, as the U.S. government had been so kind as to provide him with lodgings and a small stipend to cover transportation and food. Indeed, he explains as Bennet tries to talk to him about responsibility, it would have been rude to refuse the generosity.

During the next two days, Lydon explains many things about his recent sojourn to London, and although Bennet makes repeated attempts to get a word of sense out of him, he resists answering direct questions. Bennet is so exhausted from listening to him prattle on, he's actually grateful to return to the peace and quiet of the office on Monday morning.

His respite lasts all of forty-two minutes, for at ten o'clock on the dot—*on the dot!*—Lydon arrives to take up his post as the development department's new full-time associate. Immediately upon entering, he shakes his head and says, "Ah, John, I should take your desk now because I'm the returning hero."

Bennet feels the bile rise in his throat, but John calmly points to the chair by the window and tells him that seat is reserved for all returning heroes. Lydon scowls, Bennet bites back a scathing remark, and Meryton strolls in to welcome the returning hero with a bouquet of flowers, which he places on the folding tray table that will serve as Lydon's desk until a more permanent solution can be arranged.

"Maintenance," Meryton quickly assures him, "will bring by a proper desk later in the day or early tomorrow. Definitely by the start of next week."

The temporary workstation is quite lacking in comfort and practicality, which would have been a problem had Lydon actually sat at it, but he doesn't. Rather, he darts around the building visiting every department, including maintenance, tucked in what used to be the root cellar, to make sure the members of each team are provided with the opportunity to offer their congratulations and gratitude. Having applauded Lydon individually, the staff is invited to the museum's café at 3 p.m. to appreciate him collectively at a bash hosted by Henry Cortland Longbourn himself and covered by the *Forest Hills Times*.

Standing under a banner that says, "Welcome home, Lydon," Meryton quiets the room and raises a plastic flute of sparkling white win. "On behalf of Henry, the board of directors, the entire staff and myself, I would like to thank Lydon Bethle for saving the Longbourn at the risk of great personal harm to himself. The nobility of character he has demonstrated is precisely the sort I'd expect from myself but rarely see in others. Bravo on a job very well done. To Lydon!"

The gathered crowd, whose debt to Lydon now includes alcohol in the middle of the workday, drinks happily, and the inevitable calls for a speech fill the room. The guest of honor, who doesn't need to be asked once, let alone twice, immediately takes center stage. Lydon is Lydon still—untamed, unabashed, wild, noisy and fearless—and his ten-minute speech is a tribute to all these characteristics.

"No, seriously," Lydon says after his line about the awfulness of the FBI's coffee gets a big laugh, "if I needed a reason to stay on the straight and narrow, government-grade java would be it."

Bennet can't bear it any longer. He gets up and walks out of the room.

The next morning, as Bennet is working quietly at his desk, Lydon says with insufferable self-importance, "I never gave *you* an account of my heroism. You were not there yesterday when I told Meryton and the whole museum about it. Aren't you curious to hear how it was managed?"

"No," Bennet replies. "The less said the better."

Naturally, Lydon, who rests his hip on the edge of John's desk because his own has been found insufficiently grand, laughs at this deflating comment and launches into an explanation of how and when he'd discovered Georgia's infamy. The story has so many twists and turns, so many unexpected reveals, Bennet can't imagine how any intelligent person could believe it, let alone an intelligence organization such as the FBI, and after several minutes of listening silently to the nonsensical blather, he says, "Bullshit!"

Lydon is surprised, as is John, who looks up from his computer.

"I don't know how you managed it, Lydon, I really don't," he says, more tired than angry. "You somehow convinced the FBI that you're not a thief and a liar, and I'm happy for you because you're my brother and I love you and I don't want you to spend the rest of your life rotting in a cell. But I know you're guilty and you better hope the FBI doesn't figure it out anytime soon because the statute of limitation on theft is a decade."

"Look," Lydon says, dropping some of his swagger, "I am relieved and grateful. I am, truly. Do you have any idea how terrifying it is to have the London police bust down your door? I almost shit my pants. That was the moment, man. That's when the shit became real and I looked at Georgie and she was as white as a ghost and I knew. I knew she'd been fronting the whole time and had no grand plan and my freak-outs had freak-outs. But it's over and everything's all right. Darcy swore it was."

"Darcy!" Bennet repeats in utter amazement.

Horrified, Lydon throws his hand over his mouth. *Now* he looks guilty. "Shit. I wasn't supposed to tell anyone that Darcy was at the FBI office in London. It's meant to be a secret."

"If it's a secret," John says, "then don't say anything else about it. We won't ask you any questions."

Although Bennet is burning with curiosity, John has left him no recourse but to follow him onto the high road. "Oh, certainly. No questions."

"Thank you," Lydon says.

Bennet puts it out of his head by returning to the letter he's writing, but putting it entirely out of his head is beyond his capability, and by the end of the day, he feels as if he's about to go mad. To remain ignorant on such a point is impossible, or, at least, it's impossible not to try to get more information. Darcy had been in the FBI office in London— the very last place on earth he'd expect her to be. Possible explanations why, rapid and wild, flit through his brain, but the one he most wants to believe seems the least probable.

Unable to bear the suspense, he presents himself at 26 Federal Plaza at nine o'clock the next morning and settles in for another vigil.

CHAPTER TWENTY-FIVE

From the couch in the FBI reception area, Bennet fills out a Freedom of Information Act request, while Ida peppers him with questions about John. Although it's been almost two weeks, she's yet to forget his high cheekbones and bright blue eyes, and wanting to see more of both, she's trying to nail down a strategy for future contact.

"Does he go on Facebook a lot?" she asks. "I liked a bunch of photos he posted from Cape Cod, but I haven't seen anything recently. Does he respond to messages? Is that the best way to get in touch? Or should I post something on his feed? Does he like animal videos? I saw an adorable one with a hepped-up baby goat leaping over his brothers and sisters."

He's spared the indignity of giving her dating advice by the appearance of Special Agent Tompkins, who greets him warmly and invites him back to his office. Bennet takes a seat, thanks him for his time and immediately requests an explanation of what Lydon has let slip.

"There's no logical reason for Darcy Fitzwilliam to be involved in this case," Bennet states forthrightly. "She has no connection to Lydon or to the Longbourn. She's practically a stranger to all of us, so I can't comprehend why she would be present in the London office while this was being dealt with. If it doesn't violate any security clearances—and

I don't see how it could—I'd very grateful if you would tell me how and why she was involved."

Because it's the FBI, Bennet expects pushback for the sake of pushback. What secretive governmental organization ever revealed information without coercion? But Tompkins nods easily and explains that Ms. Fitzwilliam's involvement has been crucial to the success of the operation.

"Or I should say operations, plural, because Ms. Fitzwilliam was coordinating with the Washington office to apprehend and arrest Ms. Wickham in an operation entirely unrelated to ours in New York. Ms. Fitzwilliam had long suspected Ms. Wickham of illegal acts but had no proof, so she worked with Associate Deputy Director Miller to set up your brother as dupe for Ms. Wickham. She believed your brother's lowly position at the museum made him a likely target, a supposition that proved correct. As my team was called in after the fact by the museum to investigate the theft, we were not aware of the investigation already in progress, which is why there was so much confusion initially."

Tompkins leans forward, causing his chair to squeak, and says, "I'm sure you understand why this information has not been released. Ms. Fitzwilliam is a public figure who values her privacy and she doesn't want her name associated with the matter in any way. As I understand it, she only involved herself because she felt guilty about not having made Ms. Wickham's true nature more generally known. Apparently, earlier dealings had given her a clear idea as to the extent of Ms. Wickham's immorality, but she felt disclosing those matters was beneath her."

Bennet doesn't doubt that all the official documents connected to the case relate the same story and he knows Tompkins believes he's telling the truth, but he recognizes grade-A bullshit when it's shoveled in his direction. Darcy's motivation sounds legitimate. She probably did go to such extraordinary lengths to extricate Lydon out of a sense of guilt. But the rest is pure fiction and he wonders how she pulled it off. Wealth buys influence, and status gains access.

Perhaps Associate Deputy Director Miller is an old family friend. Perhaps he owes the Fitzwilliams a favor. Perhaps the Fitzwilliams now owe *him* a favor.

However the thing was managed, Bennet is beyond grateful for Darcy's making the effort—and it was, he acknowledges, a great deal of effort. It cannot be easy to convince one of the highest-ranking law-enforcement officials in the country to alter the facts of an investigation. How mortifying it must have been for Darcy, who holds the truth in such high esteem, to ask an FBI agent to lie and doctor records in order to make it appear as if an operation were already in progress. It must go against everything she believes, and yet she made these huge moral compromises for a young man she doesn't know and couldn't possibly respect.

Bennet wants to believe she did it for him. Given their history, it doesn't seem entirely implausible that some lingering sentiment spurred her to do what she could to fix a situation that had deeply upset him. But his vanity isn't great enough to allow himself the compliment. Whatever Darcy feels for him now, the man who harshly scorned her affection, it couldn't be equal to a good deed of this magnitude. No, she did it for the reason stated in the official documents: to assuage her guilt. Feeling she'd been wrong, she'd used the considerable means at her disposal to rectify her mistake. That she did puts Bennet—and, indeed, his entire family—in her debt, and he can't conceive how they would repay her.

Daunted by an obligation too immense to ever reconcile, Bennet rises from the chair and thanks Tompkins for his candor. Thoughtfully, he strolls down the corridor, but as soon as he sees the unoccupied reception desk—thank goodness for Ida's soy latte addiction sparing the need for further dating advice—he picks up his pace and makes a beeline for the stairs. Out on the street, he heads north on Lafayette until he hits a small park with benches and, his mind racing, he sits down to make sense of his feelings.

He's overwhelmed, to be sure, by the magnitude of the debt, for he owes Lydon's freedom, his future, everything to Darcy. With fresh horror, he recalls the harsh words with which he'd rejected her proposal and regrets every one. For himself, he's humbled, but he's proud of her—proud that she was able to get over herself and do something so kind and compassionate.

Bennet doesn't know how to proceed. Unfamiliar with the protocol for thanking a woman for saving your brother from doing ten to fifteen in a federal penitentiary, he has no idea what the proper response is. Would a card be appropriate? Flowers? Should he send her a super casual email that only alludes to her remarkable kindness? That Darcy doesn't want anyone to know about her actions has been made clear by Lydon and Tompkins, and yet he can't simply let it slide. Something is required of him. If only he could figure out what.

He's still considering the problem when he arrives at the office two hours later, but the news that Bingley is returning to the Netherfield immediately supplants it as the most consuming thought of the day. Meryton, quite in the fidgets, looks at John as he announces the news. Smiling, he explains that she'll be in town shooting for several weeks.

"Shooting?" Bennet asks, not sure if he's more amused or puzzled by the image of Bingley aiming a rifle at a flock of grouse.

"A movie," Meryton says. "A minor part only and she'll be playing a version of herself. I read about it on Deadline. She'll be staying at the Netherfield. I've already confirmed it with the head of housekeeping. Mrs. Nicholls says she'll be here on Thursday at the latest, very likely on Wednesday."

John isn't able to hear of her coming without changing color. It's been many months since he has mentioned her name to Bennet, but now, as soon as they're alone together, he says, "I saw you look at me when Meryton told us the news, and I know I seemed upset. But I wasn't. I was just self-conscious because I knew you and Meryton and Lydon *would* look at me. I promise you, Bingley's impending arrival doesn't affect me in the least. I'm over it. Entirely. In fact, I was just emailing with Ida about rambunctious baby goats and I think I'll ask her out for coffee. You remember Ida from the FBI office?"

"I do, yes," Bennet says. "She was nice and we know she loves coffee."

"Three soy lattes a day," John says, laughing nervously as he looks down at his keyboard and returns to the report he's writing.

Although John is trying to appear unruffled by the news, Bennet can easily perceive much ruffledness in the crease of his brow and the stilted way his fingers tap the keys. In his anxiety, he's deleting more characters than he's keeping. Bennet himself is unsure of what to make of Bingley's return. He wants to attribute it to a desire to see John—either with her friend's permission or in bold defiance of it—but the explanation of filming a movie is a little too concrete to be just a pretext. Unwilling to embarrass his brother, he remains silent on the topic for the rest of the day, but at six o'clock, just as they're about to walk out the door, Meryton pops into their office to remind John to send a gift basket to the Netherfield as soon as Bingley comes. "Our favorite committee chair must get a Gold Patrons Diamond welcome."

With a darting glance at John, Bennet suggests it would be more prudent to give Bingley some time to get comfortable before they harass her with museum business. Naturally, *harass* isn't the most prudent word to describe the enthusiastic and well-meaning contact of an esteemed institution such as the Longbourn, and Meryton settles into a twenty-minute lecture on etiquette, fundraising and abominable rudeness and ends on a trembling high note in which he resolves to invite her to dine there, in the trustees' dining room.

"We must have Mrs. Long and the Gouldings soon," he says, listing several high-value donors whom he hasn't heard from in a while.

Consoled by this resolution, Meryton is better able to bear his staff's stubborn refusal to agree unthinkingly with his every thought and notion and returns to his office to plan the menu.

He's still planning the menu the next day. The simple meal has been become an elegant dinner party, with Henry bringing along his youngest grandson, the first of his generation to consent to visit the museum. Although Xavier Trunbull Longbourn has no more affection for the collection than his seven cousins, he has had, ever since the Netherfield ball, a mad crush on Bingley, and this alliance of well-connected, deep-pocketed young people strikes Meryton as the ideal solution to their problems. Now, whenever he mentions the returning heiress, he does so in tandem with Henry's grandson, a development that has had the unfortunate side effect of slowly turning John ashen.

After three days, John says to Bennet, "I'm sorry she's coming. I wouldn't care—I could see her and not feel a thing—but listening to Meryton settle her future with another fellow is more than I can stand. She's not even here yet and already I can't wait for her to be gone."

His brother nods, understanding the fresh torment Meryton has unknowingly inflicted. The problem isn't his constant hawking of the fellow—neither brother believes the two will truly make a match of it—but rather all the talk of the future. Meryton's blather has opened up a frontier, and it stretches before John just as expansively as it stretches before Xavier.

Bennet tries to think of something comforting to say, but all the usual platitudes are inadequate to the situation. Counseling patience, the reassuring assertion that this, too, shall pass, is useless because John has always bided his time without complaint. No doubt he'll suffer this ordeal with the same forbearance with which he's suffered all the others in his life, and Bennet wishes that once, just once, his brother would rage against something. Or at the very least, pick up a damn phone and call the girl he's crazy about.

But he knows it's foolish to wish someone would behave against their nature and cruel to create expectations where there's no guarantee of a happy resolution, so Bennet sighs and points out the time: 3:30. They can use their discount at the café now.

CHAPTER TWENTY-SIX

Bingley arrives. Three days after she lands in New York—three days during which Meryton frets and fusses over the timing of his dinner party invite—she presents herself at the front desk of the Longbourn and says she's there to see the development department. Following regular visitor protocol, Martin issues her a name tag and calls up to confirm.

The call throws Meryton into a tizzy.

"Quickly, quickly," he says, rushing into the development office as if a large animal is chasing him. He dashes across the room, bumps his shin against Lydon's desk and presses his back against a row of file cabinets. "Bingley's on her way up. Quickly, everybody, look like you're hard at work. We must endeavor to appear to be an institution that puts millions of dollars to good use. Bennet, pick up the phone—you should be making an important call. No, John, don't look at me. Look at your computer screen. Type." Although his fingers are suddenly nerveless, John complies with the order. Unsatisfied, Meryton orders him to type faster. "And wrinkle your brow as if you're thinking over a matter of very great concern."

The only one in the office who doesn't affect busyness is Lydon—an irony that not even John, in his haze of anxiety, is insensible to, for all Lydon does is affect busyness. Now, however, he runs to the door, walks out onto the landing and looks down the stairwell.

"They're taking the stairs," he announces. "I say 'they' because there's a woman with her."

"Some acquaintance or other, I suppose," Meryton says.

"She's tall and has dark hair," Lydon replies. "It looks like Darcy. It must be Darcy."

Meryton, whose assumed task is sorting through the file cabinets along the back wall, greets this information with mixed feelings. He's not unaware of the estimated value of her assets, both liquid and otherwise, but he's equally familiar with her unpleasant disposition. The former wins out. "Any friend of Bingley's is welcome here, to be sure," he announces.

John, halting his pounding of random letters—he doesn't even have the presence of mind to type *the quick brown fox jumps over the lazy dog*—looks at Bennet with surprise and concern. Knowing little of their meeting at Pemberley, he worries that seeing her now will be very awkward for him.

Both brothers are uncomfortable. Each feels for the other, and of course, for himself, and Meryton rattles on about how busy they must look, chastising John for not typing fast enough and Bennet for not talking importantly enough, without being heard by either of them. The only one listening is Lydon, who responds to his boss's request for progress updates with remarkable detail.

"They've reached the second floor and are about to start the next flight," he says. "Now they've started the next flight."

Bennet's astonishment at her coming—at her coming to the Longbourn and voluntarily seeking him out again—is almost equal to what he felt at Pemberley, when she was so warm and welcoming. The color, which had drained from his face, returns briefly, giving his eyes an unexpected luster. In that moment, he believes her feelings for him remain unchanged. Reason returns quickly enough, for he knows such a development is unlikely.

He sits intently at work, striving to be composed, and glances with anxious curiosity at John, who looks a little paler than usual but calm. Fluttering at the women's imminent approach, Lydon shuts the door and sits down, then, thinking better of it, runs back to the entrance to leave the door open. He's out of breath and barely sitting when Bingley says, "Knock, knock."

Meryton closes the file cabinet drawer with an emphatic bang, turns as if surprised and says with all due enthusiasm, "Ms. Bingley, how delightful. Come in. Please come in. Our office is small but accommodating. I'm sure we can make room. If Bennet would just get off the phone—how rude of him to still be talking—you could have his seat."

Bennet immediately hangs up the phone, belatedly remembering to say good-bye to his fake counterpart only after he puts down the receiver, and rises to give Bingley his seat. She pooh-poohs the suggestion and insists she can stand for any number of minutes in a row. Bennet turns to Darcy to give her his seat, but she looks so serious, so cold and foreboding, with none of the warmth she had at Pemberley, and the offer dies on his lips. He sits down again to his work with an eagerness it doesn't often command.

Despite Darcy's lavish fortune, Meryton greets her stiffly, his cool tone standing out in sharp relief against the warmth with which he'd addressed Bingley, and Bennet's appalled and embarrassed. His boss has no idea that it's only due to Darcy's generosity that the stolen funds were returned intact.

Darcy, after asking how Mr. and Mrs. Gardiner enjoyed their cruise, a question Bennet answers with unintended curtness, says scarcely anything. She's standing by the door—perhaps that's the reason for her silence—but the room is so small, the distance hardly matters. While Meryton chats merrily with Bingley, asking a dozen questions about the movie she's doing, trying to ascertain, it seems to his employee, a fundraising opportunity among the cast and crew, Bennet glances at Darcy now and again. He finds her looking as often at John as at the floor and realizes she's reverted to form: thoughtful and brooding.

He's disappointed and angry with himself for feeling let down. He should've known better than to expect anything but sullenness from her. But then why has she come?

Bennet doesn't want to talk to anyone but Darcy, and yet his mind is entirely blank. He can't think of anything to say except to ask about her brother. Then he falls silent.

"It's been a long time, Ms. Bingston, since you went to London," Meryton says. "The Golden Circle Diamond Advisory Society has been languishing in your absence. It hasn't hosted a single event since you left. Things have been rather quiet, though not entirely quiet. We did have some unseemly business recently: the theft of a considerable sum from the Longbourn's bank accounts. I suppose you've heard of it. You must have seen it in the papers. It was in the *Times* and the *Wall Street Journal,* and of course everywhere online. Did you see it?"

Bingley replies that she did and congratulates him on the recovery of the misappropriated funds.

"As awful as the whole ordeal was," Meryton continues, "it was well worth it to discover the scope and depth of Lydon's—you do recall Lydon, don't you?—heroism. Despite the danger to himself, he infiltrated a ruthless gang of criminals and valiantly brought them to justice. Honestly, I don't know how he had the skill and daring to pull off such an elaborate sting operation all on his own. We're very proud of him. We might even name a drinking fountain in his honor *if* we can find a sponsor. Perhaps Ms. Fitzwilliam would be good enough to underwrite it?"

Bennet gasps in horror at the unprecedented gall of the request, and not daring to look at Darcy, he glances at Lydon, who, he's relieved to see, has the grace to turn bright pink.

"No, please, not a fountain. I mean, it wasn't exactly a *whole* gang, so, like, whatever," the youngest Bethle chokes out honestly. The demurral only ennobles him in the eyes of Meryton, who thinks the museum's savior is merely being modest and suggests that a fountain isn't good enough for so gracious a creature.

Unable to stand it, Bennet asks Bingley how long she plans to stay in New York.

"A few weeks," she says.

Meryton, who knows three or four weeks is not enough time to put together a mailing, let alone a social event, devises an extension. "When you've finished shooting your film," he says, "I beg you will come here and shoot something with us. John's been working on a short documentary on the history of the Longbourn and its collection."

The embarrassment Bennet feels on John's behalf at this patently false statement is so acute, he gladly wishes to never see either Bingley or Darcy again. His annoyance soon fades as Bingley, grateful for the subject, asks John about the film. His brother's face turns pink at the attention, but he's otherwise composed as he cites the year Cyrus Longbourn broke ground on the palazzo. Realizing rather quickly that the project isn't quite as far along as Meryton's enthusiasm suggests, Bingley smoothly switches the topic to things she knows John is interested in and, in a very short time, the two are chatting breezily. Bennet is both amazed and encouraged by how easily they've fallen into their earlier rapport.

When the visitors turn to leave after a half hour, Meryton, mindful of his scheme to pair Bingley with Henry's grandson—a scheme that seems less and less likely as he watches her interact with John—invites them to dine at the Longbourn in a few days' time.

"You owe me one, anyway, Ms. Bingston," he adds. "When you left town last spring, you promised to have dinner here. I've not forgotten, you see, and I assure you, I was very disappointed that you didn't come back and keep your engagement."

Bingley looks a little silly at this statement and says something about having been prevented by business. Then she announces she has to run because she has her first fitting for the film at three o'clock.

"Since I'm playing, per *Variety,* 'a version of myself—

that's right: I haven't shot a frame and already I'm quoting my notices!—I don't see why I can't wear my own clothes. Ah, Hollywood," she adds with amused exasperation.

As soon as they're gone, Meryton disappears into his office. He reemerges ten minutes later with several sheets of paper with two rows of boxes—storyboards, so John can get to work on his film project.

"You're already months behind schedule," Meryton notes sharply before inviting Lydon on a tour of the museum's drinking fountains to identify the one most suitable for dedication in his honor. Now that Darcy isn't present to shame him, Lydon happily falls in with the plan and suggests that perhaps they think a little bigger. A hallway, perhaps.

As soon as they're gone, Bennet runs down to the café to get an espresso—or, in other words, to think without interruption on a subject that makes him more jittery than caffeine. Darcy's behavior astonishes and confounds him.

Why, if she came only to be silent, grave and indifferent, did she come at all? No answer makes him happy, and he resolves not to think about her anymore, a resolution that's easily kept as he spots John approaching with a cheerful look on his face.

"I'm glad that's over with," he announces as he sits next to Bennet on the stone bench. "I was anxious about the first meeting, but clearly there was no reason to be. I care as little for her as she does for me."

"Yes, very little indeed," Bennet says, laughing as he dips his head into the demitasse. "Oh, man, you better take care."

"Me?" he asks, his tone as offended as it is surprised. "You can't really think I'm at risk of falling for her again?"

Bennet finishes his espresso and lays a hand on his brother's shoulder. "I think you're at very great risk of making her as much in love with you as ever."

John smiles weakly and walks up to the counter to order his own shot of espresso, and even though it's only twenty-two seconds past eleven o'clock, the pleasure of the 20 percent discount is denied him.

CHAPTER TWENTY-SEVEN

At twenty-three years old, Xavier Trunbull Longbourn is a little young for Ms. Charlotte Bingston, but given the advantages of his education—Exeter, Oxford and now Goldman—he has many of the qualifications that Darcy had once deemed necessary to earning the title of well-rounded gentleman.

When Mr. Goulding asks him about the worrying upward trend in the Shenzhen Stock Exchange, he tries to calm the older man's concerns about a bubble in fluent Cantonese. Although he's less than successful in his endeavor, Goulding's Cantonese being limited only to the ordering of General Tso's chicken, he impresses Bingley, who compliments him on his pronunciation.

That is, however, the extent of their courtship, for Bingley's eyes are focused almost continually on John during the whole affair. When the large party, comfortably assembled in the courtyard, repairs to the trustees' dining room, she waits to see which chair he takes and then snags the one next to him with such speed and grace that Mrs. Long, who was about to sit down, apologizes to Bingley for almost stealing *her* seat.

Bennet, with triumphant satisfaction, looks at Darcy. She bears it with noble indifference, and he would've assumed

Bingley has received her permission to be happy had he not seen her eyes also turn toward Darcy, with a look of half-laughing alarm.

Throughout the meal, Bingley is attentive and lively, balancing her interest in John with her social obligation to appear interested in everyone, and observing her behavior, Bennet is convinced that, if left wholly to themselves, the couple's happiness would be speedily secured. Although he knows better than to take anything for granted, the prospect makes him happy, thereby brightening an otherwise cheerless evening. Darcy is at the other end of the table, seated on one side of Meryton, which is, he knows, an arrangement that makes neither one happy nor shows either to advantage. He's not close enough to hear their conversation, but he can see how little they talk to each other and how impersonal and abrupt their manner is when they do. His employer's ungraciousness makes Bennet more keenly aware than ever of how much they owe her, and he longs for an opportunity to express his gratitude. Surely, their only conversation for the entire evening won't be the polite greeting they'd exchanged upon arrival.

Anxious and uneasy, he waits for a moment to approach, but when she's finally free, sitting quietly by herself in the lull before dessert, he's deep in conversation with Mrs. Long about a plan to build a Ferris wheel as large as the London Eye on Staten Island.

"I see the appeal, of course," she says. "All those tourists—some 1.5 million each year and counting—taking the ferry out and turning right back around because there's nothing to do. It's a smart business decision, and I'd support it if it were just about the Ferris wheel. But it's not."

"It's not?" Bennet asks.

"It's not," she says confidently. "The Ferris wheel is a horse."

"A horse?"

"A Trojan horse to get us used to seeing an eyesore in the harbor. Then, when we've grown accustomed to the lumbering monstrosity, the city will push for its real objective: wind turbines."

Her theory's ridiculous, but Bennet loves a good conspiracy as much as the next person and listens patiently as Mrs. Long outlines the mayor's eight-point plan to foist wind power on the unsuspecting people of New York City. By the time she's finished, dessert is being served and Darcy is nowhere to be seen. Bingley is also missing and he assumes the two have gone off together, presumably to the ladies' room. While he waits for their return, he picks at the impeccably turned out tarte tatin with lavender ice cream.

Darcy reappears just as the waitstaff is clearing the table and offering a second round of coffee. Bennet flicks a finger, securing a refill for himself, and decides that this is it: He will talk to Darcy now. He stands, leaving the coffee on the table to grow cold, and takes two determined steps in her direction. Before he can take a third Lydon is at his side, inviting him to go clubbing with him and Xavier.

"The party's in a super secret location in Brooklyn," Lydon says. "You need, like, a password to get in. Xavier has the hookup. We're heading out soon."

The offer's preposterous—why in the world would he want to hit the hipster scene with a couple of recent college grads?—and yet it has some appeal. His youngest brother is less likely to get into trouble with him hovering nearby. Meryton, who's abandoned his scheme to marry off Bingley to Xavier, is delighted by this promising new alliance, for a confirmed hero who's firmly attached to the institution is better than a beautiful heiress who's intermittently devoted.

"I'll think about it," Bennet says, his eyes trained on Darcy, whose attention has now been claimed by Mrs. Goulding.

"Cool. Lemme know," Lydon replies before walking away to issue the same invitation to John, who wastes no time in declining.

Bennet returns to the table, and as he drinks his coffee, wonders if he's being a fool or a deluded idiot to believe Darcy might still have feelings for him. She had put her heart on the line and been refused in the cruelest way possible. How could any woman, regardless of how proud she is, get past such a crushing blow? Indeed, the only way to handle the humiliation would be to act entirely unaffected by the event, which would explain Darcy's extraordinary affability at Pemberley.

The term, he thinks, is *overcompensating*.

By the time Darcy strolls over to Bennet, ostensibly to leave her empty coffee cup on the table, he's convinced she doesn't feel anything for him beyond a sort of residual fondness. Regardless of her emotions, he's deeply grateful for her kindness and will have no peace until he expresses it. He opens his mouth to do just that, but Darcy speaks first, offering an unexpected compliment on the quality of the dinner. She then remarks on the style and comfort of the room. Her comments are so polite and mundane, it seems inappropriate to follow them with heartfelt gratitude, like giving a flight attendant a standing ovation for pointing out the emergency exits, and instead he asks about her brother.

"Is he still at Pemberley?"

"No, he's returned to London to pack up his things."

"And then he'll come back to New York for good?"

"Yes, he starts Juilliard in two weeks."

The conversation is stilted and awkward, and Bennet, unable to bear it a moment longer, opens his mouth to thank her for saving Lydon. He has barely spoken three words—*please let me*—before Meryton volunteers him to escort the Gouldings to their car.

Bennet bites back a growl, politely excuses himself and waits impatiently as the guests make their good-byes. Henry stands near the door, a delighted glow brightening his eyes, as he considers the successes of the evening: the sparkling conversation, the delicious meal, his grandson's burgeoning interest in the museum.

When Bennet comes back, Henry is reviewing these triumphs again for Darcy's benefit, and Meryton, preferring not to engage in further conversation with Bingley's proud friend, is helping the waitstaff clear the table. In fact, he's more hindrance than help, for he doesn't know where anything goes and insists on putting the coffee cups where the salad forks belong.

John and Bingley are nowhere to be seen, but the mystery of their disappearance is immediately answered when Bennet walks into the cozy sitting room off to the left and finds the couple engaged in a passionate clutch before the fireplace. John's arms are wrapped so tightly around Bingley, it's clear he has no intention of ever letting go. Bingley, her own hands grasping the lapels of his suit jacket, obviously has no quarrel with his plans. If this tableau hadn't told the whole story, the faces of both, as they hastily notice him and break apart, would have. *Their* situation is awkward enough, but his is still worse. Not a syllable is uttered by either, and Bennet's on the point of scurrying away when Bingley squeals with happiness and propels herself into his arms for a giddy hug. Then she runs out of the room.

"Would it be appallingly smug of me to say I told you so?" Bennet asks mildly.

Although *appallingly smug* would be an appalling understatement, John is too happy to mind anything and, just like Bingley, engulfs Bennet in an enthusiastic hug. Then, stepping back, he wonders what the proper interval is between declaring one's feelings and proposing marriage.

"Surely, there's a minimum," John says.

Bennet's knowledge of courtship timelines is no more complete than his brother's, but he considers the depth and sincerity of their connection and says six weeks. A month would be too short; two months seems intolerably long. Satisfied by this logic, John takes out his phone and makes a note on his calendar. Looking over his shoulder, Bennet reads the entry: Propose to Bingley, make self happiest creature in world.

A moment later, Bingley returns with a bottle of champagne, and Meryton, following not the bubbly heiress but the bubbly itself, which costs upward of $100, enters behind her. Although nobody says a word, he immediately perceives the change and clutches the mantelpiece rather than accost the couple with his happiness. Then he returns to the kitchen to get flutes, which Bingley, in her haste to return to John, hadn't bothered to look for.

She pops the cork as she calls for Darcy. "We're having a toast," she explains, though she doesn't say why and her friend doesn't ask. Like Meryton, Darcy quickly grasps the situation and accepts the glass of champagne without any appearance of outward discomfort. Bingley makes several exuberant if not entirely comprehensible toasts to the future and the past and the present and to the effervescent spectacle of life and to the capriciousness of fate and to the persistent challenge of human interaction and, last but most eloquently, to rugelach.

Henry is clearly confused by such irregular goings-on, but Meryton's delight conveys something of the occasion's importance and the amused benefactor obligingly raises his glass with each new salute.

"Would you believe she's been in love with me all along?" John says to Bennet, his eyes trained on Bingley as she laughs at something Darcy says. "She was in love with me in April when she went to London and the only reason she didn't come back was she thought *I* didn't love her. She thought I thought she was just another donor." The surprise of this is still evident in his voice.

"A gross miscalculation, to be sure, but now we know she's not vain," Bennet observes.

A few minutes later, he's joined by Bingley, who, as if seeking approval, promises with unabashed earnestness never to hurt John. "I'm known to be flighty. I'm not, you understand, but that's how I'm perceived, and anyone who has followed my exploits during the past few months could be forgiven for thinking I'm fickle and impulsive. But I was nursing a broken heart," she says, as if that explains everything, and in a way it does. She sighs contentedly and reaches for Bennet's arm. "Oh, I'm going to be like a sister to you. You're going to love me almost as much as you love John."

Bennet honestly and heartily expresses his delight in the prospect of their relationship and submits to another enthusiastic hug. Then he listens with bemused patience as Bingley lavishes praise on John's head. Her judgment is clearly corrupted by affection, but her observations are spot-on and actually demonstrate an excellent understanding of his brother. Amused, Bennet doesn't doubt for a moment that they'll be happy together—they're both too good-natured to be otherwise.

After Bingley rushes off to tackle John, who's standing by himself near the fireplace, Meryton sits next to Bennet and gushes over the evening's triumphs, which are not limited to John's promising new relationship. Henry has agreed to underwrite the Lydon Bethle Honorary Drinking Fountain—outside the men's room on the third floor—and Xavier called *Art & Style* "interesting."

"But *not* in that bland way that indicates he couldn't think of anything else to say and was only making the comment out of an obligation to be polite," Meryton hastens to add, "although a grandchild of Henry's feeling thus obligated to an employee of the Longbourn would be a triumph in and of itself. His tone, however, was far more invested than that and implied a genuine interest in the material."

Although Bennet offers no encouragement, Meryton continues to parse Xavier's level of enthusiasm, and he watches helplessly as Darcy talks to John and then Bingley and then Henry and then John again before finally taking her leave. She says good night to Bennet using the same polite tone that she does with Meryton, which strikes the former as a rather clear indication of her feelings. She even volunteers, for Meryton's benefit, you understand, the information that she'll be going to London for ten days to help her brother pack his things.

Bennet, his emotions in turmoil—to be so close and

yet so far away from saying anything that matters—makes a hugely mundane comment about having a safe trip. Darcy nods, says thank you and looks at her phone. Then she's gone and Bennet is left to rebuke himself for not being more clever. He's not a Nobel laureate, to be sure, but certainly he can rise above benign travel banalities.

He's still chastising himself ten minutes later when he slides into a town car next to Bingley, who insists on dropping him at his apartment before they head to John's. That the international jet-setting heiress is content to forgo her three dozen rooms in Manhattan for John's 3.5 in Queens strikes him as perhaps the single most endearing thing ever, and, despite his own misery, he says good night with a curiously upbeat feeling in his heart. Sometimes things work out exactly the way they're supposed to.

CHAPTER TWENTY-EIGHT

If a silver Rolls-Royce driven by a white-gloved chauffeur is an uncommon sight at the Longbourn, it's nothing compared with a Birkin bag in black crocodile worn by an imposing society matron who shows no hesitation as she strides past the admissions desk. Guided by an assistant in practical brown pumps whose familiarity with the museum's layout had been established prior to their arrival, the lady breezes by the courtyard, turns right at the café, marches down the hallway and waits in front of the elevator for her companion to press the button.

Everyone—the entire staff, even the security guards—is in awe of such purposefulness of motion and such ostentatiousness of wealth. Clearly, the woman is loaded. Only the filthy rich can't be bothered to press their own elevator buttons.

Martin, the highest-ranking employee on the admissions desk, says they should do something but can't think of anything particularly useful, so he pulls out his phone and googles how much a black crocodile Birkin costs. As he suspects, it's the holy grail of luxury purses, and taking a screen shot, he immediately begins to compose a tweet.

Indifferent to the tumult her arrival has caused, Mrs. Catherine de Bourgh gets off on the third floor, walks down the long corridor and presents herself at the door of the development department with little fuss.

Although her entrance is somewhat matter-of-fact—no trumpets sounding in the distance, no chaise and four pounding up the drive—the inhabitants of the room stare as if the Queen of England has suddenly appeared on their threshold, their astonishment readily apparent to anyone who cares to look.

Lady Catherine does not care to look. She enters the room with an air more ungracious than her usual lack of graciousness, makes no other reply to Bennet's greeting—he isn't too startled to bid her hello—than a slight inclination of the head and sits in the rickety chair next to the door without saying a word. Bennet awkwardly summons his boss. "Mr. Meryton, have you ever met Mrs. Catherine de Bourgh…?

Meryton, all amazement and quivering excitement at having a guest of such high importance, receives her with the utmost composure. Silently, however, he's screaming, Trustee of the Metropolitan Museum of Art! Patron of the philharmonic! Sponsor of the Central Park Conservancy!

Lady Catherine makes no response and turns away from the executive director's outstretched hand. Meryton is too overwhelmed by the honor of her presence to notice the slight.

After sitting for a moment in silence, Lady Catherine says very stiffly to Bennet, "I hope you are well, Mr. Bethle. That gentleman, I suppose, is your employer."

Meryton preens happily at this acknowledgment not only of himself but of his status. Very concisely, Bennet answers that he is indeed.

"And that"—she tilts her head a fraction of an inch in John's direction—"I suppose, is one of your brothers."

"Yes, ma'am," Meryton says, eagerly holding up his end of a conversation he erroneously believes is already in progress. "That's my director of individual giving. My department associate is out to lunch, but you may have read about him in the papers as he recently foiled a dastardly plot to steal great sums of money from the Longbourn."

"You have a very small café here," Lady Catherine returns after a short silence.

"It's nothing in comparison to the many fine eateries you have at the Met," Mr. Meryton says, "but it's much larger than the Queens Art Museum's."

"This office must be extremely inconvenient in the evening. Awful in the summer—the window is full west."

Meryton assures her that no one ever works after dinner and then adds, "May I ask how your nephew Collin is?"

"Yes, very well. I saw him the night before last."

Bennet watches the exchange, completely puzzled as to why the great patroness has suddenly decided to bestow her favor upon them; a glance at John reveals he's equally baffled.

Meryton, with great civility, begs Mrs. de Bourgh to take some refreshment—in the moment, he can't recall what they have in stock: maybe bottled water? Perhaps some Girl Scout cookies?—but she very resolutely, and not very politely, declines to accept anything. Rising to her feet, she says to Bennet, "Mr. Bethle, there seemed to be a prettyish kind of courtyard on the first floor. I'd be grateful if you'd accompany me there."

"Go, go," Meryton cries, "and give Mrs. de Bourgh a tour. I think she'll like the fountain."

Bennet obeys and, sliding his phone into his pocket, leads their noble guest out of the office. As they pass through the hall, Lady Catherine opens the doors to the janitor's closet and staff kitchen, and pronouncing them, after a short survey, to be decent-looking rooms, walks on. When they get to the end of the corridor, Bennet sees not only that her assistant's waiting for her, but that the thoughtful woman has held the elevator for her. They get onto the waiting car and ride down to the first floor. Then they proceed in silence along the marble walk that leads to the courtyard—Bennet's determined to make no effort at conversation with a woman who's being even more rude than usual.

How could I ever think she was like her niece? he wonders as he looks in her face.

When they reach the fountain, Lady Catherine begins in the following manner: "You have to know the reason for my visit, Mr. Bethle. Your conscience must tell you."

Bennet stares at her with unaffected confusion. "You're mistaken, ma'am. I have no clue why you're here."

"Mr. Bethle," her ladyship replies, her tone now approaching open anger, "you must know I'm not a woman to be trifled with. *You* may choose to be disingenuous, but I'll speak with the candor for which I'm famous. Two days ago, I heard a very alarming report. I was told that you were engaged to my niece Ms. Darcy Fitzwilliam. Although I know this can't possibly be true—I'd never insult my niece by believing it—I felt compelled to come out here immediately and tell you how strongly I disapprove."

"If you know it's not true," Bennet says, his color rising, "then why bother coming?"

"To get your assurance that the report is untrue."

"Won't your coming to my humble office to see me," Bennet says coolly, "be taken as confirmation? Anyone from Page Six trying to verify the report, *if* there actually is such a report, need look no further than our Twitter feed to find it. Your presence in the museum won't pass unnoticed by the staff. Martin at the front desk, for example"—he takes out his phone and pulls up the tweet that preceded her arrival on the third floor—"has already posted a photo of your handbag."

"If!" Lady Catherine cries, without sparing even a glance at the screen. Her relationship with social media extends no farther than conceding its right to exist. "Are you actually pretending to know nothing about the rumor? Aren't you the one who started it?"

"I neither started it, nor heard it."

She nods. "And will you also confirm it's not true?"

"No, I don't think I will. Not having your reputation for candor, I see no reason why I should answer such an intrusive question."

"Your response is unacceptable. Mr. Bethle, I insist on your answering me at once. Are you engaged to my niece?"

"You've already said it's not possible."

"It's not. Unless she's lost her mind. In a moment of weakness, she might have forgotten what she owes to herself and to her family. You could have used your wiles to take advantage of an infatuated young woman."

It's hard not to smile at the accusation of having wiles—wiles, as if he were an antebellum heroine in an overwrought drama—but Bennet manages to maintain his composure. "If I have, I'd be the last person to admit it."

"Mr. Bethle, do you know who I am? I'm one of the most influential people in this city. I say the word and opera houses are built. In two days, I could cut off funding for your little collection so thoroughly the only money you'll be able to collect are coins from this fountain. Now tell me what I want to know. As Darcy's almost nearest relative in the world, I'm entitled to know her plans."

"But you're not entitled to know *mine*."

"Let me be clear: This match, to which you have the presumption to aspire, will never take place. No, never. Darcy will marry my nephew Collin. What do you have to say to that?"

"Only this: If she's already engaged to your nephew, then why would you believe she's engaged to me?"

Lady Catherine hesitates for a moment and then replies, "The engagement between them is of a peculiar kind. I'm still sorting out the details, but it will never happen if a man like you—a social-climbing office boy with no breeding or money—is determined to prevent it."

"I'm not determined to prevent it," Bennet says calmly. "Considering your nephew's inclinations, I think nature has taken a stronger stance on the matter than I could. And that being the case, why can't Darcy be with me, if that's what she wants?"

"Because honor, decorum, prudence, nay, interest, forbid it. Yes, Mr. Bethle, interest, for it's not in your best interest to proceed with this madness. None of her friends or family will accept you if you disobey me in this. You'll be snubbed and hated by everyone who knows her. Your alliance will be a disgrace; your name will never be mentioned by any of us."

"A terrible misfortune indeed," Bennet replies with a fair amount of irony, for the idea of passing unacknowledged by the imperious and pedantic Lady Catherine de Bourgh seems more blessing than curse. "But I'm sure being with Darcy would offer compensations."

"You despicable man! Have you no respect for people more important and influential than yourself! Let's sit down," she says, changing her tone as she avails herself of one of the many stone benches that line the courtyard. "I came here, Mr. Bethle, determined to achieve my purpose, and I won't be dissuaded from it. I won't give into any person's whim, and I refuse to accept failure."

"I can see, then, how very frustrating this conversation must be for you."

"Don't interrupt," she snaps. "You will listen to me in silence. Collin and Darcy are made for each other. They're a perfect match in breeding, social standing and fortune—especially the last as the fortune on both sides is large. Every member of their respective families wishes for the match and what's to thwart it? The upstart pretensions of a man without family, connections or money? Am I expected to endure this? No, I'm not. I will not. If you had any sense, you'd stick with your own kind."

"My own kind," he repeats softly, "is as good as your kind. My father is a lawyer. My mother is a college professor. We're entirely respectable."

"An entirely respectable middle-class nobody is not what I want for my niece."

"It hardly matters what you want," Bennet says.

Realizing the calmer, softer, more sensible approach has borne little fruit, her tone turns imperious again. "Tell me once and for all: Are you engaged to her?"

Bennet doesn't want to oblige her with an answer—he doesn't want to oblige her in any way at all—but he's compelled to say, after a moment's deliberation, "No, I'm not."

Lady Catherine seems pleased. "And will you promise me never to enter into such an engagement?"

He's staggered by the utter cheek of the request. "Absolutely not."

"Mr. Bethle, I'm shocked and astonished. I assumed you'd be reasonable. Don't fool yourself into believing I'll give up. I won't go away until you've given me the assurance I require."

"Then I hope you find a more comfortable chair than this marble bench, because I'll never give it. I won't be bullied into anything so ridiculously unreasonable. What I do will have absolutely no effect on Darcy's relationship with Collin. Mrs. de Bourgh, I'm afraid your argument is as poorly thought out as your visit. Clearly, you've made a huge mistake in thinking I'd be swayed by either. Darcy might not mind your meddling in her life, but I mind it greatly. So I'll thank you to drop the subject and allow me to escort you to your car."

"I'm not done," the matriarch says waspishly. "I have more objections. I know all about your youngest brother's infamous larceny—that the young man's so-called heroics were a patched-up business arranged by your family. I don't know how you pulled it off. Perhaps your father wields some influence after all, but your brother's nothing but a common crook. And is such a degenerate to be my niece's brother-in-law? It's offensive on every level."

"No," Bennet answers resentfully, "*you* are offensive on every level. Now, if you'll excuse me, I have to get back to work."

Lady Catherine stands, highly incensed. "You unfeeling, selfish man! Don't you care that a relationship with you would be a disgraceful embarrassment?"

"I'm done talking about this."

"You're determined, then, to have her?"

Bennet lets out a sigh of intense frustration. The woman is unbelievable! "I didn't say that. I'm only determined to make myself happy, not you."

"You refuse to submit to the claims of duty, honor and gratitude. You're determined to ruin her and make her a laughingstock."

"Look, you interfering old biddy!" Bennet says. Only, he doesn't say it. He might indeed be the unfeeling, selfish man she thinks him, but he's not cruel and he's not stupid. Rather, he explains calmly that her outdated concepts have no claim on him. Then he adds, "As for Darcy being a laughingstock, I think you either greatly overestimate the rest of the world's concern or underestimate its good sense."

"And this is your final word! Very well. I know now what I have to do. Don't imagine, Mr. Bethle, that this is over. I came here in hopes of having an intelligent discussion. But no matter. I will prevail by other means," she announces confidently. She continues to talk in the same manner—a field general planning her next strategy while bemoaning the failure of the current one—as they walk through the lobby followed by her assistant. In her distress, the volume of Lady Catherine's voice rises several notches, and the entire admissions staff, half a dozen security guards and a small tour group of French retirees watch in amused fascination as Bennet is berated by the imposing woman with the Birkin bag. Martin, noting how beautifully the sun glints off the pristine black crocodile, can't resist taking out his phone to get a few shots.

When they arrive at the door of her car, Lady Catherine turns hastily and adds, "I will not say good-bye to you, Mr. Bethle, or bid you good day. As you've ruined my day, I wish you no enjoyment of yours."

Bennet doesn't answer. Without saying good-bye himself, he walks into the museum. Meryton impatiently meets him in the lobby, having heard quite a few differing reports of the ruckus. In one account, Mrs. de Bourgh is haranguing Bennet. In another, he's scolding her. In a third, they're yelling at each other at the top of their lungs and elbowing tourists who get in their way.

"What happened?" he asks eagerly. "Why did she want to talk to you? Why were you arguing with her? Was it over the amount of money she wants to donate? Was the figure so incredibly large that it caused you to temporarily lose your mind?"

Bennet resorts to a lie. Relating the substance of their conversation would be impossible, and Meryton wouldn't believe it anyway. He scarcely believes it himself. "She only came to tell us Collin is well," he says, and walks toward the elevator.

CHAPTER TWENTY-NINE

Tequila isn't the solution. Almost two hours into an enthusiastic drinking session with his brother and Bingley, Bennet discovers that not even tequila shots are strong enough to make him stop thinking about Lady Catherine's extraordinary visit.

"Guacamole," Bingley says as she stares into a basket of tortilla crumbs at her friend Samantha's Mexican restaurant. "Let's get more guacamole. And chips. Lots more chips. Ooh, and some queso fundido. I'm suddenly starving."

John holds up his hand to wave down a waiter, and, making the suggested requests, assures the love of his life that the food will be on the table posthaste.

Smiling foolishly, if somewhat drunkenly, Bingley demands that he say it again.

"The food will be on the table posthaste."

"No," she says, shaking her head, "the other part."

"Love of my life."

Now the smile is all foolishness, and she leans in to kiss him. Bennet, whose eyes are turned in their general direction, hardly notices the byplay. His mind is too preoccupied with the bizarre fact that Lady Catherine actually traveled to their obscure outpost in Queens with the sole purpose of berating him into ending his engagement to Darcy. It was, he supposes, a rational scheme—maybe even a worthwhile one—if such an arrangement existed. But it doesn't, and Bennet's at a loss to understand how the rumor got started. The only possibility is Collin himself. Most likely he was teasing his aunt during a particularly officious moment.

If this theory is right, then the Longbourn volunteer succeeded beyond his wildest dreams.

Bennet shudders as he considers the further damage to be done by the nonsensical story, for Lady Catherine's intent to apply to Darcy next had been apparent. He doesn't doubt that Darcy will be more receptive to her aunt's catalog of Bethle evils, for many of them echo her own concerns. The arguments, which had struck him as weak and ridiculous, might seem full of good sense and solid reasoning to her. If she's been trying to figure out her next move, as has often seemed to be the case, the advice and counsel of a loved and admired aunt might tip the scales out of his favor once and for all. Unblemished dignity would prevail, the social order would remain untrammeled, and he'd most likely never see her again.

And so the clock has started, he thinks as the new basket of chips arrives at the table. Darcy has promised Bingley she'll be back in time for the luncheon her friend is hosting at the Longbourn in a few days. She'll either attend the event or make up some excuse to miss it. If she comes, he'll have a reason to have hope and if she doesn't....

Well, suffice to say, he'll close the book on this chapter of his life.

Bingley's friend Samantha, who owns several cantinas in the city, personally delivers the queso fundido and sits down at their table. After ordering another round of Cuervo—nothing but the best for her besties—she chats easily with John about stand-up paddle boarding and the limited supply of salted caramel ice cream on Cape Cod and the best ways to wake Bingley up in the morning. If Samantha feels any sense of horror at her friend's cavorting with someone of so obviously an inferior social standing, she doesn't let on. None of

Bingley's friends, of whom he's met several in the last week, have shown anything but delight at her finding someone who loves her wildly and treats her well.

Weak and ridiculous indeed, Bennet thinks again as he recalls Lady Catherine's vehement insistence that every sensibility would be horrified by the prospect of Darcy taking up with a lawyer's son.

Sure, he thinks, if they're living in the middle of the nineteenth century.

To be fair, Bingley isn't probably entirely up to snuff, either. She's wealthy, certainly, but her father amassed his fortune only in the last thirty years, making the Bingston clan arrivistes in Lady Catherine's estimation. This subtle snobbery might explain why no stigma is attached to her dating a lawyer's son. Poor, open-minded Bingley already counts shopkeepers and restaurant owners among her acquaintance. What's one more middle-class stray?

Unable to decide whether these thoughts provide solace or only more agitation, Bennet accepts the shot of Cuervo and downs it with enthusiasm. He knows the alcohol, which burns his throat, will offer little respite from his thoughts, but he appreciates the distraction, and when Bingley insists the queso fundido is so good, it'll blow his mind, he's just drunk enough to hope it's literally true.

Darcy doesn't bail. Instead, she arrives at the Longbourn luncheon a few minutes early, and before Meryton has a chance to tell her about her aunt's visit, a conversation Bennet dreads, Bingley asks her to run and fetch her a latte from the café downstairs. Darcy is momentarily nonplussed by the request, the expression on her face indicating that she clearly doesn't grasp the concept of running and fetching, and Meryton immediately volunteers Bennet as a substitute. He eagerly complies. Now that he's in the same room as Darcy, he suddenly wants to be somewhere else, a goal that's foiled when she announces her intention to accompany him.

Very little is said as they walk toward the elevator.

Bennet, who he hadn't expected to have a moment alone with her quite so soon, is working up the nerve to speak. He figured maybe after the lunch he'd be able to pull her off to the side, or perhaps while she waited for her driver to bring the car around. But the opportunity has presented itself, and the thought of prolonging his uncertainty is almost as unbearable as the prospect of ending it. So, as soon as the elevator doors close behind them, he says, "Darcy, I'm sorry if it embarrasses you, but I must thank you for saving Lydon. Ever since I've found out, I've been anxious to let you know how very, very much I appreciate your unparalleled kindness to my brother."

Darcy is surprised—very surprised indeed—by his statement, and she looks down at her fingers for a moment before speaking. "I didn't think the FBI would be so bad at keeping a secret," she replies in a tone made awkward with emotion.

"Don't blame the FBI. Special Agent Tompkins was very discreet, but Lydon let it slip and I couldn't rest until I knew the whole story. Let me thank you again and again, on behalf of Lydon and my parents and myself and my whole family, for going to so much trouble. I know fiddling with the official FBI record is not without risks for you, and I'm humbled by your generosity and compassion."

"No thanks are necessary, but if you must," she replies, "let it be for yourself alone. I did it only for you."

Now the elevator arrives at the first floor and the doors open. Cursing the rotten timing, and the impulse that led him to start this conversation in an elevator—an elevator, for God's sake!—he steps out of the car and turns to the left. The café is to the right but no matter. No one's actually fetching coffee anymore.

Before Bennet can think of a response, Darcy says in a rush, "You're too kind to trifle with me. If you still feel the way you did in July, please tell me so. I feel exactly the same, but just say the word and I'll drop the subject once and for all."

Bennet doesn't say anything. Heedless of the busy hallway, of the tourists strolling by and his coworkers bustling about, he takes her face into his hands and presses his lips to hers. He kisses her long and deep and with far more ardor than is appropriate for the Jessa Winthrop Longbourn Memorial alcove, and when he feels the press of the wall he realizes he must stop now or mortify them both. Heavy with resolve, he pulls away and looks into her face, her traffic-stopping gorgeous face, and says, "My feelings have undergone a radical change, and if you're free to leave here, I'd be delighted and most absurdly grateful to demonstrate just how radical a change that is."

Darcy, whose color is already high, turns a brighter shade of pink at his suggestion, which, having forgotten entirely about their errand, she immediately agrees to. She remembers the latte again fifteen minutes later as she's walking up the steps to Bennet's apartment building, a converted warehouse with pretty window boxes, and cringes with embarrassment as she imagines Bingley and John scratching their heads over their sudden disappearance. Bennet pulls out his phone, taps a few lines and hits SEND, and Darcy, reading the text over his shoulder—"Abandoned latte mission; on the trail of something more stimulating"—giggles.

Some of Bennet's euphoria dips as he unlocks his door and reveals to her expectant eyes his modest home, with its sparse furnishings, live-in kitchen and narrow bedroom. The only things it has going for it are the brilliant rays of sunlight pouring in through the southern exposure and its cleanliness. He's relieved he hasn't left the towels lying on the bathroom floor, though, truth be told, he never leaves the towels or anything else lying around.

Suddenly self-conscious, he starts to apologize for the apartment's smallness and its evident lack of luxury, and Darcy shakes her head as she laughs.

"Yes, that's right, taunt me for my small-mindedness. *That* Darcy probably would have been much taken aback by a sensible man living within his means," she says, as she walks across the room to the window. "I have lots to be sorry for, and I've done little since that day but repent. When I think about that conversation—my words, my tone, my whole attitude—I want to bury my head under a blanket. Everything you said was true, all of it. I didn't behave like a decent human being. Honestly, I'm surprised you didn't slug me when I called your uncle a huckster."

Bennet, however, is much too appalled by his own behavior on that occasion to listen to her castigate herself for hers, and he strolls over to the window to take her into his arms, for anything else is simply too much to bear.

"What'd you think of the email?" she asks. "Did it make a difference? Did you believe any of it?"

"The email, the email," he repeats softly. "The email was a revelation. Don't get me wrong: I didn't want to believe a word of it and dismissed it the first time around. But I'm not completely inured to reason, and the next time I read it and the time after that, it all started to make sense. Especially your observations about John. He *is* a cipher. It's partly his placid nature, partly his professionalism. He's not like me—he'd never hurl insults at a woman brave enough to put her heart on the line."

"You're giving me too much credit," she says. "I didn't risk anything, because I didn't know anything was at risk. There wasn't a doubt in my mind of the outcome. I really thought you'd be flattered and assumed you felt something for me in return because I was just that vain. Instead, I got the set-down of the century. It was good for me. I've been selfish my whole life, I realize that now. My parents instilled in me the importance of good values. But they also raised me with a strong sense of entitlement, to believe my thoughts, feelings and experiences are more important than everyone else's. A classic example of special snowflake indoctrination, and since we had the money and prestige to back it up, that sense of superiority was validated over and over again. People have always behaved as if the Fitzwilliams are worth a little bit more than everyone else, which taught me to care for only my own family and to think unkindly of everyone else. Worse: It taught me to think little of other people's worth in comparison to my own. And that's who I was from eight to twenty-eight and who I still would be if you, dearest, most darling Bennet, hadn't shown me the light. I've yet to demonstrate my appreciation," she adds with a wholly uncharacteristic grin, "which, having been raised with all those good values, I'm now obligated to do."

At her expression of heartfelt delight, Bennet feels his own heart trip in his chest and he finds it suddenly hard to breathe, an activity that grows steadily more difficult as she presses her lips to his and murmurs all the lovely nonsense of a woman violently in love.

Bennet's narrow bedroom is steps away, but they make it no farther than the couch, and although he has a vague sense that something more dignified is befitting the heir to the Fitzwilliam fortune, he's beyond thrilled to discover it's not required.

A celebratory toast is a must, after the afternoon's other celebratory activity has been very satisfactorily concluded—twice—and Bennet takes out a lovely bottle of Pouilly-Fuissé that he'd been saving for a special occasion. It must be said, nothing of this magnitude of special had ever registered on his radar. He digs up cheddar cheese, melba toast and some dried apricots, and lays the feast on the coffee table.

Darcy refills her glass and compliments him on the vintage.

"At the risk of sounding insufferably ironic, I must warn you not to get used to the luxury, as that bottle is not only an anomaly for me but a one-off as well. The thanks of a grateful patron. I won't be serving anything quite so elegant should your aunt come to call."

She smiles at the mention of Lady Catherine. "The poor dear. Her plan to break us up, when we weren't even together, backfired spectacularly. After you refused to give her your word, she applied to me for the same promise, and that gave me hope. You're so blunt—I knew you wouldn't have hesitated to state clearly and unequivocally your lack of interest in me."

Bennet colors slightly and laughs as he replies, "Yes, you know enough of my bluntness to believe me capable of that. Having abused you horribly to your face, I wouldn't think twice about abusing you to all your relations."

"I deserved it. Your accusations were based on mistaken assumptions, true, but my behavior was still terrible. I can't think of it without cringing."

"Excellent. Now let's quarrel over who behaved worse. The loser gets the last drop of wine," he says, holding up the almost empty bottle, "and the winner has to go rummage through the cabinets to find another bottle. I'm fairly certain there's a decent Syrah over the sink."

Conceding the game before it's even begun, Darcy moves to stand, but Bennet quickly intercedes with a firm tug and suddenly she's back in his arms and neither one is thinking about cupboards or contests or red wine.

Later, after they've finally made it to the bedroom and Darcy has admired the bright modern painting on his wall and complimented him on his taste in books, which aligns very nicely with hers, Bennet asks how she fell in love with him. "What set it off? I can understand your going under quickly, but what made you take the plunge?"

Darcy shrugs and rolls onto her side to look him in the eyes. "I don't recall."

"My handsome face didn't interest you—that we know from your honest assessment at the party. My manners were atrocious. On more than one occasion I was intentionally rude. That was it, wasn't it? You admired me for my impertinence. Be honest."

She grins. "For the liveliness of your mind, let's say."

Bennet refuses her attempt to whitewash. "We'll call it impertinence and be done with it. The fact is, you were sick of civility, of deference, of officious attention. You were disgusted with men always currying favor and deferring to your opinion on everything. So much for your fine definition of a gentleman. Privately, you hated them for always seeking your approval. I roused your interest because I was so unlike them. And this is proof of your good nature—if you'd really been the miserly person you described earlier, you wouldn't have been able to stand me."

"I'm not so sure about that, but I like that you think so."

"Stick with me, kid, and I'll have you mounted on a bronze pedestal in no time."

After a thoughtful moment, she says, "It was the pimientos that set me off."

He's nonplussed by the non sequitur. "What pimientos?"

She laughs. "Yeah, that's the thing. I don't know. At the gala benefit, you were talking to a colleague about the pimientos in the olives and there was something about your tone that appealed to me."

Bennet likes this explanation so much another hour passes before he remembers to thank her for bringing Bingley and John together. "I know that was you."

This she denies. "I merely informed her that my opinion of your brother's feelings for her had changed."

"You mean, you gave your permission."

Darcy decries the description and insists her friend doesn't require her consent for anything. "It's only that Bingley can be insecure when it comes to men—she has a lousy track record—and she sometimes relies on the judgment of others. With that in mind, I watched John closely during our visit to your office and later at the dinner party, and it was obvious how he felt. So I explained that my previous estimation of his affection was wrong, as he seemed to be utterly infatuated with her. She took it from there."

"And wasted no time. Whereas *some* people...."

The implication is clear, and Darcy, understanding at once, explains that she was too embarrassed to say anything. "I'm not like Bingley, jumping in with both feet. She's always been the outgoing one. That's why she makes such a great Golden Diamond Precious Metal Very Important Committee chair. I'm not nearly as good a host as she."

"You were the perfect host when we had dinner at Pemberley. And wonderfully outgoing. I was not. I was too horrified to be caught literally on your doorstep. I can't imagine what you thought."

"I thought it was too good to be true. It was like when I was a teenager and used to imagine bumping into my latest crush in the most unlikely places, like the airport or the movie theater. Suddenly, there you were and I was ridiculously grateful for the chance to show you that I'd changed and that I didn't resent you for rejecting me. And when that thing with your brother happened, I knew I had to do whatever I could to help—partly because I felt responsible. If I'd told people what Georgia was really like, she wouldn't have had access to the Longbourn in the first place. But also because I hated the thought of his conviction always hanging over you. My intervention was ultimately minor. The FBI actually had a file on Georgia already—some student loan scam from a few years ago—and all I did was convince Associate Deputy Director Miller to make Lydon part of that ongoing investigation."

Bennet, who's not surprised to hear Darcy downplay her involvement, thanks her again and again and again for saving his idiot brother from a miserable existence. He knows he'll never be able to thank her enough, but he's happy to spend the rest of his life trying—yes, he thinks, the rest of his life, even though they've been together for only twelve hours. He knows this is it, and as he turns off the light, he promises to take her to the best bakery in the entire city for breakfast.

She closes her eyes, rests her head on his shoulder, yawns hugely and observes how heavenly that sounds. Then, after a moment, she adds, "Just, please, no rugelach."

Oh, yeah, he thinks, grinning in the dark, the *rest* of his life.

CHAPTER THIRTY

Nobody suspects a thing. The likelihood of Bennet and Darcy hooking up is so far removed from anyone's expectations that when they both disappear at the same time neither John nor Bingley wonders if the events are related. Not even Meryton, with his endlessly optimistic schemes to bestow committee chairs on grateful heiresses, considers the possibility.

When Bennet enters the office the next morning, a little later than usual but a whole lot earlier than he'd like, John looks at him curiously and asks where he ran off to the day before. "It's not like you to go MIA, especially during a work event."

Amused, Bennet says, "I sent you a text."

"You mean that cryptic message that revealed no actual information?" he asks. "Yeah, we found that very helpful. Thanks."

Bennet shrugs and sits at his computer.

"Darcy cut out, too," John says. "It threw Bingley for a loop because she knew Darcy had been looking forward to the lunch. Just as she was starting to fear she'd been kidnapped, she got an apology. Very brief. Bingley worried the text was *too* brief, but I managed to talk her down from that. Plus, we spoke with Ms. Reynolds, who said Darcy had called to say she wouldn't be home for dinner."

As his brother talks, Bennet realizes his text was even more cryptic than he'd supposed. Next time, he'll use pronouns, although, recalling the cocktail of emotions he'd been feeling yesterday—impatient, aroused, giddy, anxious—he's surprised he managed to communicate anything at all.

"Darcy was with me," he says.

"Oh," John says, not getting it even now. He types a line of text and then looks up again. "Where'd you go?"

"Back to my apartment," Bennet replies, "to have sex."

His tone is so matter-of-fact, his brother assumes he's joking. "Very funny. What'd you really do? Go somewhere else because the café had a crazy-long line? "

"John, John," Bennet says chastisingly, shaking his head in exaggerated disappointment, "if *you* don't believe me, who will?"

His brother looks at him doubtingly. "You and Darcy? Seriously? But you don't even like her."

"You have no idea. It's been *months* since I've felt that way. In fact, in recent weeks, I've been positively pining. Fine brother you are not to notice."

Despite these assurances, John remains unconvinced, and putting all kidding aside, Bennet calmly and solemnly promises him it's true. But he can't remain somber for long and the teasing glint returns to his eye. "So what do you think? Are you happy for me? Is it as brilliant a match as you and Bingley?"

"Bingley will be delighted. She's been wanting to set you two up for ages, but I told her it was impossible," he says. "I'm still not sure it *is* possible. Are you quite positive?"

Darting a glance at the doorway, through which Meryton might enter at any second, Bennet suggests they go down to the café for coffee. Once settled there at a table, he fills his brother in on everything: Pemberley, Lady Catherine, Lydon. By turns, John is amazed, amused and appalled, and aside from reprimanding his brother for keeping so much important information to himself, he listens quietly.

"I didn't tell you some of it because I didn't want to

mention Bingley," he says, by way of apology, "and I didn't tell you the rest because I couldn't figure out how I felt. It seemed better to avoid the subject altogether. But now it's all sorted and everything's out in the open."

John shakes his head. "It's a lot to take in. I'm happy for you. Very happy for you. As you know, I've always liked Darcy and I think she'll be good for you. And Bingley will truly be over the moon. But this thing with the FBI! I can't believe that was Darcy. We owe her so much. I don't know how I'll ever repay her."

As the hour wears on, the café starts to grow crowded, and although they could spend half the day in conversation, they relinquish their table to a family of tourists hovering nearby. They decide as they climb the stairs to the third floor that they have to confess everything to their parents about Lydon's heroics. The elder Bethles deserve to know the truth.

Meryton is waiting for them when they return to the office, his expression thunderous as he takes them to task for abandoning their posts. Neither has done anything that Lydon doesn't do every day of his life, but while they were gone, their benefactor had stopped by to commend them on several recent large donations and Meryton, unaware of their absence, could provide Henry with no information about his staff's whereabouts.

Although the site of the matronly Meryton in a rage is pure comic entertainment—his cheeks puffy, his nose red, his eyes feverishly blinking—Bennet offers up his relationship with Darcy as a balm to his temper. He expects his boss's state of mind to brighten immediately, but the news has the unanticipated effect of making his mood more tragic. One employee dating an heiress is a consummation devoutly to be wished, but two?! Two tips the scales into potential desertion. With one brother tethered to the economic realities of employment, Meryton had hope of holding on to them both. Now the cause feels lost.

As there's nothing remotely humorous about a maudlin

Meryton, John and Bennet do everything they can to cheer him up, including a spot-on imitation of Collin doing Lady Catherine by Bennet. Their antics have no effect and they change tactics, assuring him with all due sincerity and earnestness that neither has any intention of leaving. He refuses to believe them, and it's only the appearance of Lydon, whose honorary spigot has been upgraded from drinking fountain outside the third-floor men's room to a trickling water feature in the rose garden, that raises his spirits. No one whose name is actually affixed to a slab of marble at the Longbourn could ever bear to abandon it.

The logic seems faulty to Bennet, especially given Lydon's track record, but he's far too smart to say anything, and eventually the office settles down. The youngest Bethle manages to put in a record sixty-four minutes at his desk before going on a caffeine run. As much as Bennet wants to say something snarky to John about it, he knows his own level of productivity, marred by a lengthy text exchange with Darcy, is hardly a model of office efficiency.

By the time Lydon returns an hour later, Bennet's plans for the evening have been firmed up, and he invites everyone to dinner at Darcy's. He even includes Meryton, hoping that seeing the glories of Pemberley firsthand will assuage some of his disappointment at having an employee who's free to run tame among them.

The dinner is Darcy's idea, an opportunity to demonstrate how thoroughly she's changed, and although it's not at all necessary, he's grateful for the gesture.

At least, he was grateful when she made the offer, but now, as he stands on the threshold of her house waiting for her assistant to answer the door, he feels nothing but anxiety—anxiety at seeing her again, anxiety that the dinner will be a disaster, anxiety that she'll realize her aunt is right. He feels so much anxiety, he actually considers turning tail and running. But before he can succumb to his cowardly impulse, she's at the door, not Ms. Reynolds, and she's giving him a kiss on the lips. It's a nice kiss, a soft kiss, and it's imbued with all the lovely implications of familiarity: intimacy, warmth, anticipation of what's to come. His heart rate slowly returns to normal; the need to flee subsides.

As it turns out, he has nothing to worry about. Dinner goes wonderfully. Darcy isn't the sort of person whose happiness overflows in mirth, but she's kind and welcoming and interested throughout the meal, and later, when they retire to the lovely drawing room overlooking Central Park for coffee, she sits on the arm of Bennet's chair rather than assuming her own. The scene—Bingley and John laughing, Lydon listening intently, Meryton too much in awe to do little more than stare blankly—is beyond anything he'd imagined, and all of it strikes him as far too beautiful to last.

And a few months later, when his parents are there and the Gardiners and Lady Catherine unbends enough to stay for cocktails—not the whole meal, mind you, just a glass of wine before the theater—he's struck again by the sensation of profound contentment and thinks once more that something so perfect can't possibly last.

And yet somehow it does.

ABOUT THE AUTHOR

Lynn Messina is the author of more than a dozen novels, including the best-selling *Fashionistas,* which has been translated into 16 languages. Her essays have appeared in *Self, American Baby* and the Modern Love column in the *New York Times,* and she's a regular contributor to the *Times* Motherlode blog. She lives in New York City with her husband and sons.